Michael Palin is an English comedian, actor, writer and television presenter. Born in Broomhill, Sheffield in 1943, he read modern history at Brasenose College, Oxford, where he met fellow comedy writer Terry Jones. Shortly after beginning a career as a writer and presenter for various TV programmes, he collaborated with Jones, Eric Idle, John Cleese, Graham Chapman and Terry Gilliam to form the world-famous Monty Python comedy troupe. Post-Python, Palin went on to write for other TV shows such as *Ripping Yarns*, as well taking on film roles such as the hapless Ken Pile in *A Fish Called Wanda*, which earned him a BAFTA Award for Best Actor in a Supporting Role. He has been presenting travel documentaries on TV since 1980, including *Around the World in 80 Days* and *Pole to Pole*; later shows have featured travels to the Sahara Desert, the Himalayas, and Brazil. In 2000 he received a CBE for his services to television. Because of his self-described 'amenable, conciliatory character', Palin has been referred to unofficially as 'Britain's Nicest Man'.

THE TRUTH

Keith Mabbut is at a crossroads in his life. When he is offered the opportunity of a lifetime — to write the biography of the elusive Hamish Melville, a highly influential activist and humanitarian — he seizes the chance to write something meaningful. His search to find out the real story behind the legend takes Mabbut to the lush landscapes and environmental hotspots of India. The more he discovers about Melville, the more he admires him — and the more he connects with an idealist who wanted to make a difference. But is his quarry really who he claims to be? As Keith discovers, the truth can be whatever we make it . . .

Books by Michael Palin
Published by The House of Ulverscroft:

AROUND THE WORLD IN 80 DAYS

MICHAEL PALIN

THE TRUTH

Complete and Unabridged

CHARNWOOD
Leicester

First published in Great Britain in 2012 by
Weidenfeld & Nicolson
London

First Charnwood Edition
published 2013
by arrangement with
Weidenfeld & Nicolson
An Hachette UK Company
London

A catalogue record for this book is available
from the British Library.

ISBN 978–1–4448–1734–8

Published by
F. A. Thorpe (Publishing)
Anstey, Leicestershire

Set by Words & Graphics Ltd.
Anstey, Leicestershire
Printed and bound in Great Britain by
T. J. International Ltd., Padstow, Cornwall

This book is printed on acid-free paper

'Gertrude, truth is a very complex thing'

OSCAR WILDE, *An Ideal Husband*

PART I

The Problem

Keith Mabbut was a writer. Of that he was convinced. He lived in London on two floors of a red-brick, gabled house in Upper Holloway. He would have preferred to have lived nearer to the heart of the capital, but needs must and he was only a short walk from Finsbury Park station and on a good day could be at the British Library within thirty-eight minutes of leaving home. He lived with Stanley the cat, and Julia, his daughter, who was nineteen and known to all as Jay. He had another child, Sam, who was training to be an actor and didn't live at home. Mabbut and his wife Krystyna, who was Polish, were separated. Mabbut's father and mother had died quite some time ago, within a year of each other. He had an older sister, Lucy, who lived in Australia.

Though he had made a career out of the written word, and indeed had a British Gas Award to show for it, he had reached the age of fifty-six with nothing resembling the success of his great literary heroes, George Orwell and Albert Camus, both of whom had died in their forties. Setting aside the clear, if unpalatable, correlation between genius and early death, he had formed the opinion that his best work was yet to come. And in a way he least expected, so it was.

1

The atmosphere at breakfast in the Stratsa House Hotel was as overcast as the skies outside. Regret seemed to have the upper hand over expectation; yesterday, rather than today, seemed uppermost in people's minds. This was certainly true in Keith Mabbut's case. He had completed his history of the Sullom Voe oil terminal and his work on Shetland was over. In three hours he would be flying out of Sumburgh for the last time.

He examined the buffet. It was always the same but he lived in hope that one day a fruit compote might appear, or a thick Viking muesli, or just anything not in a packet. Today there was less than usual. Not even a banana. He slit open a small bag of Alpen, which he tipped into a bowl, adding some yogurt, a spoonful of raisins and a dried fig.

He ordered tea and took his usual corner table by the window, looking out towards the sea.

A middle-aged couple, two single men sitting separately, and a lone female with bobbed blonde hair and a very large book were the only other occupants of the thickly carpeted, curtain-swagged restaurant and bar known as the Clickimin Suite, named after a loch on the outskirts of Lerwick. One thing he'd miss about Shetland was the joyful exuberance of the place names. Spiggie, Quarff, Muckle Flugga, Yell and

Gloup, the Wart of Scousburgh, the Haa of Funzie and the Bight of Ham. Beside these, Lerwick itself, derived from the original Norse, *Leir Vik*, meaning 'a muddy bay', seemed disappointingly mundane.

Gales had blown hard across the muddy bay this last week, but had dropped quite suddenly overnight, and instead of the customary rattling of the windows, the only sounds in the Clickimin Suite this morning were the buttering of toast and the low gurgle of the coffee machine. Up in his room, Keith's bag was packed and ready to go.

Last night the oil company had given a party at Rani's, an Indian restaurant at the northern end of the harbour, to celebrate the completion of his book, which was to be called *Triumph In Adversity. The Official History of the Sullom Voe Oil Terminal.* Commissioned by NorthOil, one of the consortium of ownership companies, to celebrate the thirtieth anniversary of the start of production at the terminal, the book had been the brainchild of the Edinburgh office, therefore never wholeheartedly endorsed by the local management, who preferred to get on with their work with as little fuss as possible. So the fact that Howard Michie, the chief manager at NorthOil, had a prior engagement was not unexpected, and it was his senior assistant manager, Kevin O'Connolly, who had been deputed to attend on his behalf. Mabbut didn't like O'Connolly at all. He was a professional Scotsman, parading a hard-bitten Glaswegian mythology as transparent as glass. There were also familiar faces from public affairs — Harry Brinsley and Sheila O'Connell, both young, bright and woefully underemployed — as well as Roscoe Gunn from Planning, tall and tedious, Laurie Henneck from Accounts, Rob Taggart, who had been taken off development to co-ordinate collection of all the material Mabbut might require, and last of all, Mae Lennox from Human Resources, who was responsible for seeing that Keith was paid and housed while he was up in Shetland.

When he had made his first visit sixteen months earlier, Mabbut had been struck by how little was known about the terminal, whose input and output had, after all, transformed the British economy. In the local bookshops there were shelves devoted to fishing and birdwatching and local music; there were three or four histories of the Shetland Bus, an operation which had used the island's fishing boats to assist the Norwegian resistance in the Second World War, but the few books on the oil industry were long out of print. The smart and comprehensive new Museum of Island Life, itself paid for by oil revenues, had several displays of Neolithic stone dwellings and only one devoted to the source of the windfall that had changed the inhabitants' way of life. The Shetlanders' reticence about their riches had rather encouraged Mabbut. Embarrassed at first by the lowliness of the commission he'd accepted, he began to see a role for himself, not as a company man, but as an outsider who could write honestly and objectively about what Sullom Voe really meant to Shetland. Pretty soon

7

he realised this was not what was required. Oil companies, traditionally secretive, were, after disasters like the spill in the Gulf of Mexico, compulsively paranoid, and NorthOil was no exception.

As security was tightened at the thousand-acre complex forty miles to the north of Lerwick, it was made increasingly clear to Mabbut that he was being paid to accentuate the positive. References to the chaotic early days of construction when an imported workforce was quartered on a desperately unprepared island, or the IRA bomb that went off on the day the Queen officially opened the place, or the two potentially catastrophic oil spills that happened near by, were discouraged or simply struck from his text. Some of the local managers had made their objections to the book personal. Not only was Mabbut seen as an outsider — what they called up here a 'soothmoother', one who had come into Lerwick harbour from its southern mouth — he also had form as that most despised of the breed, an environmental journalist.

Kevin O'Connolly prided himself on his informal, folksy style. He was a reformed alcoholic and had been a company man since his teens. As steaming dishes of biryani, murgh massallam and rogan josh were brought to the table, he clapped his hands for silence.

'Before you all get stuck into your curries, I'd like to say thank you on behalf of NorthOil to Keith and all those who've helped him produce this book about what we're all doing up here. Especially for those who were never quite sure.'

8

Laughter.

'The oil business is blamed for just about everything these days and it's nice to read some good things about ourselves, like the fact that we turned a peat bog into the biggest oil terminal in Europe within four years, and that we've kept it running day and night for thirty years. If the Greenies had their way, we'd be a peat bog again, but thankfully we have someone like Keith to tell our side of the story, and it's a great story that we can all be proud of. So on behalf of the company, and I know our managing director would join me in this, I'd like to thank Keith for doing a grand job — for a Sassenach . . . '

Nervous laughter.

' . . . in capturing the skill, the enterprise and the resilience that Sullom Voe has embodied these past thirty years. If you want to be reminded of how important our business is and how well it's doing, this will be the book for you to read. And we all look forward to receiving our free copy.'

Laughter again.

'So thank you, Keith.'

He reached down and picked up something that Rob Taggart had slipped on to his chair.

' . . . and from all of us at NorthOil, we'd like you to accept this as a wee token of our thanks.'

'A lifetime security pass!' shouted someone, which raised a good laugh; 'a Scottish passport!', which raised an even better one. In fact the present turned out to be an all-weather jacket, as worn on the rigs, with 'NorthOil' picked out in bold yellow capitals across the back of it. Not

9

something Mabbut could see himself wearing to the next Greenpeace meeting.

He gave a short reply, short because he was unable to express how frustrating it had been writing the book, knowing that every manager on the site was breathing down his neck. O'Connolly made his apologies and left shortly afterwards, giving Mabbut a powerful handshake — he was not the sort of man for a bear-hug. The atmosphere relaxed. The food was good and, knowing that the company was paying, those who stayed moved from beer to wine and even some curious Indian *digestif* that Rani produced from a back cupboard. Mabbut fell into a long conversation with Laurie from Accounts, who had lived on the island all her life and was desperate to get away and see the world. She'd never been to London, and no matter what Mabbut told her about it, she still wanted to go. As the evening wore on, those who lived out of Lerwick bade their farewells and began to drift off. Soon only Mabbut, Roscoe Gunn and Mae Lennox were left. Roscoe was a dour man on whom alcohol appeared to have no effect at all. He was, however, that even more deadly combination, a dour man who likes company, and it was long past midnight before he shook Mabbut's hand one final time and headed off into the night. Mabbut waited for Mae Lennox to settle up. As they stepped out on to Bank Lane the sky was wonderfully clear and a small crescent moon hung so sharp and bright above the bay that neither felt they could turn their backs on it. Instead they walked down towards the waterfront, where the outline of a recently docked Norwegian three-master rose against the night sky. They turned south along Commercial Street, whose solid and sturdy old manses ran parallel to the sea, which lapped gently at the flights of stone steps leading from the houses to the water.

Of all those he had met during his work at Sullom Voe, Mae was the person he'd miss most. She was in her mid-forties and had never been married, except to her work. She must have had offers because she was lively and bright and looked good, without ever seeming to put in much effort. They'd spent a lot of time together and grown fond of each other, but whereas her friendliness had been chummy rather than intimate, his feelings were more complicated.

'Walk to the Knab?'

Mae feigned horror.

'The Knab! I've to be at work in the morning, Mr Mabbut.'

'It's my last night.'

'I've not got the right shoes on.'

'I'll carry you.'

Mae snorted with laughter and looked up at the sky.

'Well, we'll go a little way more. It's a rare old evening.'

They pulled up their coat collars as they cleared the protective walls of the houses and the wind caught them straight off the water. At the top of the next hill they found cover again, in the lee of an ill-starred assortment of modern bungalows and large stone houses with pointy roofs. A roller-coaster path led down between them to a low cliff and then wound up again past a cemetery. Serried ranks of silver tombstones stretched up the slope, like a silent army watching them. Neither spoke until they'd reached the headland known as the Knab, where a small shelter had been provided as part of a tourist trail. Here they sat, looking out into the star-studded night with the silver-grey waters of the Sound rippling gently below.

Mae flicked her hair free of her collar.

'I feel like a teenager again.'

Mabbut put his arm around her, protectively and companionably, but with enough pressure to feel her compact shape between waist and ribcage.

'I can't remember that far back.'

She turned towards him.

'Are you looking for sympathy or something? Look at me. Halfway through my forties already.'

'Ah, but you still have a lot of life ahead of you, Mae. Most of mine is behind me.'

'Oh, don't give me that. What are you? Fifty-six?'

'You should know, you're the one who employed me.'

'Fifty-six is nothing.'

'It's nothing times fifty-six,' said Mabbut bleakly.

Ahead of them, a few clouds were drifting above the southern horizon.

'If someone had said to me on the journo course that, by the time I was pushing sixty, I'd be being thanked by an oil company for making them look good, I'd have left and become a toilet attendant.'

'Thanks a lot.'

'You know what I mean. It's nothing personal. Just a nagging reminder that success is something that happens to other people.'

Mae shook her head impatiently.

'There you go again, Keith. Always beating yourself up.'

'I'm not the only one beating me up. You remember what O'Connolly said when I came up with all that interesting stuff about the early days and the local council being told one thing and the oil company doing another? 'They were troublemakers, Keith, people who dinnae know a gift horse when it sits on their heed.' That's what he said.'

Mae gave a short laugh.

'We've done all right out of it.'

Mabbut snorted angrily.

'Oh, sure, but only because some of you caused trouble. Made the companies pay up. But they wouldn't let me put that in the book.'

A cloud flitted across the moon and the sea turned from silver to black.

'You know, Mae, I sometimes have this dream that I'm walking across a bridge at rush hour and everyone else is coming the other way.'

'You make things difficult for yourself. You don't have to do that. None of us is perfect, you know.'

'I'm not talking about perfect, Mae, just honest reporting. I've given them what they wanted, but it wasn't what I wanted.'

13

This wasn't what he wanted either. Not with Mae Lennox, not on his last night on Shetland. He tried a grin but didn't quite convince.

'I'm sorry, Mae. It's my despair gene. There's nothing I can do about it.'

He turned, leaning in close to her.

'I'll miss you, Mae.'

'I'll miss you too.'

He moved his arm lightly across her shoulder.

'Come to London.'

Mae laughed, a little more heartily than he'd have liked.

'Me? No. I promised my mother I'd never go south of Berwick-on-Tweed.'

'I'm not joking. I'm serious.' He pulled away. 'Come to London. Come and live with me.'

Mae stopped, laughed, shook her head then laughed again.

'Why not? It would be wonderful. We get on so well. You understand me, Mae.'

'*Why not?* Because you're a married man for a start. Are you going to keep me in a wee room somewhere?'

Mabbut was aware of the silence around them. The moon had disappeared, and the wind too.

'Just a silly thought,' he said.

She leaned across and kissed his cheek.

'We've both had a lot to drink.'

'That's why I can tell you these things, but it doesn't mean I've just thought of them . . . '

Mabbut broke off. Staring into the inky darkness, he took two deep breaths.

Mae put her hand on his.

'You're a good man, Keith Mabbut. You

14

should remember that more often.'

They sat for a moment, neither speaking. Mae peered out of the shelter.

'Weather's changing.' She checked her watch and got rapidly to her feet. 'And it's two o'clock!'

They walked back into the town. As they passed the Point, a different wind hit them, a north wind so brisk and searching they had to huddle close, which is how they were when they stopped at the bottom of the short, steep alleyway that led to Keith's hotel.

He gave her a long last hug.

'I hope we'll see each other again, Mae. One way or another.'

'Me too.'

'A night of rapture in Berwick-on-Tweed?'

She smiled, squeezed his hand and turned away, walking quite briskly up Commercial Street, her heels clicking on the flagstones. He watched her for a while, but she didn't look back.

★ ★ ★

The first flecks of early morning rain pattered across the windows of the Clickimin Suite.

'Cooked breakfast this morning, sir?'

Waking from his reverie, Keith noticed a cheerful Filipino standing beside him with a notepad.

Mabbut shook his head.

'No, no thank you.'

He peered out of the window. He could just make out the sea between the trees and the

15

garages. He was glad he hadn't told Mae the full truth about Krystyna last night, although he couldn't stop himself wondering what the effect might have been if he had.

It was three days ago now that he'd heard the news. He'd spent the morning cooped up at the terminal running last-minute checks on things like surge-tank capacity and pre-fabrication ratios, and he was heading back from the Voe when his mobile had sounded. It was Krystyna. Since the split, these calls had followed a fairly strict and regular pattern: Monday evenings around eight, basic information exchanged, emotion avoided, all over in less than ten minutes. So this was an exception. Her voice was a little highly pitched too. She had asked him if he was able to talk, and he had pulled off the road on to the cinder-track driveway of a small, whitewashed farmhouse. It had been one of the island's better days, a late afternoon breeze barely troubling the clouds in a bright blue sky.

His wife delivered her message succinctly. She had met a man. There was mutual attraction and he had asked her to go and live with him. At the moment she was still sharing a flat with their son Sam, but it wasn't altogether satisfactory and she intended to accept the offer.

Mabbut took this in, his attention distracted by a pair of sea eagles straight ahead of him, slowly dipping and rising on the air currents. He thanked her for letting him know, and with a clumsy attempt at insouciance asked why she had thought it so important to ring him now.

And that was when she had told him that she wanted a divorce.

This shouldn't have been a shock. They had been apart for so long that he'd begun to see their separation as a sort of bond between them. Not being able to live together was something only the two of them shared. The day before he'd bought her a rather expensive Shetland wool sweater. She was never easy to buy for, but this one, with its traditional wave-like pattern and delicate combination of greys and pale blues, had been just up her street. Giving it to her would have confirmed that there was still some business as usual, apart from just the children.

Not wanting to go back to the hotel, he had retraced his journey along the road as far as Brae, a village grown into a small town as a result of its proximity to the terminal. Oil money, skilfully extracted from the companies by a dogged council, had provided a new school and a leisure centre that a town twenty times its size would have been proud of. An area of bright new Scandinavian-style homes, nicknamed Toytown by the locals, had advanced up the hillside. New restaurants and shops had opened to service them. The previous winter Mae had rented one of them for Keith, so he'd be closer to the terminal on those days when the sun sank at three and didn't reappear until ten the next morning.

Instead of going straight on to the terminal, he took a secondary road to the west, across the narrow bridge that led to a rocky, red-granite island. Driving on until the road ended, he'd

17

walked the half-mile or so that led to the edge of the cliffs. He had sat down on a grass-tufted ledge and looked out to sea. Across the water lay the convoluted outlines of the islands of Papa Little and Vementry. To the west, the Atlantic stretched away, unbroken, until it reached the coast of Greenland. Gulls wheeled and cried as the waves rushed and sucked at the shiny black rocks two hundred feet below him.

Krystyna Woniesjka had been one of the students on a creative writing course that he'd taught at Leeds back in the early 1980s. Mabbut, a voracious reader from early childhood, had started writing stories as soon as he could spell. At Huddersfield Grammar he'd vied with a boy called Clive Attwell for top honours in English. Attwell had been a winner in every way and ended up with an Exhibition to Cambridge. Mabbut, the better writer, had ended up at the University of Hull, where some brooding resentment at the way things had turned out drew him towards politics. After three years as a minor firebrand he secured a second-class degree and a place at the local school of journalism. It took him a further three years to realise that his politics were lukewarm, more about reaction than action. Then, thanks to a good friend's wife, with whom he'd had a very brief affair, he found himself applying, success-fully, to be the first creative writing tutor at Leeds Polytechnic. He'd had a patchy history with girlfriends. He fell for women easily, and his choices had generally been unfortunate. He was more of a romantic than a predator, and it had taken him quite a time, and some unhappiness, before he realised that Krys was different from the rest. She was Polish for a start, the youngest of six children, and daughter of an air force couple who'd stayed on in England after the war. What had attracted him at first had not been her looks but her defiance. Unlike her English counterparts she was unapologetic about everything she did. If she'd made a mistake or a misjudgement her chin would go up and her black eyes would flare like those of some dangerously wounded animal. This put a lot of people off, but for someone like Mabbut, who was good at argument but bad at confrontation, it was irresistibly appealing. So much so that he began deliberately to find fault with her work in order to provoke the desired reaction. On one occasion she had been so angry at his comments that she had demanded a personal interview with Mabbut and his superiors to discuss her grievances. Mabbut managed to steer her away from an official hearing, but agreed to meet her out of college hours to discuss it.

It turned out that her tendency to intransigence was as much of a cover as his tendency to conciliation. With five siblings, life for Krystyna had been a constant battle, as had growing up with an unspellable Polish name in a rural English village. Finding a similar taste in books and films, they began to go out together. Physical intimacy had been the very last thing to happen, but when it did it was good in a way Mabbut had not known before and he fell very deeply in love with the difficult, contrary, utterly unique

19

woman that fate had sent his way. The attraction he held for her was more enigmatic. She didn't really discuss things like that. She wasn't philosophical or particularly curious (which made her a rotten creative writer) but his considered, more thoughtful approach to things tempered her fiery nature and with him she found that there was less to be indignant about. She looked glorious on their wedding day and he felt proud, privileged and relieved that his life finally had some meaning. They had vowed to love each other as long they both should live.

Mabbut had been staring down at the ocean without really focusing, and when he raised his eyes and looked beyond the shore, he could see that the water was covered with whitecaps. A gull-wing of dark grey cloud was approaching fast from the west. It was a dramatic sight and he was tempted to sit and watch it, but he knew these Shetland storms could beat about for hours, so he stood, bracing himself for a moment against the wind, before stumbling back to the car.

By the time he had returned to Lerwick the full fury of the storm had struck the island, so he had sat in the hotel car park, turned off the engine and watched the rain as it streamed down the windscreen.

Many times since they had split up Mabbut had prodded about in his memory, trying to dig out the moment when he knew it had all gone wrong, as if that might give him the key to make sense of all the other evidence. So far he had found nothing. There were memories of angry,

20

hurtful words, even tantrums on occasion, but none of them was The One. The only explanation he could find lay in a process that, now he came to think of it, had begun as soon as they met. They had changed their behaviour to suit each other. Krystyna had become less volatile and he had become less apologetic. This had suited them for a long time, even made them pretty good parents, but at some point it had begun to turn into something negative. Krys, as he always knew, was bright, and with the chippiness rubbed off, she was also charming and popular. Once the children were at school she began to take on secretarial work, at home to start with, then later in offices. Thanks to a colleague of Mabbut's she became first secretary and then general assistant to one of the big fish in the Transport Union. From being steadily employable, she became positively sought after, working for some important committees, poached by the occasional MP with a book to write. He, on the other hand, her erstwhile teacher, had had a much more volatile career. He had made some headway as an environmental journalist, and become quite well thought of. His exposure of a water company involved in releasing toxic discharge into a local river brought him an award and some notoriety, but when he tried to follow up this success, he found many of the old doors closed. Refusing to accept that his days of exposing major scandals might be over, he became increasingly stubborn and unapologetic — ironically, the very qualities that had first attracted him to Krystyna. So their roles changed. She became the one doing the comforting, while he became increasingly unpredictable. Mabbut put it down to the fact that life had moved on, journalism had changed and people like himself, writers with a conscience, were increasingly being crowded out by interfering proprietors and pusillanimous editors. The Thatcher years had knocked the stuffing out of people. They didn't want uncomfortable exposure. They wanted consensus and job security. And, like everyone else, they wanted more things.

After many pub lunches with an ever-decreasing band of like-minded colleagues, Mabbut had convinced himself that it was time to provoke by other means. While the bills were, just about, being paid by work for newspaper supplements and company reports, his mind began to turn to his first love, fiction. He'd taught it, he'd met his wife through it, but he'd never had the self-belief to write it himself. Instead he'd been lured back to journalism, and look where he'd ended up. Now, before it was too late, it was time to correct the course of his life.

He had started working on ideas during the Shetland winter and had come up with something that had surprised and excited him. Something bold and ambitious in scope, a project that would need time and care and attention, but which, if it worked, could be breathtaking. He had made it quite clear to his agent that this time he would not compromise truth and integrity by selling himself to the highest bidder. He would use what savings he had from selling out to business to buy the time he needed to nurture this new work.

Krys, meanwhile, had begun to enjoy the rewards of her practical good sense and efficiency, and could not understand why he could not simply buckle down and do the same thing. All that he found so stifling she found both stimulating and usefully lucrative. For a while her orderly success made her tolerant of his wayward ambitions, but as the children left school and wanted things that their father could no longer afford, she found herself having to bear more and more of the burden. The money she made from her hard work should have bought her the little luxuries she saw friends and colleagues taking for granted. Instead it was now funding a mortgage on their son's flat and a university course for their daughter. It wasn't that she didn't respect her husband any more; she no longer understood him. She had settled into life. He hadn't. She demanded practicality, he pleaded creativity. It was an argument they'd had from the moment they met. It was what had brought them together. Now, twenty-five years later, it was pushing them apart.

★ ★ ★

'Shall I take that, sir?'

Mabbut looked around him. The Clickimin Suite had emptied. The girls were cleaning, wiping and re-laying tables. He finished his tea, paid his bill and with a round of farewells to the staff, stepped out of the Stratsa House Hotel and into the waiting taxi.

23

2

'I just want you to meet him.'

'You want my approval?'

There was a pause at the other end.

'I know it's difficult, Keith, but I want us always to be honest and open with each other. Otherwise we lose everything. We end up hating each other.'

Mabbut had the phone on a long line that stretched from the bay-windowed sitting room into the hall. He had been vacuuming the hall carpet when Krystyna rang, and was about to start on the stairs, which were also footprinted with Shetland mud and sand. Strictly this should have been Beryl's work, but Mabbut had dispensed with her services two months earlier, as a cost-cutting exercise. Krystyna and Beryl had been close and he hadn't as yet had the heart to tell her. Another reason for being on the defensive.

'I'm just being honest, Krys. I don't want to meet this jerk.'

'Keith, we have been living apart for nearly two years.'

'Seventeen and a half months actually.'

'We parted by mutual consent because we weren't happy together.'

'You weren't happy.'

There was a squeal of exasperation.

'Oh, please! Let's not get into all of that again,

24

or I shall have to remember all those names you called me, and all those times you weren't there when I needed you and Jay and Sam needed you.'

'I took on too much, OK? I've said I'm sorry. Someone had to bring in the money.'

'And that was me! I spent four nights a week — *after* I'd finished at the House, after I'd cooked for you all — copy-editing reports that should have been written properly in the first place, to make enough money because you . . . '

'I know, I know. But things are different now.'

'What's different, Keith?'

'I've at last got time to take on something I really want to do.'

Krystyna sounded suspicious. 'A visitors' guide to a nuclear power station?'

A low blow, which he chose to ignore. He tugged at the phone cord, which had twisted itself around the cast-iron umbrella stand that had so delighted Krystyna when she'd spotted it in a local junk shop.

'I'm going to write fiction again.'

There was a pause.

'I was good at that, remember? When I taught you.'

'You knew a lot about everyone else's work.'

Stanley, their large, lazy black cat, appeared at the top of the stairs, looking down at him. He arched his back, stretched his legs and brushed himself against the newel post. Mabbut jabbed his left foot on the off-switch. The noise from the cleaner died.

'I'm much more confident now. Fiction's what

everyone wants these days, Krys. And I've been thinking a lot about it. I've an idea that could make big money.'

'What is it?'

'A trilogy. Set at the dawn of human history, when humans began to socialise for the first time.'

'Science fiction?'

'It's *not* science fiction!' Mabbut clouted the bottom stair so hard with the cleaner-head that Stanley scampered back into one of the bedrooms. 'That's other worlds and space and ray guns. This is historical re-creation.'

'And who's bought this? Who is paying you?'

'No one's paying me yet. That's the point. I'm deliberately not settling for an advance until I've material to show. Then I'll be in a much stronger position for film rights and so on.'

He could hear a forceful exhalation at the other end of the phone.

'Keith. Sam's mortgage payments are three months behind. Jay wants her own place. Get real.'

'OK, I understand. But right now I don't see how a divorce will help.'

'Look, Keith. It's confirmation of where we are. I can't live with you and you can't live with me. I have a good job and I've met someone who cares about me and about the children and at last I have some chance of getting my life back together.'

'And what about me?'

'You'll be free to write your masterpiece without having to worry about me.'

'But I like to worry about you.'

'Look. All I'm asking is that we act like grown-ups. I can tell you lies or I can tell you the truth. The truth is that I've met someone I want to spend the rest of my life with.'

Silence.

'What's the matter?'

'That is so painful.'

'But it's the truth. What do you want me to say?'

'Anything. Just don't call it the truth.'

'He's a good man, Keith.'

'I'll take your word for it.'

'Just come and meet him.'

'I can't. I'm too busy. Honestly, Krys, I'm not interested.'

Mabbut put the phone down. His breathing was fast and short, as if he'd come up from under water.

★　★　★

'She's known him for a bit. He was an MP, I think. He's on committees, that sort of thing. She met him while she was temping.'

'I didn't know your mother was temping.'

'That's because you never bothered to ask.'

It was evening and he was at the kitchen table, absently flicking through the pages of what turned out to be yesterday's *Evening Standard*. Jay had prepared supper for the two of them, as always a little stronger on the lettuce than he would have preferred. As she moved around the table she reminded him so much of her mother.

27

Brisk, darting movements. She wore her dark hair close cropped, which suited her slim figure and accentuated her wide hazel eyes, the only feature that indicated he might be her father. He closed the paper and tossed it towards the recycling box.

'So. What's he . . . this man . . . what's he like? Her new *friend*.'

'What d'you mean?'

'Short, fat, old, young. Rastafarian.'

'Rex? He's OK.'

'*Rex?* Who calls themselves Rex these days?'

'He's about your age. Maybe older. Bit of a tummy. He was probably quite good looking once. Sam and I think he might have a false eye.'

She giggled and scooped some food from a dish.

'Plate?'

Mabbut held it out and received a dollop of something.

'Weren't there supposed to be sausages with this?'

'Sausages? You must be joking. You know I don't do sausages.'

They ate together in silence. Jay with fork in one hand, her mobile in the other.

'He's quite posh,' she added finally.

'Posh?'

'Yes, you know, he's a bit lah-di-dah. 'Awfully good' this and 'awfully good' that. Knows everybody. Sam does a great Rex.'

'Well, I'll remember that.' Mabbut sank his fork, all too easily, into something maroon and semicircular. 'If Sam ever deigns to speak to me again.'

Jay shook her head. 'Dad. What's bugging you so much? Coming back to see us all?'

'No, darling. It's just that your brother — my son — seems to have an issue about telling me anything about anything.'

'Maybe he thinks you'll disapprove.'

'Disapprove? Where does all this disapprove stuff come from? I'm just interested in what you all do.'

'That's what I mean.'

'Not in a judgemental way. I try to be encouraging. Have I ever stopped either of you from doing what you want to do?'

'You weren't exactly over the moon when Sam decided to join the drama centre.'

'And I've been proved right. Look at the people he's met there — a more terminally sullen group of miserabilists it'd be hard to find. I mean, they're supposed to be actors! They couldn't even communicate with the postman . . .'

'Couldn't even communicate with the postman!' Jay mimicked. 'God, Dad. You and Rex would get on well.'

'I'm sorry. I just want everyone to be happy, that's all.'

'We are, Dad. Sam's happy being an actor. Mum's happy with Rex and I'm happy with Shiraj.'

'Shiraj? Who's Shiraj?'

'He's a lovely, sexy, funny boy who thinks I'm the best thing that's ever happened to him.'

29

'And?'

'We're friends.'

Mabbut paused mid-mouthful.

'When did this all happen?'

'When you were up in the frozen north.'

'Where's he from, Shiraj?'

'He's Iranian.'

'That sounds interesting. Does he live here, work here?'

'Well, I wanted to ask you about that, Dad. He's looking for somewhere to live. Till he . . . till he . . . '

'What?'

'He's a refugee. He can't go back home.'

'Why not?'

'They arrested two of his brothers. The police. He managed to get out through some contact in the Foreign Office, but if he goes back then they'll arrest him too.'

'On what grounds?'

'His father's a journalist. Wrote something he shouldn't have.'

'The truth, probably.'

'You'd like him, Dad. You really would.'

Mabbut took this in. He was intrigued.

'Sounds a lot better than Rex Lah-di-dah.'

They both laughed.

'So, will you meet him? He's living on someone's floor and I'd really like to . . . well . . . help him. Soon.'

For the first time that evening, Mabbut felt better. At least someone still needed him.

'What about the day after tomorrow? Let's have dinner.'

'Thanks, Dad.'
Jay leant across and kissed him.
'And I'm glad you're back. Honestly.'

★ ★ ★

Mabbut was doing the washing up when, half an hour or so later, Jay went out, staring into her mobile as she pulled open the front door. Hands in the sink, Mabbut glanced out of the window into what passed for a back garden. At the stained and rusting trio of garden chairs, the beds that needed weeding and the bushes he should have trimmed back weeks ago. His daughter was in love. As far as he knew, for the first time.

He'd intended to spend the evening clearing emails, clearing the desk, clearing NorthOil out of his system, so that at nine o'clock the next morning he could enter his new life with seamless ease. But as he turned to climb the stairs he found himself paralysed by a sudden shock-wave of self-pity: because of Krystyna, who he was about to lose, and Mae, who he would never see again. And Jay, who'd found another man. It was a short, sharp feeling of abandonment which paralleled some distant memory. Of people walking away from him, and the fear that they would never come back. The sensation was painful enough to make him grab the banister rail and hang on to it for quite some time. When it had passed Mabbut steadied himself, breathed deeply and made his way carefully back to the sitting room. Here he picked up a half-drunk bottle of red wine and the remote control for the television and sank heavily into the sofa with a long and heartfelt sigh.

When he awoke the bottle was empty. On the television two politicians were being grilled about plans to extend an airport, in a studio that looked like a military command centre. One MP insisted categorically that it was a very good thing as, all in all, the bigger the airport, the less its overall environmental impact. On a huge screen behind him appeared the words 'Less Environmental Impact'. His opponent argued categorically that it was a very bad thing as the bigger the airport the more people would die from the effects of pollution. The huge screen switched to 'More Deaths from Pollution'. After some searching, Mabbut located the remote under a cushion and flicked off the television.

He sat for a while, taking in the room in which he and Krystyna had shared so much of their life. He remembered the running argument about where the sofa should go, Krystyna adamant that it belonged in the bay, he equally adamant that it should face the window so you could see out. Which had brought up the whole question of what there was to see. To him, Reserton Road N19, a modest street of three-storey Edwardian terraces with brick walls, white-stuccoed window surrounds and steep roofs with pointed gable ends had been a great find, and he was happy that he had acquired such a place in an area that had not become too posh or gentrified. For Krystyna this was exactly the problem. In her pragmatic Polish way she could not understand why anyone would want to live in Reserton Road N19 if there were half a chance of living somewhere posh and gentrified. For Mabbut, North Holloway was somewhere he would be perfectly happy to spend the rest of his life. For Krystyna it was a low rung on the ladder of advancement. Which is why she preferred to have the sofa with its back to the view. In the end they had compromised and the sofa presently stood at right angles to the window.

Opposite the sofa was an old pine sideboard. On top of it were gathered all the old family photos. Mabbut's eye fell on them now. In one Sam, eight or nine maybe, was being squeezed by Krystyna, with Jay on her other knee, pouting stagily. Next to this photograph, in a silver frame badly in need of a polish, was a more formal study: Krystyna in a long black dress at the Dorchester, arm tight around him as he clutched the phallic plastic flame that was the British Gas Award for Environmental Journalism. Behind that, as if in the background, was a picture of Rita and Graham, his mother and father, taken on one of their trips.

When his dad had retired from what used to be called the Egg Marketing Board Rita had galvanised him into action. They had become role models for the Saga generation: walking the Pennine Way, the Pembroke Coast Path and Offa's Dyke in the same year. Maybe she'd known there was a problem ahead, but she never let on and appeared to be as shocked as they all were when his father's illness was discovered. In

33

his last year this sparky, irritable man was reduced to being a spectator of his own decline. With his sister Lucy in Australia, the filial responsibility had fallen almost entirely to Mabbut. Ironically, he'd been inspired by his parents' sense of adventure to try to see more of the world himself. But just when his agent landed him a juicy, reputation-restoring commission from the *Sunday Times* to cover the Arianca dam project in Argentina his dad had entered the last, long-drawn-out stages of his cancer. There could be no question of his leaving home. Looking back now, it was not his father's death as much as his mother's sudden, completely unexpected deterioration soon afterwards that cost Mabbut the momentum he needed, and sent him instead into the arms of big business.

He stared for a while at Rita and Graham. They smiled back at him, the hoods of their anoraks ever so slightly raised by the breeze. They both wore expressions of such irrepressible cheerfulness that he allowed himself to feel a pang of jealousy that they had come through their working lives to find such a place of contentment.

3

The next morning, much to his surprise, Mabbut awoke without any of his usual anxieties; his mind was clear and he felt an extraordinary sense of liberation. Duty done, money earned, he was at last free to begin what really mattered to him. What, at some deeply needy level, had mattered to him since he had first looked at a book. To write stories. To be a writer of fiction. This was the first day of a new life, the day when an imagination cooped up for far too long could break free at last.

Mabbut's story was based on the premise that when man first emerged from Africa a tribe had split from the rest and mated with the very last of a line of trans-terrestrial beings. They had adapted so well to their surroundings that in a few generations they had developed an extraordinary and sophisticated way of life, and as they were far from the main migratory routes they were able to build a sort of prehistoric Shangri La, safe, secure, harmonious and progressive. This was the land of Albana, where a moral code based on co-operation and conciliation had evolved and where violence had no place. Then came the day when this haven was discovered by the outside world and the people of Albana had to learn cunning and cruelty to survive. They became, in time, a feared and destructive people. But two or three escaped and made their way through astonishing perils to keep alive the Ancient Truths, the arcane knowledge of Albana.

In his tiny study, off the landing at the top of the stairs, Mabbut drew up the blind and welcomed in the chilly morning light. He settled himself at the computer, interlocked the fingers of both hands, then sipped the remains of his coffee, cleaned his glasses, blew his nose, eased a blackberry pip from between his two front teeth, sighed heavily and began. And that's when the phone rang.

In later years he wondered whether, if he'd turned the phone off as he'd intended to, all the things that subsequently happened to him would have happened at all.

Out of habit he picked up the receiver. There was a pause, a pause long enough for Mabbut to know exactly what sort of pause this was and whack the phone down before anyone could start to sell him anything. The phone rang again, almost immediately. This time there was no pause.

'You just put the phone down on me.'

'How was I to know it was you? You didn't say anything.'

'You didn't give me a chance.'

'You don't usually need a chance.'

'I'm ringing with the best news of your life and you put the phone down on me.'

'I thought you were trying to sell me something.'

'I am, dear boy, I am. And when you hear what it is, you'll want to buy it.'

Mabbut's glance was caught by a movement

outside the window. From within the cloud of ivy that covered his neighbour's wall, a fox appeared, withdrew, then reappeared, this time sloping off along the wall and dropping down into the garden next door.

'I've just started the novel.'

'We need to talk. Lunch?'

Mabbut adjusted his chair.

'It's a trilogy. I can't take breaks.'

'Goldings at one?'

'Look, this has to be something hugely important. It's my first day. Lose this and my whole — '

'It could be hugely important. Trust me, Keith. Would I lightly take an author away from his book?'

★ ★ ★

The bus dropped Mabbut by the university and he cut through past the electronic showrooms and the Yum Yum Sushi House until he found himself outside the familiar green door of Goldings Dining Room. It was always a surprise to find it still there, with its bland façade of green-painted panels, and its name scrawled in italics, like a signature. It was warm enough today for two spindly tables to have been squeezed on to the pavement. He found his agent inside, at a table as far away from the sun as possible. She was ensconced with her mobile phone and a glass of red wine. She acknowledged Mabbut distractedly, and carried on talking.

Mabbut smiled at the Croatian waitress, a strikingly beautiful girl who he sensed was unhappy.

'Red?' she asked, glancing at Silla's half-empty glass.

'Better not.'

The waitress shrugged and gave that awkward sideways grimace which was the only thing Mabbut didn't adore about her.

'I've started my new book. Don't want to lose concentration,' he explained.

She laid a mat on the table and looked up at him.

'What is it about?'

'It's about the first men on earth.'

The waitress frowned.

'And women?'

'Yes, yes, of course. Women too.'

There was a pause, as if everything that needed to be said on the subject had been said.

'What you want, then?'

'Coke, please, Martina.'

Silla, ear still clamped to the phone, shook her head vigorously, wagged her finger and mouthed 'wine'.

He shook his head.

'No, not today.'

Silla repeated the gesture, this time overriding Mabbut and appealing straight to the waitress. By the time Keith had protested again the glass was on the table in front of him. The Croatian gave one of her inexplicable but deeply appealing half-smiles.

'The special of the day is rigatoni.'

She turned away.

Silla Caldwell covered the phone and hissed at him.

'Sit down. Stop hovering!'

Mabbut smiled grimly and pulled out a chair, grating it almost deliberately along the unevenly tiled floor.

His relationship with Priscilla Caldwell went back twenty years to the days when he had, for a short time, been one to watch. Indeed, he had appeared in the 'Ones To Watch' list attached to a Sunday newspaper article about a new, fearless breed of journalists, none of whom anyone could remember now. Silla liked young men with radical tendencies, and despite the fact that she was Home Counties metropolitan and he a wary Northerner they'd always got along pretty well. She had done her best to nurture his investigative tendencies, but when the well had dried up she'd used her contacts to find him work in the steady if unspectacular world of company commissions. Mabbut was not success-ful enough to claim her whole attention and she was not close enough to him to be part of the rest of his life. On this basis, their chummy but undemanding relationship had ticked along nicely. Until today, when Mabbut sensed that something had changed. Her big green eyes were wider than usual and her sturdy, broad features betrayed an unfamiliar bounce. Silla was excited.

She laid her phone on the table, throwing it a meaningful glance as she did so.

'That was Ron Latham.'

He frowned.

'Ron Latham. Urgent Books. Used to be with Waddilow and Bowler until they became Herald and Barker. Did the Flapjacks.'

Mabbut knew the name, but from the business, not the literary, pages.

'He's one of the biggest players now. Stacks of money behind him.'

Mabbut's eyes narrowed. Silla clinked her glass against his with such abandon that it was clear it wasn't her first.

'And he's after you.'

'What for?'

But Silla was off again, leafing through the menu then waving at the waitress.

'Let's order,' she barked.

They both chose the day's special. He drank his glass of wine and half the bottle she later ordered. She remained almost coquettishly mysterious about the matter in hand, and only politely interested as he expanded on his novel, so they talked about this and that, and a small fight outside the Spanish club farther down the street provided some unexpected entertainment. An hour later Silla switched on her phone, and kissed him briefly.

'I'll see you tomorrow morning.'

'Look, Silla, you've torpedoed my first day on *Albana* — '

'On what?'

'*Albana*. The *novel*! Remember?'

Silla pushed back her chair and stood up, smiling crisply.

'Not a good title, by the way.'

She waved the bill.

'Albania or Nirvana. You can't have both. Excuse me!'

The lovely Croatian switched off her mobile and came towards them.

'It's a working title.'

'We had one bottle of water. The rest was tap, I think.'

Mabbut persisted. 'I can't let you sabotage my second day.'

'There. Two San Pellegrinos. We only had one.'

The waitress looked down at the bill for some time, as if trying to decipher ancient runes.

'OK. I change.'

Silla reached for her coat.

'The life of a writer is unlike any other, Keith. It's lonely, it's unpredictable, it's blown by the winds.'

'So?'

'A writer's mind must never be closed. It's his duty to be curious and my duty to feed that curiosity. Think of it as the start of a big adventure.'

She gave him a brisk, breathy hug.

'Meeting's at eleven. Pick you up at ten.'

'I'll take the Tube.'

She frowned.

'They're in darkest Southwark, darling.'

For Silla public transport was a foreign country. She shook her hair, pulled on a beret and smiled reassuringly.

'I'll send Hector.'

Which was exactly why Mabbut had suggested taking the Tube.

4

Silla Caldwell was one of the few writer's agents who still employed a driver. This was partly to do with an old-fashioned concern over image and partly because a year or so previously she'd totalled her own car after a carafe too many with a Swedish thriller writer. No one had been hurt and it was quite likely she would have got away with it had the car she'd hit not had a policeman in it. With a deftly mixed cocktail of charm and remorse Silla had avoided public opprobrium and all who knew her reckoned she'd been very lucky indeed. Apart from the loss of a colourfully eccentric Alfa Spyder, the only real penalty she'd incurred was the arrival of Hector Fischer in her life.

And it was Hector Fischer's large, close-shaven, ever so slightly perspiring head that Mabbut could see from the back of the BMW as they sat becalmed in the Russell Square one-way system.

'She was no good for him,' Hector insisted, in his menacing Austrian accent. 'No good for him at all.'

Silla was deep in a phone call, so Mabbut felt duty bound to respond.

'So what did he do?'

Hector's eyes flicked up to the mirror and focused on Mabbut, like someone peering into a house through the letter box.

'What did he do? What would *you* do?'

The traffic edged forward. Keith, whose attention had wandered during the early part of the story, shook his head equivocally.

'I've no idea.'

'You've no *idea*! A woman you've helped out of the gutter turns and spits on you, and you've no *idea*!'

Fischer braked sharply to avoid killing a frail elderly person who was making their way over a designated crossing.

'I tell you what I would do,' he shouted over the blast of his car horn. 'I would have kicked her out and changed the locks! That would be my idea of what to do!'

They turned into Doughty Street. When he'd first arrived in London, Mabbut had come down here to pay homage to Charles Dickens, who'd lived and worked in one of these houses.

'Every time she sobbed a tear and shook her bum he took her back. 'Oh it's OK! Don't worry! I'll look after you! Put your head on my shoulder. There!''

After all these years, the amount of history in a single London street was still something to marvel at.

'I would have said there was only one place for that head. On the block!' Hector chuckled grimly and accelerated towards a traffic-calming platform ahead of them.

'On the block!' he repeated with satisfaction.

Silla finished one call and started another. Mabbut decided to feign sleep.

Urgent Books occupied the first two floors of an old tobacco warehouse on the south bank of the river between Southwark and London Bridge. It had been brusquely converted for a quick sale at the height of the property boom and despite its cast-iron columns and sturdy brick walls the change of use had rendered it virtually indistinguishable from a host of similar commercial developments which had sterilised a once quirky riverside.

Automatic glass doors gave access to a wide open-plan reception area, a curious conjunction of marble tiled floor and whitewashed brick walls. A curving glass staircase led up to a gallery and a bank of lifts serving the upper floors. Mabbut and Silla were halfway up the stairs when a wiry, athletic man strode out on to the balcony above. Silla waved. He nodded back at her with a wink that could have been a twitch. Or just a wink.

Ron Latham didn't fit any preconceived idea Mabbut had of a publisher. He had very black curly hair and an almost unnaturally clear complexion, such as you might see on a waxwork. His shirt was collarless, and worn tucked into snug-fitting black jeans. He wore a pair of rimless glasses, so thin that they almost could be mistaken for part of his skull. His age could have been anything between twenty-five and forty-five. He greeted Silla with a kiss and Mabbut with a firm grip from a surprisingly soft hand.

'Ron Latham. I'm the CEO. Everyone calls me Ron.'

He smiled mirthlessly and led them through an open-plan office, past twenty or thirty consoles from which no one looked up. At the far end was the only room with a proper door: steel with a hardwood finish. Latham held it open and beckoned them into a conference room with a wide picture window overlooking the Thames. Mabbut caught sight of a train rumbling over the bridge to Cannon Street station before Latham pressed a remote control and blinds clicked into place.

'Sorry. Bit bright. Coffee?'

A complete breakfast had been laid out at one end of the glass-topped conference table. Latham poured coffee and stretched his arm out over the spread.

'There's juice and pastries. Croissants. Whatever you want.'

He didn't make it sound tempting.

Latham and Silla talked a little of mutual friends and the ups and downs of the market. The two of them seemed comfortable together. Mabbut looked about him. At one end of the room stood an easel from which hung sheets of paper, ruffled almost imperceptibly by the softly humming air con.

Considering this was a publishing house, there were very few books to be seen. Maybe this was the shape of the future. The world on a screen. Mabbut was old fashioned in these matters. He used a mobile and a computer, neither very competently, but when he was on the road his

45

first point of contact remained his notebook and pencil.

As he reached for a croissant, Mabbut caught Latham's eye. Latham smiled crisply, professionally. Maybe he was nervous too, for when he spoke it was with a touch of unconvincing matiness.

'I've known Priscilla since she worked the show-biz pages at the Chronicle group. I like her, because she's always gone her own way. Never followed the herd.'

Mabbut was about to reach for the butter, but thought better of it.

'So when this came along, she was the first person we went to for a recommendation.'

Mabbut looked across at his agent. Her expression gave no hint of her trademark hard-nosed scepticism. Instead she stared back at him with a look of bright anxiety, like a mother who was taking her child to the doctor.

Latham finished his coffee and put his cup back on the table. He smiled.

'She thought of you.'

'For what, exactly?' asked Mabbut.

'Something quite exciting.'

Latham indicated a row of chairs and at the press of a remote control, a screen purred down from the ceiling.

'This is super-confidential, but it'll give you some idea of what we're after.'

He flicked the remote and the room darkened. Suddenly the screen was illuminated and an arresting image appeared, a figure walking from left to right across what looked like stony scrub

46

in some hot country. The camera zoomed in and revealed an imposing middle-aged to elderly man with a mane of thick greying hair.

Mabbut recognised the man even before the title caption came up.

'Hamish Melville,' intoned a sententious voice-over. 'Aged seventy-five. Anthropologist and activist.' A series of close-ups showed a large head and a strong face with eyes deep set beneath the brow, as if they were peering out from the mouth of a cave. The face was not so much handsome — the nose and cheekbones were too prominent for that — as it was mesmerising; the way John the Baptist looked in Renaissance paintings, an impression strengthened by hair worn long and tangled. Various film clips followed. Usually shot on the move, with Melville striding through the bush, or surrounded by a group of tiny tribal people, or, in one case, sitting cross-legged with a group of fellow protesters in front of a police line. Place names clicked up on the screen: Bangladesh, Brazil, Borneo. All the environmental hot spots.

The presentation was clinical and factual, but to Mabbut it was fascinating stuff. In an age of universal access Hamish Melville remained an enigmatic maverick. The Action Man of the environmental movement. Mabbut was familiar with the background. The cancellation of the million-dollar Puerto Jainca dam project and the saving of the Akwambe lands in the Niger delta were just two of Melville's successes, yet the man himself was famously reclusive. He rarely gave interviews and when he did they were more

47

likely to be for a school magazine than a national broadsheet. Apart from his hit-and-run campaigns, his legendary influence on everything from conflict resolution to economic development stemmed from two books and the occasional address, delivered, more often than not, to a convention of rickshaw drivers rather than a UN assembly. For journalists of Mabbut's generation this combination of the inspirational and the subversive was a constant source of speculation. They admired and envied Melville's unique ability to stay out of the headlines and yet remain extraordinarily effective in pricking consciences. To see these glimpses of the great man — working on a farm, riding a train, swimming and laughing in some frighteningly turbulent river — was almost like watching footage of some old communist icon.

The last sequence was quite different. It was a montage of maybe a dozen shots of Melville in urban locations, caught on what looked like a CCTV camera, leaving an airport, entering a building, on the steps of a government facility, shaking hands with movers and shakers. In some of them Melville wore a suit. In one, getting into a large car, with security men holding the door, he was carrying a briefcase. On this last, incongruous image, the commentary drew to a conclusion. 'Who is the real Melville? And where does his power lie? *Melville. The True Story.* An Urgent exclusive. Coming to you next Christmas.'

The words faded and slowly the lights came up. Latham reached for the remote. The screen ascended, disappearing soundlessly into the ceiling. Almost simultaneously the blinds folded back and daylight flooded the room.

'That's interesting stuff,' Mabbut murmured. He glanced towards Silla. 'But why are we . . . er . . . why are we watching Hamish Melville home movies?'

Latham raised his immaculately trimmed eyebrows.

'More coffee?'

Mabbut shook his head. Latham stood, refilled his own cup, added sugar, glanced briefly towards the door then turned back again.

'We, that is, Urgent Books, want to commission a book on Melville. Everyone loves him, everyone respects him. He's admired all over the world. By the people whose land he saves, by the conservationists and the ecologists, as well as a hell of a lot of people who don't agree with what he's saying, but like the way he says it. *And* he has an international profile.'

Latham walked towards the window, stirring his coffee.

'He isn't government, he isn't UN. He's not a bureaucrat or a politician. He's never accepted an honour or a medal. He's one of the last of an almost extinct species — the free spirit, the lone wolf. The guy who does what he thinks is right and argues about it afterwards. He's an inspiration to some, a bloody nuisance to others. Yet the real Hamish Melville is a mystery. We know jackshit about the man himself. How he lives, works, operates. What he really wants to achieve. That's the gap we want to fill.'

Latham turned and looked at Mabbut.

'And?'

'And we want you to fill it.'

This was so completely not what he'd expected that at first Mabbut could come up with no reaction at all. He needed a moment to decode the complex mix of excitement and unease that had suddenly come over him.

'*Me?*' Aware that his voice sounded shrill, he paused and came down an octave. 'I mean, why me?'

'As you can imagine, Melville isn't the sort of man for a celebrity biog or a memoir. He'd run a mile from a star performer. He'd sniff out anyone with an agenda. It's happened before. Good journalists, top writers have tried to get close and failed miserably.'

'So why would I be different?' asked Mabbut.

Latham moved towards him. He was talking faster now, like someone homing in on a target.

'Silla's filled me in on you, Mabbut, and I hope you won't mind me saying this, but you don't carry any intimidating baggage with you. You're not a celebrity, your name is hardly a household word. Your . . . ' His brow furrowed momentarily. 'Your record is solid but unspectacular. Even, possibly, a little dull. But you can write. She's shown me your stuff and it's fine.'

Somewhere behind him, Mabbut heard his agent clear her throat. Latham continued.

'You've been a journalist. You know about deadlines. You know about sources. And environment is your thing. You exposed that water company. You're used to working under the radar. But most of all, Priscilla tells me you're basically an honest man, a straight guy. Someone we could depend on.'

Keith stole a glance at Silla. She smiled back. But he wanted more than that. Some guidance, for God's sake, as to how he should be dealing with all this.

Latham pulled out a chair and sat down close to Mabbut.

'We'll make it worth your while, of course.'

Mabbut felt claustrophobic. He didn't like this place, he didn't like this man, and he had been in the business long enough to know that publishing houses were not charities.

'But we're not a charity, Mr Mabbut. Your part of the deal is to produce the book, start to finish, in six months flat.'

Mabbut felt a rising panic.

'I'm writing a novel . . . '

'The company wants this to be one of our lead titles for next Christmas, so I need it by April at the latest. For legal checks, rights sales and so on. And I will need complete confidentiality. If anyone asks, you're writing an overview of environmental movements.'

'But I'm writing a novel,' Mabbut repeated.

Latham leant closer to him.

'What's really important is that you look at every aspect of the man. I mean *every* aspect. We don't want a fanzine, Mabbut. We want the truth.'

Latham stood. He repositioned his chair carefully at the table. A martinet, thought Mabbut, not bright but neat. Likes things just so.

'Silla and I can discuss the details.'

Ron Latham extended his hand to Mabbut, and they made their way to the door.

'Good to meet you, Keith.'

Mabbut wanted to get his thoughts in order, to express clearly and unequivocally what his position was, but he couldn't think how to do it. Nor, it seemed, was he going to be given the opportunity. He gave a last, instinctive look towards Silla. She nodded back eagerly.

'Call you,' she said, half standing and motioning towards the exit.

Latham was already at the door, holding it open for him.

'I hope you're as excited as we are.'

5

The glass doors of the Urgent building quietly slid shut behind him. Mabbut stood in the small brick plaza. Around him office workers were occupying the steps and unpacking lunches. He felt confused. Out of place. A purposeless man in a purposeful world. He turned left, then right, heading instinctively towards the river. When he reached Bankside he picked his way through the cross-current of ambling tourists and keen-eyed joggers and found the reassurance of a bulky granite wall. He leant out over the parapet and looked at the river. It was high tide and a stiff breeze was sloshing the water about. The horn of a passing barge blasted out, like an elephant in pain.

Mabbut stared across the river, his eyes moving east to west across the oddly assorted clumps of buildings that made up the north bank. Hardly welcoming. The towers of the City held their own secrets. The ivy-clad walls of the Inns of Court protected their inmates from curious glances. The smooth stone bulk of the Ministry of Defence and the carved and curlicued Houses of Parliament, accessible only by special pass, took up another half-mile of London's private riverside.

A pair of runners thudded by behind him.

Cities, he thought, especially capitals, give the impression of being open and busy and full of people going here, there and everywhere, but at heart they're closed, conspiratorial places. He knew this because at one time it had been his job to prise out information from behind the high walls, to infiltrate the defences of impenetrable institutions and find someone somewhere who was accountable. At one stage his zeal had been ambitious, almost evangelical, until he over-stepped the mark. Called powerful people liars, paid informers inside the company, showed that good, decent people with families, friends and Masonic colleagues had been prepared to tolerate bad practice rather than frighten their shareholders.

As far as Mabbut was concerned his ends had always justified his means. Looking back now, the award he'd won for the water story probably hadn't helped. It had stirred envies, made him look smug and self-righteous in some people's eyes. It certainly made people close ranks against him. But he had been a good journalist, that was for sure, and he had bitterly resented having to make do with crumbs: corporate vanity projects, official histories, publicity puffs of one kind or another. Writing a book about Hamish Melville sounded too good to be true, and that was what worried him. Why would a sleek, smooth, plausible man like Ron Latham have any interest in an iconoclast such as Melville? And the other thing that really rankled was the way the two of them, especially his own fucking agent, for God's sake, had dismissed the novel. Well, he'd prove them wrong. *Albana* distilled what he had wanted to say for so long. In *Albana* the big

54

issues would take centre stage, and the piffling cover-ups and compromises of modern life would be put firmly in their place. It would be a big story on a big canvas. Universal and compassionate. Saying everything he wanted to say. No compromise needed.

His phone rang. Silla sounded breathless. She was obviously on the move.

'Where are you?'

'I just took a walk, along the river.'

'Good news. Ron likes you.'

'How could you tell?'

'What?'

'How can you tell what a robot thinks?'

'Don't be frivolous. All I've got to do now is iron out a few contract details, and I'm pretty sure you've got the job!'

'Silla, Silla. Slow down. Who says I *want* the job?'

There was a pause on the other end of the line.

'What d'you mean? What else are you going to do?'

'I have a novel to write!'

'Your science fiction thing?'

Mabbut aimed a kick at the wall. 'It's *not* science fiction, it's historical re-creation. Documentary drama.'

'But it's still fiction. This is for real, Keith. And, what's more, I think I can get you real money for it!'

Mabbut looked down. At his feet, a pigeon, quite oblivious to the passing crowds, was worrying away at a stub of discarded falafel.

'Silla, I told you what I want to do now. You may not have listened, but I did tell you. I don't want to be a hired gun any more. I have my own plans and I've taken the decision to concentrate all my time on my novel. This is the only way I will ever produce anything of my own. If Urgent like me that much then let's talk to them about *Albana*. An advance wouldn't hurt.'

Somewhere in the background he heard Hector's raised voice. Silla giving instructions. A door slamming. Then her voice, again, a little muffled at first.

'Keith, are you still there?'

'I'm here.'

'There is no way that I am going to get a penny for a science fiction story.'

'It's not — '

'But if I can get what I think I can get for the Melville book, you can write whatever you like for the rest of your life. *Shit!*'

He heard a squeal of brakes, the blast of a horn and a cry of anger.

'Sorry. Red light. Man in front being pedantic. Look, I'm your agent, Keith. My job is to get you work. And believe me, that has not always been easy. Now I'm just inches away from the best deal I've ever got for you, and I am not going to walk away from it. I took you on because I knew you were good. This is your chance to prove it. There is no 'either or' here. This is a great deal. Trust me.'

The phone went dead. Mabbut slipped it into his pocket, pulled up the collar of his coat and set off in the direction of London Bridge station.

56

When he got home, Mabbut checked for phone messages. There were none. He made himself a plate of toast and a cup of coffee, which he carried back up to his study. Having put down a bowl of fresh water for Stanley and wondered, not for the first time, if his cat might be hydrophiliac, Mabbut settled at the keyboard and, adjusting his chair to Position Three — straight back, forward tilt — he set to work detailing the physical appearance of Albana, the world that would confront the first men as they emerged on to the wide and windswept plateau on which their lives would be played out. He enjoyed conjuring up the vista of hard limestone stacks, crumbling gullies and wind-worn cliffs still bearing the scars of some mighty eruption.

For at least twenty minutes the images spilled as fluently into his mind as if he were describing the walks he used to take with his father round Ingleborough and Malham Tarn. Then he realised that he was indeed describing the walks he took round Ingleborough and Malham Tarn and not south-eastern Turkey, where his story was putatively set. Rather than delete everything he'd just written Mabbut reasoned that there might have been a time when southeastern Turkey could well have resembled Ingleborough and Malham Tarn, and in any case, who would know? There was one further problem. When at last he came to name this great forbidding wasteland, his original thought of calling it Da-Naa sounded all wrong. Like a holiday beach

57

in Thailand. What he needed was something with more resonance, something both epic and evil. Mordor had just the right ring to it. Which was probably why Tolkien had come up with it in the first place.

Once Tolkien had come into his mind, Mabbut froze up completely. Middle Earth was a no-go area for him. That way fantasy lay, and he simply mustn't let himself be led down that insidious path. All right, there were similarities between his vision and Tolkien's, but Tolkien was old hat. *Albana* was certainly about the struggle between good and evil, oppression and independence, but it was about so much more besides. After some thought he rechristened the wilderness Uyea, and hoped that no one would know it was one of the Shetland Islands.

It was late afternoon when he finally admitted defeat. He rubbed his eyes and stared out of the window, which needed a clean. He was letting the house go. Krys would never have allowed it to get this far. He stood up, stretched and looked down at his work. This time yesterday morning, he was embarking on something strange and unpredictable, but at least it was a work of fiction. Thirty-six hours later what was strange and unpredictable was his own life. His wife had a man, his daughter had an Iranian refugee and he had an offer to write a Christmas book about a living legend. Yesterday's certainties had become today's confusions. What he needed was someone to talk to.

He wanted to ring Krystyna, but that would involve all the other stuff. The same with Jay.

Sam would be at the theatre. He could suggest a late supper, build a few bridges. Yes, that was an idea. Father asks son for advice. A way to start talking again. He took out his phone and scrolled through the names. Then he stopped, scrolled forward, and after the briefest of hesitations, pressed once and pressed again.

'Hello, Tess.'

6

Tessa was Mabbut's secret. And as far as he knew, he was hers. They'd met on a night bus about six months ago. After a noisy Irish couple had got off at Highbury Corner, they'd been the only two left upstairs. They'd smiled at one another as the noise of the raucously arguing couple receded down the stairs. Vibrating from that nano-second of contact they'd sat there, separate but aware, as five stops went by. All the way up the Holloway Road, past the Emirates stadium, under the bridge that carried the East Coast railway line, past the Odeon cinema on one side and the Beaux-Arts building on the other, both staring straight ahead. As he stood to get off, she'd stood too. It had almost felt choreographed as he followed her downstairs, and stood waiting behind her as the stop approached, the warning signal bleeped and the doors folded open.

They'd fallen in step with each other and began to talk as if it were the most natural thing in the world. He found out that she'd been celebrating a colleague's birthday at a club in Leicester Square. She found out he'd been at a quiz night at a pub in Clerkenwell. As they turned off the main road, he had followed her to the door of a four-storey block of council flats.

Nine times out of ten, maybe even ninety-nine times out of a hundred, this would have been a very silly thing to do, but it turned out to be so easy and uncomplicated that neither of them could see a reason not to do it again. Their relationship was undemanding. It was of the here and now. They enquired very little about each other's past. He knew she was about five years younger than him, divorced, with one grown-up child who was living in the northwest. She worked part-time at a children's nursery and led a busy social life. He was fairly sure he wasn't her only partner, which was quite a comfort. Outside of sex, their lives remained completely separate.

It shouldn't really have happened, and it certainly shouldn't have lasted, but here he was, six months on, turning off the main road towards her apartment building, because she was the only person he wanted to be with right now. Even Mae Lennox, whom he dreamt about on a weekly basis, wouldn't have been the one for him tonight. He needed the welcome embrace of anonymity.

Tess's voice crackled out of the intercom. 'Come on up.'

And the metal gate swung open.

* * *

Tessa enjoyed the physical side of things. She was well built, a little overweight, but in good shape for her age. For her, sex was like a playground, full of different rides; some breathtaking, to be enjoyed with yelps and shrieks, others more traditional, but all to be tried at

61

least once. Her small bedroom was cluttered with knick-knacks: mugs from Ramsgate, Eiffel towers, polar bears and royal wedding teacups. Russian dolls, wooden puzzles, miniature candlesticks and little rubber elephants, all of which could be sent flying in the course of a night.

When Mabbut awoke, light was coming through the curtains. He lay for a while, wondering what it was about this room and this woman that seemed so necessary to him. He concluded that it was because he could walk away and come back whenever he wanted. There were no expectations and therefore no consequences. And no lies. He dozed briefly until his mobile sounded. The first bars of Beethoven's Fifth jangled beside him. It was just after eight in the morning.

Mabbut reached for the phone and swung himself out of the bed.

'Hello?'

'Am I interrupting the creative flow?'

He walked out into the living room.

'Very funny.'

'Things are moving fast. A contract's arrived. I don't want to keep these boys waiting.'

Silla was in steamroller mode.

'Can you come in, dear boy? If at all possible.'

She laid on the sardonicism.

'After you've been to the hairdresser perhaps? Before the gym? Maybe combine it with a visit to the chiropodist?'

'Just a minute.'

He searched around for his clothes.

'I'd like to get it signed. It's quite a lot of money.'

'Ah!'

Mabbut winced with pain as his foot made contact with a tiny glass rabbit.

'Are you with somebody?'

'No, I'm just . . . I've just put the milk on. Hang on a minute.'

'Only I rang the house and you weren't there.'

'No. I went to see Sam last night and stayed at his place.'

'How was it?'

'What?'

'The play.'

'Oh, it was good. You should go and see it.'

She lowered her voice.

'The contract is looking good. Best I've seen in a while. But it has confidentiality clauses hanging on it like a Christmas tree, so just for now keep schtoom. Even with Sam, all right?'

'Oh, sure! *Sure!*'

'If you could make it here in an hour or so. There are things we need to discuss, and though I love Ron dearly, he's not renowned for his patience.'

'Look, Silla. We have to talk about this.'

'OK. In an hour. My place. And say 'hi' to Sam.'

The phone went dead.

Tess called out from the bathroom.

'Another admirer?'

Mabbut peeped through the curtains. Outside he could see children playing, or hanging about.

'My agent!'

He heard the toilet flush, and a moment later Tess joined him, piling up her long red hair as she walked.

'Something exciting?'

'I must get dressed.'

'Don't be so formal.'

He made to sidestep her but she was too quick for him.

'I do breakfast, you know.'

Mabbut was enveloped.

'Tess, I promised I'd be at my agent's in half an hour.'

He felt her warmth as she pulled him close.

'Look, I've got to get — '

'They're over there.'

She indicated his clothes, heaped on the red armchair like a small deflated pyramid, then stood back and finished pinning up her hair.

'It was nice of you to call last night. I was beginning to think you'd lost the spirit of bachelorhood.'

Mabbut pulled on his underpants and reached for his shirt. As he started to button it up, a thought struck him and he paused.

'Can I ask you something, Tess?'

She eyed him cautiously. 'Try me.'

'D'you read a lot?'

She put her head to one side.

'Try to. So?'

'When you do,' he said, sitting down on the chair and rooting around for his socks, 'do you prefer fact or fiction?'

'Oh, fiction every time. I hate facts.'

64

'Why?'

'Facts are just facts.' She shrugged dismissively. 'They don't amount to a row of beans. If you want the truth, read Jane Austen.'

7

Mabbut got off at Queensway on the Central Line, checked his watch and walked to the nearest coffee shop. As he stood in line for a *macchiato* he looked at the customers sitting at their tables: one or two alone, reading or staring at their phones, a couple holding hands, a group gathered around a laptop. All much younger than him, most of them preoccupied. What would excite them most? To know more about Hamish Melville or to be transported back sixty thousand years to the dawn of human history?

He sat down and sipped his coffee. Usually after a night with Tess he felt good. Comfortable, adjusted, whole. This morning something was troubling him and he couldn't quite put his finger on what it was. He watched through the window as a telephone engineer, protected by a screen of red and white fencing, opened a terminal box and systematically worked his way through the cables inside. Mabbut observed him with a certain amount of envy. This was a man at work. Doing a job, tracing a problem, dealing with it, ticking it off on a worksheet and moving on to the next one. His tasks for the day were quantifiable, definable, achievable. If only writing could be that simple.

★   ★   ★

Priscilla Caldwell Associates operated out of Silla's flat in a mansion block off Bayswater Road. Apart from some secretarial help three days a week, she ran the business herself from her kitchen table. This morning she was as animated as Mabbut had ever seen her. She almost skipped as she opened the door, phone to her ear, nodding agreement as she led him through her timber-floored sitting room with its eclectic mix of Corbusier chairs, leather sofas and pine dressers, to a long refectory table spread with sheaves of paper. With one last nod and a grunt of acknowledgement she clicked off the phone.

Her big eyes appraised him.

'Sorry to ring you so early.'

Mabbut detected a dusting of disapproval in her voice.

'I've managed to get a good deal from Latham. A very good deal. And I'd like to pin this down before their feet start to chill.'

She took a wine gum from a bowl, then pushed it towards him.

'Look, Silla, you may have decided about this, but I haven't.'

She made no appearance of having heard what he said. Instead, she licked her index finger and began to flick through one of the documents on the table.

'Silla, listen to me. I have made a plan for next year and it doesn't include Ron Latham or Urgent Books.'

His mobile buzzed. He glanced down. It was a text from Jay.

*Where were u Dad? We were supposed 2 have
dinner, right?*

Oh God, he'd completely forgotten. And why?
Because his new reordered life had been fucked
up by Ron Latham.

Silla selected one of the sheaf of papers and
held it out to him.

'Contract. In less than two days, what I'd
normally have to wait two months for.'

He took it from her.

She stabbed a finger at the pages he was
holding.

'Sixty thousand on signature, sixty thousand
on delivery and sixty on publication. And I'm
trying to push them into some kind of cut of
foreign rights. They think they can sell this
worldwide.'

Mabbut's head ached and his mouth had gone
dry. On his contracts 'Sixty thousand' usually
meant the number of words.

'What's the catch?'

She shrugged and pushed back a lock of hair.

'Must be delivered in six months max, direct
interview material from Melville himself, and
quite a tough little rider about publisher's
approval. But you're new and Latham's paying
you well. You'd expect them to protect
themselves.'

'Protect me. Tell them we need more time. Tell
them six months is impossible.'

'I don't think that's a good idea,' said Silla,
drily.

'I'll need to check this, Silla. I need to check it
carefully.'

'Since when did you check a contract?'

This hurt. It had been so long since there'd been a contract worth him checking. Silla softened.

'I've been over it three times this morning, dear boy.'

He dropped the papers back on the table.

'Silla, aren't you the weeniest, teeniest bit suspicious of all this? Does it not strike you as odd that all my previous contracts have taken weeks to finalise, and suddenly along comes the biggest one ever and they want it sorted out in twenty-four hours. I mean, this just doesn't happen.'

Silla took off her reading glasses, rubbed her eyes, and slowly shook her head from side to side. She looked tired. Mabbut had the distinct feeling that she too might have been up all night, albeit for different reasons.

'I've never had a fight with a client for getting them too much money, Keith. This just doesn't happen either.'

'It's a perfectly natural question. Why am I suddenly worth all this?'

'OK. If it makes you feel better, it's not you who are worth all this, it's the book. Latham has decided that this is what he wants. He wants the Melville story. He is convinced it could be a big earner. He also knows that Melville is pathologically opposed to having a book written about him — which incidentally adds more than a touch of spice to the project. So in order to get this book, he has to play a different game. He has to stalk his prey.'

'You're talking Ronspeak.'

Silla held up her hands.

'Dear boy, hear me out,' she said with an edge.

A ginger cat sidled into the kitchen and stared malevolently at Mabbut.

'That means no press releases, no fanfares, and no juicy rumours about some big shot signing up with Urgent to tell the Melville tale. Ron knows that for this to work, his tactics have to be completely the reverse.'

She tapped the papers on the table.

'And I supply him with the magic ingredient . . . '

'Hair dye?'

'The best author we can find with no established record of success.'

Mabbut threw back his head and laughed.

'That's good, Silla. I should put that on my business cards. *'Keith Mabbut. Author. No established record of success'.'*

Silla stood up. She ruffled her hair and flicked on the kettle behind her.

'It could be worse, Keith. Crap but successful. That's a much longer list.'

Mabbut let out a deep sigh.

'It's unorthodox, dear boy, and I know that beneath that prickly radical exterior lurks a tight-arsed Yorkshire conservative. But believe me. For once, this is *good*.'

The kettle began to hum. Mabbut turned away, but there was no escape. Even the cat was staring at him expectantly.

'What is this, Silla? The moment of truth?'

Silla held out a pen.

'Enjoy it, old boy. Make up for all those moments of untruth.'

'Untruth?'

'All those times you've blamed me for leading you into things you didn't believe in. What did you call them? 'Parish magazines for blue-chip companies'. Official histories of pumping stations. Profiles of the chairman. I know you think I'm a cynical old cow, but while I happily admit the pleasure I get from screwing money out of tight-fisted corporate accountants I wouldn't share a taxi with, I'm genuinely proud of this one. Hamish Melville is one of the few good men left, one of the rare people I want to know more rather than less about. And for some wholly inexplicable reason you have landed the dream job of satisfying my curiosity.'

She tapped one of the typed pages.

'And my greed.'

She dropped the pen in front of him.

'I honestly believe this is far and away the best thing you will ever do.'

Mabbut looked at Silla. Her dark but well-cut hair framed a sturdy, strong-boned face. A face that was both lively and inscrutable. The face of a survivor. He knew that face and he knew that look. She wasn't going to back down. Well, neither was he. Not yet.

'I'm sorry, Silla.'

Behind her, the kettle surged, climaxed, and faded.

8

It was nearly two o'clock that afternoon when Mabbut turned off the Edgware Road and, checking his daughter's message one final time, searched for the name Harveh in a row of cafés and shops brimming with sweets and pastries. Outside some were tables where short-haired, broad-shouldered men sat playing draughts and smoking narghiles. He spotted the slim incongruous figure of his daughter, waving to him, almost silhouetted by the bright lights of a café's interior.

Harveh was small and very busy and it was a moment or two before he picked out a young man dressed in Western clothes looking anxiously in their direction. Jay raised her hand towards him and Mabbut was aware of her attention slipping away from him to this awkward, diffident boy — yes, he *was* a boy — who rose to meet her.

'Dad, this is Shiraj.'

The boy's dark eyes met his. They showed little animation. Jay rested a hand on his shoulder. He smiled at her and, for some reason, shook his head.

'Shiraj. This is my dad.'

Mabbut reached out and they shook hands. It was no more than a touch of hands really, hardly a shake.

'Sorry I couldn't make it last night,' said Mabbut.

They all squeezed around the table and a waiter brought tea. Shiraj looked so young and so vulnerable; his daughter's awareness of this and her response to it was something that touched Mabbut. She'd always been open and generous with her feelings — he'd regarded this as both her greatest strength and her greatest weakness — and Mabbut felt a tug of envy at the artlessness of her affection.

They ate sherbet and drank pomegranate juice. Shiraj had sharp, birdlike features and jet-black eyes that were constantly on the move. He had been studying English at college in Tehran but had come under suspicion for spending time with Kurdish groups. He had been arrested, asked for names he couldn't give, and then beaten up pretty badly and warned not to return to the university.

'Were you any threat to the government?'

Shiraj smiled thinly.

'If you are a Kurd in Iran then you are always a threat. Guilty until proved innocent.'

'You're a Kurd?'

'No, sir.'

'Then why get involved with them?'

'Dad, if you knew how these people were treated you'd . . . '

Quietly but firmly, Shiraj laid a restraining hand on Jay's arm. It was an oddly grown-up gesture and Mabbut felt bad for misreading him as a boy.

'They happened to be my friends, sir, and they needed my help.' He looked Mabbut in the eye. 'I was not a martyr. I wasn't a Kurdish

73

nationalist. They were my friends and they were in trouble.'

'They stubbed cigarettes out on their arms, for God's sake!'

Shiraj looked around in some alarm as Jay's voice rose.

'And they'll do the same to Shiraj if our stupid fucking government sends him back! He needs help, Dad.'

'Please, sir, I'm fine. There are people who can help me.'

'Dad's a journalist. He has contacts.'

Mabbut suddenly felt protective towards his daughter. With her innocent, untested idealism. Her frank and generous support for this man she'd only just met. And her loyal and totally unjustified belief in her father.

'I would like to be a journalist,' Shiraj said quite decisively. 'All my friends want to be journalists.'

Mabbut looked around the room. At every table were men deep in conversation. Eyes staring into eyes, arms constantly rising and falling, hands in perpetual motion, fluttering and turning with sharp and delicate gestures. Everyone seemingly engaged in the most important argument of their lives. It wasn't quite the same in the Dog and Feathers. Was it the lack of muddling alcohol, or was it just that these people had more to discuss? Or that the customers in a place like Harveh were in someone else's country, and there was so much that mattered.

'Do you write for a newspaper, sir?'

'Me? No.'

Mabbut didn't quite know where to go from here. *A History of Sullom Voe Oil Terminal* wouldn't cut much ice, but this eager young man needed something.

'I write books mostly.'

Shiraj nodded. His serious dark eyes rested on Mabbut.

'He's writing a novel,' said Jay, proudly.

Shiraj's brow furrowed. 'What is this novel?'

'Yes, tell us, Dad. I haven't a clue what it's about.'

Mabbut wanted to give a fluent, enthusiastic answer, but the unfamiliar smells of herbs and rosewater and fresh-baked bread, combined with the intense chatter of people talking in a language he didn't understand, made him feel a sudden wobbling of resolve.

'It's a story,' he said to Shiraj.

'Is it true?'

'No, that's the point. It's a story . . . like *The Arabian Nights*.'

Shiraj's brow furrowed. 'That was a long time ago.'

'Yes, well . . . '

'You should write about what is happening today.'

Mabbut noticed Jay give Shiraj's arm the lightest of touches.

'With respect, sir, I could tell you some true stories you would not believe.'

Mabbut thought of Tess. How had she put it?

'Sometimes you can tell the truth better through stories,' he replied.

75

Shiraj leant towards him. His tone remained even, but he spoke a little faster.

'Forgive me, sir. With respect. There are too many good people telling stories, when what we need is to tell the world the *facts*.'

Jay crooked her finger and scoured the last of the sherbet from the rim of her glass.

'He's right in a way, Dad.'

Youthful idealism had always irritated Mabbut, especially when it was fluently expressed. He'd been a martyr to it himself. Vietnam, Watergate. Civil rights. The world's problems, which he and his friends were convinced could all be sorted out from the safety of Hull University. He felt Shiraj's eyes flick back to him, and as the boy leaned in he caught the faintest scent of jasmine.

'You were a journalist, sir?'

'I was.'

Shiraj tapped the table, emphatically, as if this proved his point.

'Then I must tell you the story of my people and you can write about it. In my country no one will write this. They will be arrested, like my father. He was a journalist, and my brothers were trying to find him, and they have been arrested.'

Mabbut nodded. More people squeezed on to the table. The café was busier than ever. He felt his own enthusiasm being appropriated by this eager young man. It was not only wearing him out, it was making him feel inadequate.

'If you don't mind I must go.' He rose and shook the young man's hand. 'It's been good to meet you, Shiraj. I'll . . . I'll do what I can.'

76

Jay caught up with him as he stepped into the street.

'Sorry, Dad. I could see you were feeling hassled. It's just that he's been through stuff he could never talk about and now he's in London everything matters to him. All at once.'

Mabbut turned back to the café. Through the windows Shiraj caught his glance, smiled uncertainly then looked away.

'I guess he could use the spare room. And . . . well, we'll take it from there,' said Mabbut, giving Jay a kiss.

As he crossed the road, he saw her skipping back into the café.

★ ★ ★

By the time he got back to Reserton Road it was late afternoon. That dark hour for any writer. He checked the cricket. No play, rain. There was a message on the answerphone which he could listen to either straight away or after an hour's writing. He listened to it straight away. It was his soon-to-be-ex-wife. She and Rex would be dining at 'a little bistro he knows' in Chelsea. She pleaded with Mabbut to come and 'just say hello'. In disgust, Mabbut switched off the message.

The phone rang again, almost immediately, but it wasn't Krystyna.

'OK, dear boy. This is what's happening. I've told Urgent about your worries about deadlines and the novel and how much it means to you, and instead of just telling us to piss off, which they were entirely within their rights to do, they are prepared to discuss these concerns with you.'

'Silla.'

'Just hear me out. Ron Latham has agreed to meet up tonight at his office.'

'Silla.'

'Go through all your misgivings one by one and he will give you absolute reassurances on all the points that concern you. I'll be there too and hopefully we can put your troubled mind at rest.'

Mabbut felt assailed and confused. After the oddly disquieting chat with young Shiraj he wanted time and space to think. The last thing he needed was a return to Urgent's bleak and spiritless office and the hard sell from Latham and Silla.

'He'll meet us at seven thirty. OK?'

Mabbut took a deep breath.

'No, Silla. It's not OK.'

'What d'you mean? We let this whole thing drop? We watch while someone else gets the commission? This could be our last chance.'

Mabbut switched the phone to his other hand. His parents smiled at him from the sideboard. A perfect storm of options was swirling about him, and he had to take one of them. Fast.

'Tell him I've got something more important to do.'

Silla's voice rose. 'More *important*? How's that going to go down? 'I'm sorry, Mr CEO of major publishing company, but the author of *The Official History of Sullom Voe*'s got something more important to do!''

Mabbut cleared his throat.

'It happens to be true. It's a very important dinner.'

'Dare I ask? Nelson Mandela, the Dalai Lama?'

'With my wife, if you must ask.'

He put down the phone and after a long, deep breath, rewound the answerphone and wrote down an address.

9

It was certainly more than a bistro. So discreetly appointed was it that he'd walked past three times, thinking it some kind of electrical substation. There was no sign, but incised into a smoked-glass strip beside the hammered metal door were the almost indecipherable words 'Atelier Gaston Quartz'. The door required two hands to prise it open. As it swung to, Mabbut found himself running a gauntlet of mirrored glass leading to yet another door. He was preparing himself to heave this open when it slid to one side with a hiss. He found himself in a carefully dimmed steel cave in which were set some twenty tables, black glass on silver chrome, only one of which was occupied. Krystyna was sitting with her back to him, so it was her companion whose eye he caught first. A tallish, disappointingly good-looking older man with a high colour. Flecks of white hair, streamlined at the temples, and a well-fed frame tucked neatly into a three-piece suit. It crossed Mabbut's mind that this might have been what Krystyna's father looked like.

Krystyna appeared strained, but seemed to be relieved to see him. Stiffly she embarked on the introductions. Her companion rose from the table, smiling amiably, and grasped Mabbut's hand before lapsing back into his seat. He beckoned Mabbut to do the same, with a gesture of elegant largesse, as if he owned the place.

'Rex owns the place,' said Krystyna.

Rex gave a self-deprecating smile.

'Actually it was opened by a Ukrainian. Frightful crook. Went belly up a year ago so we took it over. We came up with the name Gaston Quartz and it's taken off. Chef's from Inverness.'

Mabbut looked dubiously at the surrounding gloom.

'It picks up. The high-rollers like to eat late. Glass of champagne?'

Before Mabbut could refuse, he became aware of activity, of dark figures emerging from the shadows, briefly catching the light, then disappearing again. Somewhere a door opened and closed with the merest sigh.

Krystyna looked tired. Oddly enough what little light there was around the table shone obliquely on her, accentuating the Madonna-like combination of oval face, long straight dark hair with touches of grey, high cheekbones and the wide, thin-lipped mouth he knew so well.

'Rex and I are, hmm,' she had to clear her throat before carrying on, 'going to New York on Sunday.'

From nowhere a crisply hissing champagne flute appeared beside him, and there was a momentary lull as the other glasses were refilled around the table. Rex Naismith seemed quite unembarrassed by the situation. He beamed at Mabbut, thanked the waiter and raised his glass.

'Cheers!'

Mabbut mumbled. Krystyna barely raised her glass.

Rex drank appreciatively, rolling the champagne round his mouth before setting down his glass.

'Krystyna tells me you're a writer. I admire anyone who can write. I come up with the odd speech or two but not the imaginative stuff.'

Like a chess player before a big game, Mabbut had rehearsed his moves on the way there, but the one thing he hadn't prepared for was amiability. He nodded, intending to look blank, but it came out as surly.

'What the *fuck* are you doing with my wife?' is what he really wanted to say.

'It's never easy,' is what he actually said.

'I know quite a few chaps who are harbouring little masterpieces. And of course dear old Cloudesley Marshall actually had one published. It was a thriller, very James Bond. Lots of sex. Which is something one wouldn't normally associate with Cloudesley. He used to run the Boy Scouts.'

Mabbut felt like a rabbit caught in headlights. Bereft of a strategy to make them talk about what they should surely be talking about, he could only listen. Krystyna, Polish and practical, took refuge in arrangements.

'We shall be in New York for some time. Then we go to Ottawa.'

Rex grimaced.

'Frightful place. Bloody cold and all the buildings look like elephant turds. But we're supposed to be nice to Canada these days. All sorts of things brewing. Know about the Athabasca tar sands?'

Mabbut nodded. Here was something he did know about. Once.

'I was an energy correspondent.'

'Well then, you probably know far better than me what's going on there. Millions of dollars being spent buggering up the place, environmentalists up in arms, and quite rightly too, but they are passing an awful lot of business our way. We still have a lot of mining expertise and thankfully it's appreciated out there. Anyway, I have to go and make sure we're being nice to everybody and not letting Hamish Melville do the rain dance on them.'

Mabbut looked up sharply.

'Hamish Melville? How does he come into it?'

'Well, you know Hamish. Everyone knows Hamish. If there's a pie, his finger will be in it somewhere.'

Krystyna frowned and asked, 'Isn't he some kind of unofficial ambassador? Goes where the government daren't go?'

Rex raised his eyebrows.

'Oh, Hamish is as Hamish is portrayed. A super chap, but he doesn't always have the bigger picture in mind.'

'How d'you mean?' asked Mabbut.

'Well, he has his own agenda. The tar sands aren't absolutely unpopulated, and in the north-west, by the Yannahook river, there's a group of bods called the Sahallas. Indians. First Nations, they call them now. Not that many of them and a lot seem quite happy to go and work in the casinos in Calgary. But there's a hard core that money won't shift. These people are like a

83

magnet to Hamish and he's been up there, well, how can I put it, 'advising them of their rights'.'

This riled Mabbut. 'That's fair enough, isn't it? If it's their land.'

'Well, in theory, yes.'

'It's their moral right.'

'Forgive me, but I've had this argument with Hamish many times. Yes, these people have rights. But there's an awful lot of land and very few of them living on it. Our view is that they can still lead decent lives, uninterfered with, on part of the land, and let the rest be . . . er . . . developed. That way everyone benefits and they get a damned decent royalty for their people.'

Mabbut took another sip of what was, even in his limited experience, a very fine champagne.

'You know Hamish Melville, then?'

'Inasmuch as anyone knows Hamish, yes.'

Rex drank rather delicately, thought Mabbut, for a big man.

'Long ago, in the mists of time, I had the privilege of representing the people of Bletchley and South Beds in Her Majesty's Parliament. I'd travelled a bit and spoke a couple of languages so I found myself a comfortable little spot in the FCO — Foreign and Commonwealth Office as it then was . . . '

Mabbut was aware of Krystyna adjusting her position, looking quickly from one of them to the other, and he knew that she was willing the conversation on, as if this shared interest might help them avoid confrontation.

Rex smoothed a corner of the tablecloth.

'At that time, we're talking nearly twenty years ago now, Hamish was on the payroll. Roving brief sort of thing. He'd a background in the military and the City — not an unusual combination — and of course he had this wicked charm. So . . . '

At Rex's almost, subliminal nod more champagne appeared from the gloom.

'He became most useful to us in a number of delicate situations. Hostage talks, raids on installations, that sort of thing. He was very successful, a sort of latter-day T. E. Lawrence. Major — John Major, that is — wanted to bring him into government, quite high up too, but Hamish wasn't interested. He wasn't political in any way. And quite possibly because of that he began to pull away from anything official. Rarely came back to the country and from what one could tell he began to use what he'd learnt in a more . . . well . . . international sphere. In '97 I lost my seat, which was quite a relief to be honest. My wife died the same year, which was also quite a relief.'

His delivery was finely paced, assured. This was a man who was used to being listened to.

'So, quite suddenly, at the grand old age of fifty-nine and a half, I found myself footloose and fancy free. Like a lot of Tories who got the push in '97 I picked up a few directorships, dabbled in hedge funds — all sorts of wickedness — and also went back to my first love, which was poodling round the globe. Every now and then our paths would cross, usually in some bar or at a friend's place. Hamish avoided embassies like the plague. He sort of went native, but he always knew exactly what he was doing.'

'Which was?'

'Helping people everyone else ignored, basically. And making a fair nuisance of himself in the process.'

'Which he's still doing.'

'As far as I know.'

Rex looked across at Krystyna. This time it was more than a glance — an unhurried look of unmistakable warmth. He lightly, affectionately, took her hand and with the other summoned a waiter from the shadows.

'Stay for a bite with us?' he said.

It was the touch of her hand as much as the 'us' that hit Mabbut hard.

'No, I won't. Thank you.'

He pushed back his chair and stood up. Aware he'd done so rather too quickly, Mabbut took care placing it neatly beneath the table. Anything to avoid looking at Krystyna.

Rex too stood, and held out his hand.

'I'm glad we've met.'

Mabbut nodded. He wanted to speak, but found himself unable to. The two men shook hands and Mabbut turned, his eyes passing over Krystyna's without engaging. He located the exit and walked down the mirrored corridor that led him to the entrance. He pulled hard at the heavy black door, like a man trying to escape a fire. Only when he pushed did the door swing open and release him into the street.

And it was there, on the corner of Furness Gardens and Fulham Road, that a tsunami of self-pity swept over him. Tears came: pathetic, unbidden and unstoppable. Two special constables strolled by and, seeing him, looked quickly away.

★   ★   ★

The 43 bus dropped him on the corner of Lodge Street, a five-minute walk from the house.

Mabbut fumbled for his keys — far too many on the ring — and pushed open the front door. The hallway was dark, but he could see a sliver of light beneath the kitchen door and hear voices. He switched on the hall light and clattered about a bit hanging his coat up, but he still made Jay and Shiraj jump apart when he entered the kitchen. It seemed innocent enough. They were just close, not doing anything.

Jay was all brittle brightness.

'Hello, Dad. We've just made some food.'

'Sausages?'

Shiraj looked at Jay, concerned until he saw her break into a smile.

'I promise, Dad, I'll get some tomorrow. Great big thick, beefy-venison-pork-sage, everything you like. But you can cook them.'

'Can't wait.'

'Have something now. Shiraj has made carrot and yogurt soup, and it's delicious.'

'No, I've already eaten,' Mabbut lied. 'And I've some work to do.'

He looked from Jay to Shiraj. Shiraj put his hand to his heart.

87

'Thank you, sir, for allowing me into your home.'

Mabbut nodded.

'Goodnight, all.'

★ ★ ★

'Dad?'

Jay's voice made him jump. He was at his writing table, in a halo of halogen, bent over his work, miles away from the world.

'Hi, love. How are you?'

She came across to him. He felt her arms resting lightly on his shoulder.

'I'm fine. How are you?'

Without turning, he reached for her hand.

'I saw your mother tonight.'

'I know. She called.'

'Met him. Tyrannosaurus Rex.'

'And what did you think?'

'I liked him . . . yes, I liked him.'

Then something gave again, and for the second time that evening emotion got the better of him.

'I liked him, Jay. That's the bloody trouble! I *liked* him.'

Mabbut raised both hands up to hers.

'Oh, shit!'

'I'm sorry, Dad. I really am.'

'Don't be sorry. She's happy. He's a nice guy. You're happy. He's a nice guy. I'll get over it.'

It took him two or three deep breaths before he regained control.

His daughter squeezed his shoulders, and they

were silent for a while. When he'd composed himself Mabbut leant forward and adjusted the screen in front of him.

'This your novel, Dad?'

'No, no. It's just some info on someone.'

Jay peered at the screen.

'Hamish Melville.'

'You know him?'

'Of course, Dad. I'm not completely stupid.'

'I thought he'd be a little out of your age range.'

'Melville? He was a hero at school. Fighting the big boys. Siding with the locals. Tramping off into the middle of nowhere. He won a Year Six debate for who they'd most like to see running the country. Why are you looking him up?'

'Someone . . . someone's asked me to write a book about him.'

'*A book about Hamish Melville?*'

'Yes.'

'Wow! That's fantastic, Dad. Are they going to pay you?'

'Oh yes. Quite a lot.'

'Are you going to do it?'

Mabbut leant back, rubbed his eyes and stared at the screen.

'I don't know. I don't know what I'm getting myself into. I keep telling myself that all I really want to do is write my novel. That's what's new and exciting. Then I talk to you and Shiraj and even bloody Rex and the whole thing suddenly seems . . . I don't know . . . intriguing.'

'Intriguing?'

Mabbut grinned and shook his head.

89

'The publishing company's keen, but I don't trust them. And Melville hates journalists.'

He gave a bleak smile.

'Bad man wants book written. Good man doesn't want book written. It's the sort of thing that makes the ears prick up.'

'So what's stopping you?'

'I don't know exactly . . . You. Sam. The family. It's a tight deadline and would mean my going away again. If I do it properly.'

Mabbut sighed.

'I've been away too long, too often. Your mother's right. I've been bad at being a father and bad at being a husband. I've got to put some time in. Make some repairs.'

Jay squeezed his hand and giggled.

'Dad, you sound like the Odd Job Man.'

Despite himself, Mabbut laughed at this. The Odd Job Man was a part of family folklore, a character they'd met on holiday in the Lake District who had a compulsive need to fix things. He was constantly under tables and up small ladders, taking perfectly efficient things apart and putting them back together again. One day his wife revealed that he was having treatment for the condition in Preston, but long before that his place in the pantheon of Mabbut family heroes was assured.

'Seriously, you're like Sam.'

Mabbut frowned. 'Me? Like Sam?'

'You're both really good at what you do, but you're always the last to see it.'

He smiled. 'Have we got a picture of him?'

'Sam?'

'No, the Odd Job Man. I'd like to see him again.'

'I'll have a look. There must be one somewhere.'

And they both laughed at the memory. A shared laugh. Unreserved, and for a moment at least, infectious.

★ ★ ★

Mabbut lay awake into the small hours. Another sleepless night that had started with too much unhealthy imagining of Krystyna with Rex began to refocus around Melville, the book and something Shiraj had said. Something about too many good people making up stories, as if it were a waste of their talents. Mabbut knew he could do the book and do it bloody well. So what, exactly, was stopping him? Was it just the suspiciously large amount of money he was being offered?

He sat up, switched on the light. Then he switched it off again. He could think more clearly in the dark.

When it really came down to it, what was bugging him about the Melville book was not its subject, but the crass way Ron Latham was approaching it — thinking he could achieve anything with his chequebook. Melville was a sophisticated operator. This project would need intelligence rather than wads of cash to find the man behind the smokescreens.

As Mabbut chased these thoughts around his head he became more and more convinced that

91

things could be different if he were to take the initiative in the hunt for Melville. He knew about tenacity. He'd won an award for it once. He also knew that the way to crack a story was not unlike the way detectives approach a crime. To catch Melville one would have to use Melville's own tactics. Go underground. Work below the radar. If he were free to do it his way, then he could make the book work.

The alarm clock showed 2.30 when Mabbut finally gave up the struggle to sleep and, pulling on the dressing gown Krystyna had given him for the last birthday they'd spent together, he sat down at his computer to plot a guerrilla strategy.

Over the next two hours he tried to pick out the likely trouble spots that Melville might be drawn to, bearing in mind the issues on which the man was known to hold strong views. There was no shortage of ideas. If it was indigenous people threatened by 'development' that attracted him, then Melville could be almost anywhere in the world. In Papua New Guinea 312 local tribes, some as yet uncontacted, were sitting on resources that the Indonesian government, backed up by their army, was determined to extract. In Botswana the Kalahari Bushmen were being denied access to their wells, or simply been driven off their land to make way for a three-billion-dollar diamond mine. There were issues over oil extraction in the Peruvian jungle, titanium in Kenya, copper smelting in India, diamonds in Zimbabwe, hydroelectric schemes in Brazil, even beauty spots in Shropshire threatened by coal mining. Mabbut scanned endless websites which tracked revelations about global greed: Forest Watch, Tribal Information Forum, Freedom to Know, Hate Oil, Leave Us Alone, Protect Or Die, Godwatch, the Danish Women's Environmental Action Group. By dawn his eyes were stinging but a plan of action was beginning to form in his mind.

He showered and made himself an early breakfast. Toast, a bowl of fruit and strong coffee. He took his second cup upstairs. There was no sound from either of the other two bedrooms. Pushing his door to, he sat at his desk and dialled Silla's number.

She sounded husky and defensive.

'Silla Caldwell.'

'I'll do it.'

For some reason this led to a prolonged attack of coughing at the other end.

'Now you tell me. Latham's just left on a plane to Sydney, for Christ's sake.'

'Doesn't matter. All I need is travel expenses and for Ron to stay in Sydney for as long as possible.'

10

Sam Mabbut was tall, and took after his mother in looks, with jet-black hair and strong cheekbones. Girls loved him, not so much for his cheekbones as for the soft, shy sadness of his eyes. He had a slightly wavering voice which he saw as a drawback and others saw as distinctive. Though Sam had an uncomfortable relationship with his father, he was glad to have been born the son of a writer and took this obligation seriously. For the last year Sam and two other young men had been writing plays and poems under the collective name of No Hope Theatre, and it was their latest work that was being given its world premiere in a private room above the Dark Lady pub in Chiswell Street. All the family had turned out, including, Mabbut noticed, both mother and father.

Krystyna may have been here out of maternal affection, but Mabbut was here out of duty and guilt. He had little time for No Hope's repertoire, but if he was going to be wrapped up in the Melville project, this might be his last chance of seeing his awkward, prickly son for a while.

'Arse,' intoned a voice from the blackness, pretty much on the dot of 8.30. 'Arse that illuminates the world.' A chord rang out. A single key-light hit Sam's curled up figure as it lay whimpering on the floor. Fake shit fell from the ceiling on to the audience. For what seemed an interminable amount of time, Sam's character engaged with various threatening figures, both verbally and visually. It was a bravura performance but Mabbut found that his mind kept wandering and, despite his best efforts, his eyes gently closing.

In the second half fan heaters were turned on as the action of Arse transported the audience to a Turkish gaol. Mabbut felt uncomfortable for Shiraj, but the boy was watching with rapt attention, his fingers locked in Jay's.

At the end Mabbut had a moment or two with his son. Sam, who had an awkward habit of never opening a conversation, flicked the hair from his eyes and gave his father an ironic or possibly just uncertain smile.

'You were great. But occasionally . . . '

'You don't have to say anything, Dad. I know you don't do polemic.'

'You stick to your guns. I admire that. You don't try to please everybody.'

Sam nodded towards the departing audience.

'We seemed to please most people here.'

With Sam, free speech was a one-way thing. The truth was that, apart from one or two loners lured up from the bar by the title, ninety per cent of Arse's audience consisted of friends and family of the cast.

At that moment Krystyna, obviously in a hurry, squeezed between them. She kissed her son with an unequivocal warmth that irritated Mabbut. As if she were the only one who understood him.

'Fantastic! You boys are so good. Meet you downstairs?'

She cupped Sam's pale cheeks in both hands, kissed him again and with a wave turned and headed for the door. Mabbut watched her go, then gave his son a brief hug.

'Must get together soon. I'll think of something. Give you a call.'

He caught up with Krystyna as she hurried down the stairs. A cold draught blew in from the half-open fire exit.

'Drink?' he asked.

She paused, looked rather severely at him for a moment, then as he held the door open, walked past him into the bar.

'White wine spritzer?'

As if he needed to ask. It had been her drink of choice for thirty years. He'd rather hoped that Rex might have educated her palate. The bar was crowded and noisy, as these places always were.

He put the drink in front of her and pulled up a stool. For a moment it felt like old times; it was something they always used to do, and he smiled at the memory. They had once made each other happy.

'What's that?'

She pointed accusingly at his glass as if it might be evidence of infidelity.

'A large Scotch.'

'Since when?'

'Since I saw *Arse*.'

'It was great.'

'No, it wasn't.'

'Sam and the boys told me they wrote it in a week.'

'Felt like it,' he said, irritated less by her opinion than by her assumption of inside information.

'It was strong stuff.'

'It was repulsive. Be honest.'

Krystyna shrugged. 'What were you expecting, *Mary Poppins?*'

'I don't see why I should have to take responsibility for the Armenian genocide, that's all.'

'Not you. Us.'

'No Rex tonight?'

'He's at the Mansion House.'

'Underground station?'

'No. The Mansion House. For the Lord Mayor's Dinner.'

Krystyna sipped her spritzer, but having established a points victory, she softened.

'It was good of you to come last night. I know it can't have been easy for you. To meet Rex.'

There was a pause.

'What am I supposed to say, Krys? That he's a better man than me?'

Surprisingly, Krystyna put out her hand and touched his arm.

'Don't be stupid. He's different, that's all.'

'Rich, witty, well connected . . . '

She shook her head dismissively. Mabbut smiled.

'And that's just me.'

She laughed, a quick, defenceless laugh. Such a rare thing between them these past few years.

It was like striking a match in a darkened room.

'I wanted to let you know, I've taken on a book. Something I didn't tell you about. It's well paid, but it does mean I shall be away travelling again.'

'That's good, isn't it?'

'Is it?'

Krystyna looked at him carefully.

'What are you trying to say, Keith?'

'Come back.'

She shook her head and looked away.

'Come back. Before it's too late.'

'Don't be silly. We both know it won't work.'

'Only one of us knows.'

'Keith, I am saying this once and for all. We parted for good. We agreed. Rex wants to marry me. I want to marry him. If you respect me, let me go. We can still be friends. And he likes you. He got on well with you.'

Mabbut finished the whisky in one fierce gulp and thumped his glass down on the table.

'Thanks, but I'm not taking that bait. If you want an endorsement from me, forget it. He's yours, not mine. He may love me like a brother, but to tell you the truth, I'd be happier if I never saw him again in my life.'

11

In retrospect, it had been a foolish thing to say, thought Mabbut, as Rex approached, shook his hand and settled himself at the table of a discreet Italian restaurant on the corner of Horseferry Road.

It had taken a few days for Silla to sort out the details with Latham. She had, she said, managed quite cleverly to present her client's indecision, bordering on ingratitude, as nothing more than a weighing up of two major offers, without, of course, admitting that not a cent had been committed to the novel by any publisher. They had then moved on to Mabbut's concerns over research and his insistence that he be able to plan his own moves. Latham had argued that he was paying and it was up to him to call the tune. He had already begun to assemble a team of bright young graduates to help with research. Silla got him to agree that they would remain London-based, leaving Mabbut free to track down Melville abroad. Latham replied that he personally would lead the team and make relevant enquiries as to Melville's movements, ensuring that Mabbut had somewhere to start. Mabbut had told Silla that this was absolutely not acceptable, whereupon she finally blew up, gave him a lecture about gratitude, opportunity, unselfishness and other priorities. The contract was finally signed at her office late one evening over a takeaway curry.

Mabbut was then faced with the unpalatable fact that sitting at the top of the list of those 'personal' contacts he could call on to begin his search for Melville was his wife's new lover. He had swallowed this bitter pill, along with a hefty dose of pride, and had written to Rex Naismith in confidence, outlining his plans and requesting any advice he might have. Within a few days Rex had come back with 'one or two bites' and suggested that they meet up.

Mabbut had been the first to arrive at the modest trattoria five minutes' walk from Parliament Square. A few moments after he'd sat down Rex loomed through the door, to be met cordially by the portly owner, with whom he engaged in some prolonged and convivial banter — in Italian — before handing him his coat and proceeding to the table. He shook Mabbut's hand and smiled apologetically.

'Hope you don't mind coming down to my neck of the woods.'

'It's fine.'

Mabbut, wrong-footed by Rex's incorrigible politeness, sounded unconvincing.

'Krystyna tells me that you both saw Sam's play. *Bottom*?'

'*Arse*, actually.'

Rex leant back, laughing generously.

'She enjoyed it very much.'

'Yes, she did,' was all Mabbut could think of to say. 'Thank you for seeing me.'

Rex waved this away.

'Not at all. I'm on a committee for

interdepartmental efficiency savings so any interruption is to be grasped with both hands.'

'When we last met, you said that you knew Hamish Melville.'

Rex nodded. Mabbut noted, with obscure satisfaction, that his companion was a little out of breath.

'And you tell me you're writing a book about him.'

'It's all rather hush-hush.'

'Of course.'

A waiter hove into view.

'Drink to start with, sir?'

Rex beamed happily.

'A glass of wine could be my saviour. What about you?'

'Fine.'

'Bottle of the house red.'

As the waiter went away, Rex explained his choice of restaurant. It was small, family-run and so unobtrusive and unpretentious that it was popular with politicians who appreciated privacy. Which was why it was always busy. Mabbut took a quick look around.

'Except today,' added Rex. 'They're still in recess.'

The waiter returned and Rex tried the wine.

'Not bad. Italian farmyard. Nothing complicated.'

With a quick nod from Rex, the waiter poured two glasses and left the bottle on the table.

'So, how can I be of help? The book sounds interesting.'

'Except that my publisher is a control freak.

101

His idea of helping me is to gather up a team of previously unemployed media studies graduates who are supposed to be out there 'gaining me access'. But as I told you in my letter, that is not how I like to work. It seems to be the perfect way of alerting the entire world to the fact that the hunt is on. Which is why I . . . well . . . I wanted to talk to you.'

Rex raised his glass.

'Good health.'

Mabbut responded awkwardly. They were not meant to be friends.

'Your instinct is absolutely correct,' Rex went on. 'Hamish is notoriously touchy about privacy. I don't know the exact details, but they say that there are only a half-dozen people he trusts. Like him, they're all highly educated, multilingual and totally loyal. Beyond that, there is a sort of sleeping network of sympathisers he can mobilise in pretty much any country in the world. Many are just locals, but Melville always makes sure they have access to state-of-the-art communications. A barefoot army with laptops. Breaking into his network isn't going to be easy. Certainly not by conventional means.'

Rex picked up the menu.

'Shall we order?'

They both went for the special. Rex was expected back at his committee and Mabbut was aware that already that morning he'd had two messages from Latham, fresh back from Australia.

Rex broke the end off a bread roll.

'I gather from Krystyna that you earned your

102

spurs on the investigative front. Some award, she tells me.'

Does she? And what else? Mabbut thought to himself.

'Oh yes, I was a big star. Fifteen years ago.'

'How so?'

'Got a tip-off that arsenic waste was being dumped in a river in the Midlands. Worked my way through the evidence. Couldn't find anything. Company with unblemished record. Then a child died. Not even in the area — in a village miles away, in what used to be Westmorland. By pure coincidence I was tracking through company records one last time when I came across the name Saxilby, which rang a bell. It was the same name as the boy who'd died. I followed it up, found that he'd died of liver malfunction. Odd in a boy of twelve who was previously healthy. Turned out that before his parents split up he lived right beside the stream that drained from the factory. That was the link I needed. After that it was all down to chemical testing. Bingo. Arsenic sulphide discharges over a period of three months. The company knew about it but hushed it up. And that child wasn't the only casualty.'

Rex nodded as he listened. 'That must have been a damn good feeling. I mean, to nail the buggers.'

Mabbut smiled. 'Yes, it was a good feeling.'

'Then what?'

'Nothing like that ever came my way again. Within the industry there were those who felt I'd been underhand.'

'And had you?'

'I . . . er . . . I paid some money from my paper to the boy's mother to get access to his medical records. It was more or less the only way of getting at the truth but it meant that, in addition to my British Gas Award, I was given a bollocking by the Press Commission, and journalism being the business it is, that was what most people remembered.'

Their food had arrived: two plates of linguini, gently steaming.

'And since then?'

'I worked on whatever came along. A bit of ghost-writing, editing, then company commissions to pay the bills. Sleeping with the enemy, you could say.'

'So when this Melville book came up . . . '

'I was surprised, to say the least. Still am. Great subject, good money. Just difficult people to deal with.'

Mabbut felt comfortable with Rex and there was no longer much point in fighting it. In fact Rex was the first person he'd been able to talk to like this for a very long time. He smiled ruefully.

'I was toying with not doing it at all. There is another project I really want to do.'

'Ah. The science fiction story.'

'Historical re-creation.'

'Yes, Krystyna's told me about it.'

Mabbut's ears pricked up. 'And?'

For once Rex was hesitant.

'She . . . she thinks that, of the two, you're better off going with the non-fiction.'

For a while they both ate. An American family

104

came in. Mother, father, grandmother, two teenage children, all identical, apart from their age and gender. They stood there awkwardly, the grown-ups debating among themselves while the two children looked back at the door.

Rex sat back, then dabbed the sides of his mouth, before laying his napkin to one side. He regarded Mabbut thoughtfully for a moment, then leant forward and dropped his voice.

'I've talked to a few people since I got your message — it's all right, I gave no names — and I have it on pretty good authority that Hamish is currently in the subcontinent. There's something brewing there which sounds completely up his street. Big industry, local tribes. Very much Hamish's stamping ground. I still have a vested interest in knowing what he's up to, but you'll understand that I can't be seen to be betraying confidences. I'm still too close to Westminster.'

Mabbut nodded.

Rex checked his watch.

'Talking of which, time flies.'

He finished another mouthful, pushed his plate to one side, then reached inside his pocket and handed Mabbut an envelope.

'You'll find a key and an address in there. When you go, be sure to take some ID. Passport, driver's licence. All the details I could find will be in there waiting for you. Sorry about the George Smiley bit, but I have to be seen as fragrant.'

He smiled encouragingly.

'I hope it'll help you find him. All I can say is

move fast, because you can be sure he'll move a lot faster.'

'Thanks, Rex.'

'And Keith, my name must be kept out of this, completely.'

'Why are you helping me?'

'I was a friend of the old bugger. I admire him. I think he's an unsung hero, and we're short of heroes these days.'

Rex left with a jaunty farewell as if they were old school chums who'd just enjoyed a reunion. Mabbut paid the bill and took a bus to St John's Wood. Following Rex's instructions he found a long low building which looked as if it might at one time have been the property of the nearby church. Now there were iron grilles over the lancet windows and a large sign had been stuck across the arched doorway bearing the name of the Capital Storage Company. At reception Mabbut identified himself using his driver's licence. A door automatically opened and he followed an elderly man with a limp down a passageway to an open area flanked by strongbox vaults. The custodian retired and with the key Rex had given him Mabbut opened one of the strongboxes. Inside was a white A4 envelope with his name on it. He signed the relevant forms and, slipping the envelope into his shoulder bag, he took the 274 bus and headed home.

Mabbut sat in his workroom at Reserton Road. Open in front of him were various documents: names, addresses, street maps and beside them the *Times World Atlas* that his father had invested in using some of his retirement money, and which, in the end, he'd never used. Mabbut barely lifted his head until his phone buzzed almost an hour later. It was a text message from Ron Latham confirming that Melville had been located, as suspected, in northern Brazil. But Mabbut's finger was elsewhere — tracing the course of the Mahanadi river as it snaked its way through the Eastern Ghats and out into the Bay of Bengal.

PART II

The Solution

1

Mabbut sniffed the air with satisfaction. Biju Pitnaik airport at Bhubaneswar, ancient capital of Kalinga, was a pleasant surprise. Gone was the fuzzy disorientation he'd felt as he was processed off the London flight in the glass and steel-trussed anonymity of Delhi. Here in Bhubaneswar, cosseted by a warm, damp breeze off the Bay of Bengal, disembarking passengers walked from the aircraft to the terminal through a garden of low, clipped hedges and well-tended flower beds. In among these were set terracotta figures of the better-known deities; Ganesh the elephant, Hanuman the monkey, Shiva and Vishnu. The garden led to a small, friendly arrivals hall hung with lanterns and brightly coloured banners, as if for a festival.

Mabbut took up position beside the baggage belt. Above him a brightly lit ten-metre advertising panel depicted a family, all of whom, from baby to aged grandparents, were looking dreamily heavenwards, smiling identical happy smiles. Below them, picked out in silver lettering, ran the strap line, 'Dalween Banking: For a Better India'.

Mabbut stared down at the inert rubber strip as if willpower alone might set it in motion. Some of the overlapping slats were half peeled away, revealing piles of rubbish beneath: a discarded shoe, plastic bags, stained newspapers,

111

something dark and amorphous, its damp sheen reflecting the neon above. Craning his neck, he looked towards the exit, trying to pick out the man who was supposed to be meeting him among the crowd of expectant faces squeezed up against a steel barrier. Several khaki-uniformed policemen stood around, lathis in hand.

Mabbut considered his options. Provided the baggage arrived and his was amongst it, and provided his man was there to meet him, then he could go to work immediately, following up the leads he'd been given. The only cloud on the horizon was the oppressive presence of Ron Latham. Even from five thousand miles away Mabbut could still picture the calculating stare with which Latham had fixed him as they had said their farewells in London. Latham knew that Mabbut had not told him everything about the contacts that had led him to India, and he knew that Mabbut knew he knew. Hence this cat and mouse game, with Latham ostensibly allowing Mabbut to conduct his own investigation while insisting on organising the flights and hotel and requesting that the hotel provide a guide. Silla had successfully fought off Latham's demand for daily updates, however, arguing that if Mabbut's plans to find Melville were to work he should be free to follow leads as and when they came up. Mabbut had reiterated her point, saying he had to be as light on his feet as possible, and presenting Latham with an appearance of calm confidence. It had seemed so easy in London. Now that he was in India he felt a lot less sure of himself.

'Mr Keith, sir!'

By now Mabbut had retrieved his luggage, worked his way through the crowd at the exit and found himself standing before a tall, moustachioed, slightly stooping man with thick glasses, a dark blue tie and an immaculate white shirt tucked into freshly pressed chinos. Mabbut felt uncomfortable. His shirt was damp and sweaty and the light cotton trousers he'd chosen for a pre-monsoon climate were already corrugated at the crotch. The man stepped forward and hung a garland of marigolds around Mabbut's hot neck. Then he stepped back, brought his hands together and gave a short bow.

'Namaste.'

'Namaste,' replied Mabbut, returning the bow, as instructed in his Lonely Planet guide. His companion spread out his arms to encompass the throng of meeters and greeters.

'Welcome, sir, to paradise on earth.'

He snapped an order and a frail, elderly man in a dhoti appeared and took hold of Mabbut's suitcase.

'You can wheel it!' Mabbut called after him, but it was too late. The man had already hoiked the case up on to his head and was sprinting towards the exit.

The moustachioed man bowed again.

'I am your guide from the Garden Hotel, Bubhaneswar's premier establishment for the discerning visitor. I am here to attend to your every need.'

Mabbut controlled an impulse to remonstrate, but it was too late. His companion stepped to

113

one side with another low bow, ushering Mabbut ahead of him as if the days of the Raj had never ended.

On the way in from the airport, as green paddy fields and stagnant creeks slipped by on either side, Mabbut learnt that his guide was called Farud and that his field of expertise was Hindu temple architecture from the sixth to the twelfth century.

'At one time there were seventeen thousand temples here.'

Mabbut nodded. He suddenly felt very weary.

'It is our good fortune that there are still five hundred remaining.'

As they drew up outside the hotel, three turbaned men stepped forward and grasped the doors. Short of having his name shouted out, Mabbut could hardly have effected a less discreet arrival. Once check-in was completed and further garlands and welcoming drinks had been taken, Mabbut was escorted to a room on the eleventh floor and shown, at some length, how everything from the television to the trouser press worked. When, at last, he was left alone, he locked his door and lay down on the bed.

Some time later, after an hour's sleep and a shower, Mabbut wandered downstairs for a beer.

Farud sprang up from a chair and intercepted him eagerly.

'Sir. Shall we go? It is a little cooler now. This is a very good time for the temples.'

'Look, Farud, it's been a long trip from London and I'm quite tired. Maybe tomorrow would be a better time to see the temples.'

Farud adjusted his glasses and extended a hand towards the door.

'But there are many to see. It is best to start now. Please.'

Sensing that it might be best to maintain the guise of a tourist, Mabbut acquiesced. The first of the six temples they saw that afternoon was fifteen hundred years old and undeniably beautiful. The walls were covered with lively likenesses of musicians, dancers, elephants, gods and goddesses, all in their own little panels. Mabbut would have been quite happy just to follow his guide's footsteps, but Farud would have none of this. He was a master of the interactive.

'Do you know how many gods and goddesses we have in the Hindu religion?'

Mabbut's tired brain ran through the names he'd mugged up during the flight.

'Er . . . ten? Twelve?'

'Three hundred and fifty million!'

'Ah.'

'Every single family has its own gods, you see!'

Farud then explained that the temple they were in was one of the first to be built when Buddhism was overthrown by resurgent Hinduism in the fifth and sixth centuries.

'You would think that Buddhism and Hinduism were very different, would you not, sir?'

Mabbut dutifully took the bait. 'Yes, I would.'

'Well, you would be wrong. At that time they were very close to each other. In fact many people believed Buddhism to be a part of Hinduism, so when they converted to Hinduism

115

they built temples for their Buddhist statues.'

'Right.'

'So where did they keep their statues before that, sir?'

'In their homes?'

Farud threw him a look of scorn. 'No! Under the trees.'

Mabbut couldn't help noticing the absence of any other white visitors on the temple circuit. This didn't trouble him immediately. If anything it added to the feeling that, despite a sense of almost dizzying weariness, he was seeing something new and wonderful and very different from anything the rest of his life, spent entirely west of Suez, had prepared him for. At the same time he realised that it was not going to be easy to be inconspicuous. Occasionally he cast furtive glances around him, as if at any moment Hamish Melville might come striding into view. He feared that if the great man sensed the presence of another Englishman, he would vanish for ever.

The afternoon wore on and Farud continued his erudite and expansive explanations of the evolution of the Jagamohana, the Natir and Bhoga Mandirs and various other elements of Hindu architecture.

'And the trident on top of the tower, sir, what does that signify?'

'That we are near the coast?'

Farud swung his head from side to side with delight.

'No! It is the temple of Shiva, the creator. And if it were a temple of Vishnu, what would appear up there?'

116

'An elephant?'

'No! If it were Vishnu, the symbol would be a wheel!'

'I think I should get back to the hotel, Farud. I must make a call to London before it gets too late,' Mabbut lied, weary of being the foil.

'It will be eleven o'clock in the night in the UK.'

'Yes, and I must tell my wife I've arrived safely,' he lied again.

'Ah-ha!' Farud winked conspiratorially. 'The wife. Of course.'

★ ★ ★

The next morning Mabbut slept off some of his jet-lag, and, having deferred Farud until late afternoon, he set to work on a plan of action. Matching all the information he'd gleaned in the last hectic week in London with the various leads he'd collected from Rex Naismith, everything seemed to point to a nondescript guest house that was said to be Melville's base in the city. But when Mabbut showed Farud the address, the man's face darkened and he shook his head.

'This is not a good place, Mr Keith. This is far from the airport. Many poor people stay here.'

'Well, I'd like to see it. A friend recommended it.'

Farud nodded obligingly but the look in his eyes spoke volumes.

They set off in the late afternoon. The shiny white Toyota 4×4 supplied by Farud's company seemed increasingly out of place as they left the wide boulevards of the city and bounced across railway tracks into a labyrinth of narrow, twisting back streets. Bodies spilled around the car. Mabbut had never seen so many people on the street — the only comparison he could think of was the Holloway Road on a night when Arsenal were playing at home, except that these crowds were not on their way to anywhere else. This was where they lived. There was no elevated sense of excitement urging them on. If anything, the common emotion was resignation. Faces stared into the windows, their eyes unblinking and vacant.

'Where are all these people coming from, Farud?'

'They are always here, Mr Keith. Coming and going, you know. This is a very poor area.'

They moved deeper into the old part of town, their driver, like all the other drivers, leaning on his horn, adding his contribution to the constant, discordant cacophony of the street. It was not a cacophony of complaint, or even of purpose, just an acknowledgement of a shared existence. Children squeezed between their parents, sitting two or three to a motorbike. Stooped old women moving at a snail's pace. Boys with a dozen egg-boxes on their heads. Meandering cows, skin stretched tight across spiky haunches. All were given their space on the road. And, despite the noise of all the horns, no one seemed to get out of anyone else's way.

Nothing had quite prepared Mabbut for this. It was the India he had heard, and read, about, but now it was real, he found it exhilarating and alarming at the same time. For what seemed like hours the Toyota inched its way through endless narrow bazaars until Nirwan the driver — a large, broad-shouldered, endlessly patient man — pointed out an arched gateway set a little way back from the road, and quite incongruous among the shacks selling fruit, wicker baskets and gleaming piles of pots and pans. 'Hotel Farhan, Foodings and Lodgings' read the faded sign above the entrance. Beneath it had been painted, more recently, 'P. Singh, Prop'. Nirwan swung the wheel, blasted his horn one last time and passed between cracked and mildewed pillars into a small courtyard. A black cockerel strutted irritably across their path.

Farud was not at all comfortable. He registered his displeasure by being even more curt than usual with Nirwan, who could clearly have felled him with one blow had he so wished.

'Stop here! Not *here*! There! By the door.'

The building now occupied by the Hotel Farhan had clearly been around for a while. It was almost square, with a shallow pitched roof, stone walls trimmed with laterite and rooms on three floors. Indeed, its proportions were not unlike those of a Georgian rectory. The windows on the lower level were shuttered and barred. Between them was a doorway of surprisingly elegant design, with stuccoed columns on either side. From it emerged a tall man, light of colour, with a grey, military moustache, and a shiny bald head. He wore steel-rimmed glasses and was naked to the waist.

He looked with some disdain at the car, its

119

driver and its passengers. Mabbut felt embarrassed and wished he'd asked Farud to drop him outside in the street, where their approach would have seemed less invasive, but it was too late for that. Farud got out and talked to the man, wobbling his head a lot and glancing over at Mabbut. Then he climbed back into the car, shut the door and wound up the window.

He looked serious and when he spoke it was in a strange and formal tone, like a policeman advising someone of their rights.

'Sir Keith, if it is your wish to stay here, there is a room free. It will be two hundred rupees a night. There is water and a toilet close to the room. They do not have a cook. He is gone.'

He nodded in the direction of the bony proprietor.

'But he will make some food for you. He speaks a little English.'

Mabbut was confused, and more than a little dubious. He rooted about in his notebook to check the address he'd been given.

'This is 28 Awanati Road?'

The driver nodded. Time seemed to stand still for a moment. The proprietor waited in the shade of the doorway, flicking away flies with a cotton towel. A dog appeared in the yard, barked fiercely then collapsed on the ground, panting with the effort. Mabbut knew they were all waiting for his decision. The sensible course of action would be to return to the Garden Hotel and start again, yet the name and the address matched what he'd been given. And he had to start somewhere. He looked again at the dingy yard, with the emaciated dog and the strutting black cockerel and the pile of paper and dust half swept into a corner.

'Tell him I'll take the room.'

2

Mabbut unpacked his things, and finding nowhere to put them, packed them away again. Apart from a low bed with slightly damp sheets, the furniture in his room was limited to a chair, a small table stabilised by wedges of tightly folded newspaper and a chest of drawers with no drawers in it. A bulky air-con unit above the door burst into action and shuddered to a halt at frequent intervals, as if it were trying to cough something up. After a while Mabbut turned it off and relied instead on a wooden-bladed ceiling fan that swirled silently, languidly and largely ineffectively. To combat the disorientation he felt, he took out his notebook and began to write down everything that had happened to him since his arrival in India.

When he finally looked up from his work it was evening. Farud had returned to his office, so Mabbut decided to take a walk in the thronged street outside the hotel. The air smelt of spice and incense and dung. Scooters fizzed around him, motorised rickshaws snarled their way through, an occasional gaudily decorated truck pushed past, horn blasting, while cows emerged from side streets, wandering into the thick of it all with serene indifference. A bicycle bell clanged behind Mabbut and he quickly stepped aside to avoid being impaled on the six-foot lengths of steel piping slung across the handlebars. Once he'd accepted the confusion Mabbut began to feel oddly safe and comfortable. The rough and tumble of humanity offered its own sense of security.

Then a sudden sharp cry from farther up the street cut through the ambient noise. Mabbut stood on tiptoe, craning his neck for a better view. A crowd was converging on a tilted autorickshaw. He could hear shouts, raised voices, people thumping the roof of the vehicle. He half walked, half ran to join the group of onlookers. Anger and argument filled the air as arms were raised and fists clenched. Apportioning blame seemed to be more important than helping the injured. A woman lay moaning on the ground. Beside her, a young man in shirt and jeans was cowering from the blows and kicks that were raining down on his body. Some bystanders were making an attempt to pull away the assailants and Mabbut pushed forward to join them. As he did so he felt a tight pressure on his arm and heard a soft but authoritative voice.

'Don't get involved.'

Mabbut wheeled round to find himself being gently, but firmly, led away from the scene by a tall, rangy white man wearing loose cotton trousers and a kurta. Though his face was partially obscured by a mane of lank grey hair, the jut of the jaw, the long straight nose and the deep-set eyes were unmistakable. Mabbut's mouth went dry. It was, undoubtedly, the man he'd come to look for.

*   *   *

They sat at a table farther up the street, away from the angry crowd. Beside them a boy with thick dark hair and almost jet-black skin pumped a pair of bellows to arouse the fire beneath his saucepan. Stirring the milk and tea together and adding a touch of fennel and cardamom, he brought the mixture to the boil then carefully deposited the contents into two small glasses which he set before them. Mabbut smiled his thanks. His companion picked up his glass without acknowledgement and took a careful sip.

'They're a volatile lot,' he said, staring off into the street. 'They get upset pretty quickly.'

Melville spoke crisply, almost curtly, his tone softened by the merest hint of a Scottish burr.

'No good at bottling it up.'

He turned to Mabbut and paused just long enough to make him feel uncomfortable.

'Unlike us.'

Mabbut nodded appreciatively. His glass was almost too hot to hold so he took a sip swiftly, hoping Melville wouldn't notice that his hand was shaking. Unsure what to say next, he looked back towards the scene of the accident, where arms and voices were still being raised. He sensed Melville's eyes on him.

'Here for long?'

Mabbut shrugged unconvincingly.

'Me? No, just a few days.'

'Interesting choice of hotel.'

Mabbut felt increasingly hot and flustered. He cleared his throat.

'I like to get off the beaten track,' he replied. 'Meet the real people, you know.'

'Ah, the real people. Yes.'

Melville leant back and, gathering his long grey hair in both hands, he drew it into a bunch at the back of his head and held it there for a moment. It seemed an oddly careless gesture for a man of his age and made Mabbut feel a touch more comfortable. There was so much he wanted to ask, but he was aware that he must not rush things, must control any tendency to gabble. There would be plenty of time. But then, quite suddenly, Melville stood, dropped a twenty-rupee note on the table, spoke briefly in Hindi to the boy and hoisted a bag on to his shoulder. He smiled down at Mabbut, who rose too, rather more clumsily.

Melville extended his hand.

'Well, good luck,' he said. 'And be careful. This is a tough part of town.'

And with that he nodded — not to Mabbut, but to someone behind him.

As Mabbut turned, he saw a battered green jeep detach itself from the crowds and move towards them. There were two or three people inside, all locals by the look of it. Melville gave a faint smile.

'The real people aren't always what you want them to be.'

Without a backward glance, Mclville pulled open the passenger door, climbed in and with a salvo of horn blasts the jeep headed off up the street, turned a corner and was gone.

★ ★ ★

Back at the Farhan, Mabbut sat at the rickety table in his room. He was both embarrassed and surprised to find that his hands were still shaking as he opened his notebook. The tip-off about the hotel had worked better than he'd had any right to expect. Thank God he'd not been put off taking the room. He had not only made contact with Melville on his second day in India, he had found him without any help from Latham. Less satisfactory had been his own reaction to his subject, more star-struck schoolboy than hard-nosed reporter.

He had sort of assumed that subterfuge wouldn't be necessary, that if you admired someone as much as he did Melville then you'd be bound to get on. He had never really entertained the thought that Melville might not like him, or might not want to talk to him. Which of course was highly likely. This was a man with a pathological dislike of media scrutiny. A man no journalist had been able to get near to. But at least he was in the right place, Mabbut reflected. What he needed to do now was to prepare himself a lot more carefully before their next encounter.

From his window he looked down on a narrow, hard-earth alleyway on either side of which were low houses with long thatched roofs whose eaves provided a shady space in

126

which women and children were preparing for the night. A beetle of some sort had crawled along the cracked plaster outside and was struggling to climb over the window frame. After several attempts it heaved itself up, ran along the sill and disappeared into a crack in the wall. Mabbut remained for some moments staring at the space. Then he took a deep breath, closed his notebook, pushed back his chair and stood up. He felt a welcome if uncharacteristic surge of self-belief, which he credited to the beetle. This was his Robert the Bruce moment. He would eat, wash, sleep off his jet-lag and by tomorrow would be refreshed and ready with a proper strategy for winning Melville's confidence. He had been caught with his trousers down this afternoon, but it wouldn't happen again.

It was a moment or two before he realised that someone was knocking. The raps sounded again, more insistently this time. Mabbut moved swiftly across the room and pulled open the door. The tall, strangely aristocratic figure of Mr Singh, the half-naked proprietor, stood there, his eyes flashing quickly around the room before returning to Mabbut.

'How is your room, sir?'

'It's fine, absolutely fine. Thank you.'

'It is my best.'

'Well, I appreciate that.'

'And this you must light in the evening.' He handed Mabbut a green coil on a black stand. 'For the mosquitoes.'

'Thank you.'

'There is a toilet and shower at the end of the passage. It is shared.'

Mabbut nodded.

'That's fine with me. I see I'm not the only British guest,' he added, rather pleased with himself.

Parval Singh shook his head.

'No. No British ever come here.'

Mabbut faltered, then pressed on.

'I . . . er . . . I was recommended this place by someone who said their friend Mr Melville sometimes stays here.'

Mr Singh looked puzzled, and shook his head.

'But I just met him in the street outside. A tall white man wearing Indian dress.' Mabbut waved his hands around. 'Lots of hair.'

Singh's frown lifted.

'Ah, Mr Steiner. Yes. He's from Belgium.'

Mabbut risked a long hard look at Mr Singh. He returned Mabbut's gaze evenly.

'Well, he sounded English to me. Maybe when he comes back to the hotel we can ask him.'

Mr Singh shook his head.

'He is not coming back to the hotel, sir. He's gone.'

'Gone?'

'Mr Steiner has gone. Checked out. Left.'

There was a noise from the floor below. A door squeaked then slammed shut. The sound of footsteps receded down a passageway. Mr Singh mopped his neck with his cotton towel.

'Do you have your passport, please?'

Mabbut went back inside his room, rooted about in his jacket, then handed it over.

Mr Singh turned to go.

'I make you dinner in one hour.'

Mabbut followed him into the narrow passageway. It smelt of cinnamon.

'Excuse me. The gentleman. The . . . the Belgian gentleman. Do you know where he's gone?'

Mr Singh shook his head. 'I don't know. Mr Steiner comes and goes.'

Below them footsteps returned.

'One hour. In the dining room?'

'Can I eat outside?'

Parval Singh smiled firmly.

'No.'

* * *

Mabbut ate alone in the dining room, a gloomy space at the back in which the atmosphere was not enhanced by a strip-light which kept flickering every now and then as if it were about to expire. Mr Singh was nowhere to be seen. A plate of rice and dhal was brought in by a young boy Mabbut had spotted earlier, shooing dogs from the yard. Mabbut asked him for a beer, but none appeared. His plate was then removed and replaced, a moment or two later, with a white saucer on which there was a banana and a small, squashy orange. It was marginally cooler down here than in his room, so Mabbut lingered over his fruit, trying to decide what he should do next. Find out why Melville was calling himself Steiner for a start. Having finished both the banana and the disappointingly tasteless orange, he stood up and, instead of taking the stairs, crossed the empty reception area and headed towards the front door. The balmy heat of the night and the sound of the streets rose to meet him, as did a myriad of subtle but distinctive scents. In the little yard where Farud had dropped him earlier there was now a crowd of crouching figures. Despite the great heat some were shivering, pulling blankets around them. There were lights in the gloom and Mabbut caught glimpses of liquid and foil. Some figures turned towards him but their eyes were unfocused and they quickly turned away.

The night was so hot when Mabbut returned to his room that he was forced to activate the air con, whose convulsive thumps and shudders brought him a semblance of cool air at the cost of some dreadful dreams. He was stumbling through a forest, falling to the ground and being dragged onwards by some unseen force when the grating cry of a cockerel plucked him from the nightmare. He groped for his travel clock on the floor by the bed. Indignation was added to discomfort when the clock told him that it was half-past three. The cock sounded again, just below the window, then a dog barked and another dog answered from farther away, a donkey shrieked, and soon a whole arrhythmic animal chorus filled the night. Mabbut lay staring at the barely revolving fan, unable to recapture any of the elation of the day before. His mind was full of negatives. Melville was gone and Mabbut was clearly being told, in as many words, not even to think of following him.

He heard voices below the window; the slow, subdued chatter of families rising before dawn to prepare for the day ahead. Since leaving London he had kept his mind firmly on the job in hand, deliberately trying to keep at bay other, less welcome, trains of thought. But the voices below, and the intimate sounds of a family waking, brought his own fractured family to the forefront of his mind. Mabbut thought of his daughter, head over heels in love with someone he hardly knew, and Sam, receding into the distance. Most of all, he thought of Krystyna. In particular the new dilemma posed by his relationship with Rex Naismith. Rex, more than anyone, had helped him in his quest to find Melville, and yet at this moment Rex was probably climbing into bed with his wife. And he was completely powerless to do anything. Apart from think about it. Which, now, of course, he could not stop doing.

Mabbut switched on the light, walked to the window, shook out his sweat-soaked blanket and picked up a book, but nothing could comfort him.

It was only as dawn broke that sleep, irresistible sleep, finally embraced him.

3

He was woken by a loud hammering on the door. Light and noise streamed in from outside. The hammering stopped and he heard Mr Singh shouting, 'Sir! Sir! There is telephone for you. Downstairs!'

It was Farud. He sounded concerned.

'It is the feast day of King Rama. If we go to see the Temple of the Sun, we must go very early.'

'I don't think I'll see the temple today, Farud, if you don't mind.'

'The giant chariots process at midday, Mr Keith, but you would not have to follow them with everyone else. We shall have a balcony in the old palace. There will be water for you and some small food. I will make sure I get you there. I think maybe we can be with you in less than one hour. Please be ready.'

'Farud, *please*. I. Don't. Want. To see. The temple. Today.'

But the line had already gone dead.

Mabbut went back to his room. He found his mobile but realised he didn't have Farud's number. He sat down on the bed and tried to think. If Steiner/Melville really wasn't coming back to the guest house then Mabbut's first task had to be to find him before the trail went completely cold.

He washed as best he could in the tiny

bathroom along the passage, dressed then went down to breakfast. As he went by the reception area he saw, to his surprise, three very white men. They were dressed casually, but not cheaply, in heavy checked shirts and jeans. One was staring hard at a BlackBerry, another stood near the door, looking out at the yard with barely concealed disgust, while the third, an older man who seemed to be the leader of the group, was talking to Mr Singh.

'Mr Steiner left yesterday, sir.'

'We were supposed to meet him here. Today.'

They were Americans.

'I'm sorry, sir. He is not here.'

'Did he leave any message for us, any word where he might be?'

'I think he was going to Kolkata, sir.'

Two of the men exchanged glances.

'Calcutta?'

'Yes, sir, I think he is doing some business there.'

'Where does he stay, d'you know?'

'I can't tell you, sir.'

'You *can't* tell me, or you don't know?'

'I don't know, sir.'

'You don't have a sister hotel in Calcutta?' asked the man with the BlackBerry.

'Great Undiscovered Shitholes of The World,' muttered his companion.

The older man took out a wallet and leant across to Mr Singh.

'A name would be helpful,' he said quietly.

It was at that moment that all three of them became aware that there was someone else in the hallway. Four sets of eyes turned on Mabbut.

'Er . . . breakfast?' he asked Mr Singh brightly.

Mr Singh seemed grateful for the diversion.

'Yes, sir.' He indicated the dining room. 'I will come through.'

To Mabbut's surprise three or four tables were occupied. All by Indians, all of whom seemed to know each other. They were young to middle-aged men, who probably worked in business. They slouched on their chairs, listening and laughing every time the fattest one talked. The plate of sweet pastries on the table in front of them was rapidly diminishing.

Mabbut finished his banana and this time he left the orange. The room had emptied. He checked his watch. Farud would be here in half an hour and he would lose another day looking at temples. He was thinking what to do with a sticky sweet cake he regretted biting into when Mr Singh appeared at the doorway. He looked in Mabbut's direction for quite some time, forcing Mabbut, out of politeness, to take another bite of the titbit. Mr Singh came over to his table and sat down.

'Good breakfast, sir?'

'Yes, thank you. Very . . . very tasty.'

Mr Singh reached into a pocket.

'Your passport.'

'Oh, thank you.'

The proprietor sat watching Mabbut eat the cake. When it was finished, he leant forward and spoke quietly.

'Why are you here, sir?'

Mabbut was caught unawares. He was still

trying to frame a response when Mr Singh spoke again, and as he did so he cast a swift glance out into the hallway.

'No one like you comes here by accident.'

'I assure you, I'm just the kind of person who prefers a place like this. Somewhere I can find the real people, the real India . . . '

Mr Singh leant back and looked at Mabbut the way Melville had looked at him when he'd last burbled on about wanting to find the real people.

'Sir, forgive me, but I think we must be honest with each other.'

Mabbut was aware for the first time of an electric clock ticking softly on the wall.

'What do you want with Mr Melville?'

Mabbut nodded slowly. Be honest, he thought, but how honest?

'Hamish Melville is someone I admire and when I heard that he often stayed here I thought it was a good enough recommendation. Give it a try, I thought.'

'Heard from whom, sir?'

'Someone in London, who admires him as I do.'

Mr Singh leant back as if calculating his next move. Then, abruptly, he called out to the kitchen.

'Vinoo! Chai!'

He regarded Mabbut a moment longer. He seemed to be in no hurry. Indeed, the longer he paused the more his authority seemed to grow and the more Mabbut's confidence diminished. A clatter from the kitchen brought a welcome

135

diversion, and they both looked round as the tousled boy who had served Mabbut the previous night brought out two glasses of caramel-coloured tea and set them on the table.

'You like Indian tea, Mr Keith? I have black tea if you prefer.'

'No, this is fine. Thank you.'

Mr Singh picked up his glass, held it for a moment, then set it back on the table.

'Mr Keith. It is not well known that Mr Melville stays at the Farhan Guest House. Forgive me, but if you know this information then it is from someone close to him, or from someone who means him harm.' He spread his hands. 'Please?'

'I mean him absolutely no harm,' Mabbut protested vigorously. 'How could I? He's a legend. A hugely influential figure for anyone who . . . who . . . cares about the world.'

The proprietor nodded gently and waited expectantly. Mabbut knew the game was up. He cleared his throat.

'I was hoping to make contact with Mr Melville to tell him how much I admired him. That's all.'

'You're an admirer?'

'Absolutely.'

'You're not a journalist?'

The spicy tea made Mabbut cough, conveniently presenting him with a split second breathing space.

'I was once a journalist, a long time ago,' he said cautiously.

Mr Singh's head moved, almost imperceptibly, to one side.

'You won an award.'

'How did you know that?'

Mr Singh smiled and nodded towards the kitchen.

'I have a computer out there, as well as a kettle.'

Mabbut nodded. 'Of course.'

'You stood up for the underdog, Mr Keith.'

'Well, it was a while ago, and it didn't do me much good.'

Mr Singh narrowed his eyes and lowered his voice.

'There are also people poisoning the water here, you know.'

'Yes. I read some of the background. Big industry in rural areas. No safeguards.'

Mr Singh glanced out at the hallway again. The Americans had gone. He seemed relieved.

'You have heard of Astramex?'

The name rang a bell. It had come up in his research.

'Astra Mining and Exploration?

Singh nodded.

'Are they the ones poisoning the water?'

'And doing many other things besides, sir. Many very bad things. But they are a very big company. They have offices in Dubai, New York, Brussels. Here they work far from the cities. They build their plants up in the hills, away from prying eyes.'

He looked thoughtfully at Mabbut for a moment.

'You should investigate them. You could have a scoop.'

Sensing Mabbut's wariness, Mr Singh sat back and his face relaxed into a smile.

'As you may have guessed, Mr Keith,' he tapped the passport, 'Mr Keith Mabbut, I am not a hotelier.'

He looked quickly over his shoulder as a man and a woman came in. He half stood then watched as they went to their table.

'Vinoo!'

When the boy came out of the kitchen, he turned his attention back to Mabbut.

'I was a lecturer at the university here. My studies concerned the social conditions in our province, particularly the impact of industrial development on the *adivasi* — the original inhabitants, tribes who have lived in the interior for two or three thousand years. They are a very ancient Proto-Australoid people, and their way of life is now threatened by the mining company. My work came to the attention of Mr Melville and we have become quite close. Like you, I believe him to be a great man. One of those rare people whose gift it is to change many lives. For this reason he has enemies . . . '

He paused, appearing once more to be on the point of making some decision.

'Mr Keith. I don't know you but I feel that you are a good man. I read some of your articles online.'

'Really?'

Mabbut's astonishment clearly amused him.

'Oh yes, one can find anything if you know

138

where to look. Even in India.' He smiled. 'I was impressed. You wrote with feeling, Mr Keith.'

Mabbut took a sip of his chai. By now it was tepid.

'You haven't posted anything for a long time. What happened?'

'I made enemies too. And I had a wife and family to support.' Mabbut gave a short, dry laugh. 'Protest doesn't pay the bills.'

Mr Singh nodded earnestly. He picked up his tea then spoke to Mabbut with quiet passion.

'Last July I was asked to leave the university. Conflict of interest. Support the *adivasis* or support the new science building. To be called Astra Hall. I made myself *persona non grata* for choosing the *adivasis*.' He smiled, but Mabbut thought he detected the merest flicker of anger in the back of his eyes. 'This is my university now.'

Mabbut returned the smile then looked at his watch.

'When is your man coming?' asked Mr Singh.

'Very soon, I'm afraid. He's taking me to see more temples.'

Mr Singh sighed.

'And very beautiful they are. The finest in India.'

He lowered his voice.

'But they will always be here. Which will not be true of our tribal peoples out in the hills if Astramex get their way. If you like I can give you information and the name of some contacts who would be only too pleased to tell you what they are going through. I think this is a story that would interest you. And it needs to be told.'

'Thank you. I'm sure you're right.' Mabbut paused. 'But I'm not here as a journalist. I'm just a tourist who's keen to meet Mr Melville, if that's possible.'

Mr Singh nodded, giving Mabbut the briefest of smiles.

'The two are not incompatible.'

He stood and picked up the glasses from the table.

'You are a good man, Mr Keith, but a very bad liar. With your permission, I shall draw up an alternative tour for you. It will give you the chance to see something different.'

Mabbut opened his mouth to protest, but there was something unobtrusively persuasive about Parval Singh and he was intrigued. Beneath the humble appearance Mabbut sensed the powerful intellect and sharp focus of a genuine radical. What he was doing in a place like this seemed inexplicable, but he was prepared to give him the benefit of the doubt.

When Farud arrived Mabbut was up in his room packing. While Nirwan dusted the bodywork of the Toyota, Mr Singh took Farud to one side and explained the new itinerary he had drawn up. Farud nodded grimly, his face tightening as he listened. He looked up accusingly as Mabbut came down the stairs.

'This is not what I would have chosen, Mr Keith,' he said. 'Not at all.'

4

They were a few hours out of Bhubaneswar. Farud, so loquacious the previous day, was barely speaking to Mabbut now. It was abundantly clear that Farud found the whole new direction of their tour beneath him. He was a temple man. A highly qualified architectural archivist and historian with a wealth of knowledge available, for a relatively modest sum, to like-minded clients. He was not an outback man, or an adventurer, or a humper of heavy things up steep slopes. He was a scholar. Only this morning he had secured, after considerable effort, privileged access to some of the more erotic corners of the famous Black Temple of Kanark, thought by many to be the finest example of Hindu architecture in the entire country. There would be nothing like this up in the hills. But he was a professional. The fact that he had been persuaded to abandon the glorious temples and explore instead the aesthetically threadbare interior was because he was also a good company man and as far as the company was concerned the client was always right. This, and a small, personal down payment for the extra inconvenience, had secured his agreement.

They had left Bhubaneswar mid-morning, Mr Singh having produced two copies of his new itinerary and in return taken Mabbut's mobile number as a contact. After collecting supplies

141

and fuelling up the car, they had headed out on the less busy back roads.

For most of the day they rolled along through a flat and fertile plain.

Paddy fields, awaiting the second harvest of the year, stretched away in brilliant shades of green. The villages were frequent and attractive, with long houses, many of them thatched. The shops were busy and craftsmen worked away by the side of the road, fashioning baskets or mending bits of agricultural equipment. The women and children were mainly to be found beside the water tanks, large ponds dug in the centre of the village, which served as communal baths, washing machines and quite possibly sewers. There was little sign of modern technology, though Mabbut noticed the occasional satellite dish. Out in the fields, rice cutting and sowing were still done by hand, and building materials such as bamboo and laterite, a reddish-brown toffee-like stone, were moved about using wooden bullock carts. This new dimension to India was very appealing to Mabbut: a rural way of life persisted here, unfussily, organically and, from what he could see, efficiently. It was a living thing, as attractive to him as any temple. Not even Farud's pantomime sulk could prevent him surrendering to a buoyant and quite unfamiliar sense of wonder.

They had lunch at a dhaba, a roadside shack, beside a sluggish river, in whose shallows women were doing their washing, constantly readjusting saris that slipped from their shoulders, while

142

farther downstream, near the hefty chunk of concrete that served as a bridge, young men were cleaning their motorbikes. Two or three other customers ate with quiet concentration, breaking off every now and then to talk to the patron. In a corner, high on a wall pasted with pictures of the gods, a cricket match played on a silent television screen. Mabbut ate his thali with enthusiasm, wiping his tin tray clean with the last piece of chapati.

They turned off the main road and followed a slow and tortuous route which wound up from the coastal plain into low hills covered with trees and straggly undergrowth. As they moved farther away from the sea, the soft sedimentary rock gave way to smooth, sometimes monumental granite boulders. The road surface deteriorated, the settlements became fewer and the paddies smaller and less busy. With one last flourish, the sun swelled into a huge red ball then tucked itself away behind the hills. The light faded fast and the car fell quiet. Even Nirwan, who was wont to engage Farud in long, disputatious conversations, seemed aware that this was a time for silence. In the hills, way ahead of them, something caught Mabbut's eye. He wound down his window and felt a warm blanket of air envelop him. There was a line of lights in the forest, stretching like a giant necklace from the crest of the hill down towards the valley and then up again to meet the ridge.

'What are those lights, Farud?'

Farud spoke to Nirwan in Hindi.

'They are fires, sir. Lit by the local people.'

143

Nirwan added something.

'They make ash, sir. For cultivation. They are very simple people.'

They were still climbing when Nirwan swung the wheel round and they turned into a driveway. Farud spoke into his mobile in Hindi and when they pulled up in front of what looked like an Alpine chalet, two men in white kurtas stepped forward, peering into the vehicle. Farud imparted only the bare essentials.

'This is Government Guest House Number Forty-two.'

Mabbut stepped out of the car. There was a sharp moist smell coming from the trees and the air was perceptibly cooler.

'Who normally stays here? It seems very out of the way.'

'Tourists.'

'Tourists?'

'Those for whom historical architecture is not enough. Those who would rather see people who have not changed in two thousand years.'

Farud spoke brusquely, almost dismissively, as if this was not a subject he wanted to discuss at any length. Issuing a string of orders to the staff, he gestured at Mabbut to climb the steps that led to a veranda hung with empty birdcages. In the far corner a goat was quietly chewing away at the corner of some coconut matting.

Farud disappeared into a room behind the reception. Mabbut heard voices raised. After a while Farud re-emerged, patting his brow with a handkerchief.

'There is a problem with the rooms. They did

not expect anyone tonight and the generator is too small. This is the problem with places such as this. They require notice and,' he exchanged a sharp glance with Mabbut, 'we were unable to give it. You have a room,' he said to Mabbut accusingly, 'I shall have to share with Nirwan.'

★ ★ ★

Mabbut was struggling to unpack his things by the dim glow of an old standard lamp when the light went out altogether. He heard Farud's voice and another angry exchange ensued. Mabbut was feeling his way over to the door when it flew open, striking him sharply on the side of the head. The man bustling in with a hurricane lamp gave a shriek of horror.

'Oh, sir, so sorry,' he protested, adding unnecessarily, 'I have light for you.'

Behind him, Farud appeared, quivering visibly.

'There will be no electric light for a few minutes. The generator has been removed to the kitchen so that they can prepare our food. This is the problem, Sir Keith, if I may say so, with changing plans. I would not have brought you here. Is your head damaged?'

★ ★ ★

Mabbut dismissed his worries, and before long they were eating a simple meal of rice and various vegetable curries in a cavernous room farther up the hill. There were no other guests and a huge central strip-light discouraged intimacy. Two beers had been produced and Farud was talkative again.

'To my mind, Sir Keith, there was no finer flowering of art and architecture than in the days of Ashoka, and yet we know that human sacrifice was common at the time. Hundreds, if not thousands, of people were killed at the monarch's whim, yet their religion was Buddhism. These things did not take place under the Hindu rulers who followed, and who, incidentally, did not persecute the Buddhists but rather absorbed them into their religion, which is why you see so many symbols of the elephant in Hindu temples and why there are so many similarities in the motifs both religions use. It is indeed a lifetime that is needed to study these things, not if I may say so one day and a half.'

The light above their heads gave a brief shudder and died.

'Ah. That is the end of dinner.'

Farud spoke matter-of-factly, without looking around.

'It is very typical of these places.'

There was a bustling from outside and two men, the same two who had done everything, including cook the meal, appeared with lamps.

The older of the two, who had a fine-featured face and a habit of sucking in sharply through a gap in his teeth, smiled broadly at Mabbut.

'Your room all ready now, sir. Very comfortable. The light is good.'

He beckoned Mabbut to follow him. Farud hung back.

'I will see you at eight thirty in the morning, Sir Keith,' he said, adding, without enthusiasm, 'I will try to find something of interest in this area.'

★ ★ ★

After taking a cold shower, Mabbut opened the window. A pleasant scent of jasmine wafted in but there was not a breath of wind. He took out his notebook and jotted down some details of the day. Then, having cleaned his teeth and taken some moments to decide whether he should lie on top of the sheet or beneath it, Mabbut stretched himself out on the low bed and fell into a deep sleep.

In his dream he was in thick jungle again, only this time with Farud and Krystyna, and Rex Naismith, who was wearing Highland dress. They were clawing and clambering their way through an impenetrable wall of vegetation. The ground shook uncontrollably, sending rocks and boulders raining down on top of them. They struggled ineffectually across the mossy bark of trees as the roar of the avalanche grew louder and louder until it was directly above them and around them and the forest canopy was suddenly split apart as a single gigantic slab hurtled towards them. Mabbut's eyes sprang open. He lay rigid with fear, his heart pounding. The oddest thing was that although the images had gone, the sound remained. And it was real. The walls *were* vibrating. As he listened, the rumbling slowly faded away.

A hideous figure confronted them as they walked a little way off the road towards a bleached white shrine.

'That is Kali,' Farud said, pointing. 'The black mother goddess.'

The statue's mouth was open in a vicious snarl, around her neck hung a noose of human skulls, and in her left hand she bore a bloody, dismembered limb.

'She is good.'

'Good?'

'She is the consort of Siva, the creator and the destroyer. She is destroying evil.'

'She looks terrifying.'

Farud laughed drily.

'So? Evil is terrifying. The destructive force is part of the creative force. Siva and Kali control the power of the universe. Siva is good, Kali is the avenger. Look here.'

Farud led Mabbut through a low archway to the small temple inside the shrine. Set into the walls was a series of roughly painted pink posts sticking up from the ground.

'These are the linga. The lingam is the sign of Siva. And look here.'

In the second wall were a number of alcoves depicting scenes in which the lingam was being applied to the yoni quite vigorously and from many different angles. Farud, who struck Mabbut as possibly being a bit fastidious about such matters, seemed quite at ease with this cornucopia of copulation. Mabbut was struck by the irony of it. At home such explicitly sexual material would not even be displayed in cling-wrap on the top shelves of newsagents, let alone on the walls of religious buildings, whereas India, a much less sexualised society, seemed quite able to celebrate the erotic, provided it appeared in a temple.

'You will find that there are not many temples like this out here. The people who live in the hills are very primitive. They are animist, you know, and there is little work of any quality.'

Mabbut walked around, looking at the walls. The perkily poking couples awakened all sorts of memories. Painful, in the case of Krystyna, happy in the case of Tess, complicated in the case of Mae. Reaching sexual maturity in the late sixties, on the cusp between liberation and guilt, Mabbut had initially erred on the side of guilt. However many times he was told it should just be fun, sex, for him, had implied a commitment, inseparable from an emotional relationship. To be honest, looking back now, he had made a meal of it. And in somehow trying to restrain his lust, he'd only made things worse. Fumblings, ill-timed lunges, dark gropings and desperate withdrawals. How different from the breezy figures on these walls.

Good, quiet, thoughtful sex had come only with Krystyna. She was Catholic rather than catholic in her tastes. Monogamy for her was not a choice, it was a duty. This had had a relaxing effect on Mabbut, who, while defending promiscuity on political grounds, discovered himself to be much happier with constancy. And with sex and work in harmony they had been the perfect couple, having intercourse at a slightly higher frequency than in most newspaper surveys. So what had changed? Had it been the setbacks in his working life that had affected their sex life or the very repetitiveness of their sex life that had made him somehow dissatisfied with his work?

As their sex life slowed, without explanation, falling below the national average, Mabbut justified this as normal enough; that was what happened to married couples as they got older and physical sex became less important. When he and Krystyna separated, sex, or the lack of it, was never mentioned, it simply wasn't an issue. Now, here, on a hot day on a high hill in eastern India, Mabbut realised that both of them had been lying. She had found sex with Rex (he was fairly sure) and he had found sex with Tess. In a way, the desire for new partners made them equal again. But then if they were to be truly equal he would have to admit that Tess was certainly less to him than Rex clearly was to his wife. A true equivalent would be the enigmatic Mae, for whom his feelings were not primarily about passion, or short-term relief — she was the only other person he'd ever considered spending the rest of his life with. The revelation that someone apart from him had wanted to spend the rest of their life with Krystyna had hurt him very much. Until that revelation he had always felt that he could step back from the brink and somehow reclaim her. But how hypocritical was that?

He took one last look at the carefree cavortings on the wall of the shrine. Rather than taking comfort from the innocent joyfulness, the little drawings made him aware of everything he'd lost.

Behind him, he heard a heavy clearing of the throat. He turned abruptly to find Farud eyeing him with a mixture of amusement and disdain.

'Would you like to stay longer, sir?'

Mabbut cleared his own throat in what he hoped was a business-like way.

'No, no. Let's go.'

When they reached the car, Mabbut took out his copy of Singh's hastily typed notes. He unfolded the page, struggling to read the names.

'The Masoka Hills?'

Farud nodded. 'Of course, sir.'

They set off. The day was growing hotter and Mabbut gladly accepted the guilty pleasure of the air con as they pulled on to the road, heading north-west and still climbing.

After a long phone call Farud turned back to Mabbut.

'I have found a small village near the Masoka Hills which we can see and where we can spend the night.'

He sounded less than enthusiastic.

'It is a village of the Masira Kidonga tribe. It will not be comfortable but I have made sure that you will have suitable accommodation. Nirwan will erect a tent.'

Through the afternoon, progress became increasingly slow as the road surface deteriorated, the tarmac often reduced to nothing more

151

than a gesture, a thin strip on the crown of the road. It was almost dusk and Farud was looking anxiously at his watch when they were all flung forward as Nirwan braked sharply, blasting the horn. They had rounded a bend to find a convoy of ten-wheeled flatbed trailers parked beside the road in front of them. Lashed to each one, and secured by steel cables, were colossal circular turbine drums, twenty metres long and rising five metres high. The drivers of the trucks, wearing dhotis and greasy striped kurtas, squatted in front of their vehicles and watched with detached amusement as Nirwan was forced to mount the opposite bank to get past them.

'What on earth's all that, Farud?' Mabbut asked.

'It is machinery,' he shouted above the scream of the engine. 'For the refinery. At Kowprah.'

The wheels of the Toyota spun wildly before Nirwan switched to four-wheel drive and re-established the car's grip on the slippery mud. The onlookers spat betel juice on to the ground and laughed. As they passed, Mabbut noted the lettering stencilled on the side of each of the colossal drums: 'Astramex Corporation'.

Farud followed his gaze.

'The Masoka Hills are rich in minerals. They are very important for India.'

'Why are the trucks parked there?'

Farud consulted Nirwan.

'They are waiting to move. The convoys are so big that they are only allowed to move during the night.'

During the night, thought Mabbut. And he

152

thought of the nightmare that had awoken him in Guest House 42. Maybe those vehicles had been behind the sound of the avalanche.

★ ★ ★

They were still driving as darkness fell. Mabbut stared out of the window, trying to make some sense of the landscape, but all he could see was the outline of trees against a fading sky. This was the time of doubt, when travellers should be safely at their destination. In the city there were lights and people but out here in the countryside, there was nothing but darkness.

'We are not far off now, sir, believe me,' said Farud, without turning.

It was two hours later when Nirwan finally pulled the car off the road on to an uneven dirt track. Suddenly there were people ahead, shielding their eyes against the headlights, children in shorts and T-shirts prancing in and out of the beam. The car slowed and a middle-aged man in a sarong with a cartridge belt slung across his shoulders approached, shouting at the children and raising his hand. Farud looked distinctly nervous. Nirwan wound down his window and talked with the man. There was, in the Indian fashion, much head-shaking, before the man opened the back door and slipped in beside Mabbut. He began issuing vehement instructions to Nirwan.

'Farud, is this the village?'

Farud didn't answer straight away. In fact, he didn't answer for some time. And when he did it

153

was without his usual confidence.

'I think this is not the village. It is another village.'

* * *

Under instructions, Nirwan drove the car into what seemed to be the centre of the settlement. Around them were the indistinct shapes of mud-walled houses. The curious crowds who'd greeted their arrival were being held back by a small group of youngish men and women wearing what looked like army fatigues. They wore expressions of solemn excitement and something told Mabbut that these people were no more welcome here than he was. One or two were armed. The older man, who appeared to be their ringleader, climbed out of the car and motioned for Mabbut to follow him. Mabbut leant forward to consult Farud, and even before the man with the cartridge belt started shouting at him he knew from the widening of his eyes that his guide was more than anxious. He was terrified.

The three of them were bundled out and pushed at gunpoint towards the concrete steps of a house. A low timber door was thrust open and they found themselves in a cramped, dimly lit interior. Rolls of bedding lay on the ground and in a corner were more weapons, AK-47s mostly, stacked neatly upright, one against the other. There was a not unpleasant scent of sandalwood. The man from the car issued more orders and Mabbut, Farud and Nirwan were pushed down on to their knees. Farud had begun to whimper. One of the women, with deep black eyes in a pretty, oval face, seized some fabric and began to tear it into strips. Through the half-closed door Mabbut could see three or four men searching the Toyota. They found something and held it up to the light from their torches. Then Mabbut's head was jerked backwards and his eyes blindfolded. He heard Farud talking fast and beseechingly. Then there was a sharp hiss and he went quiet. Mabbut cried out as his arms were wrenched behind his back and his wrists tied. There was some voluble discussion, then the sound of soft footfalls heading for the door.

When he heard the door close, Mabbut whispered into the darkness, 'Farud?'

There was no answer.

He whispered a little louder.

'Farud?'

Farud's voice came back, small and fearful.

'I told you we should not have come here. This is bad country.'

'What's going on?'

'We are in deep trouble. These people are Naxals.'

Mabbut had read about the Naxalites. They were Maoists, named after the place called Naxalbari, north of Calcutta, where the movement had begun. Anti-capitalist, anti-government and to the left of the left, they frightened the life out of everyone, including those they were trying to help. The authorities had just issued bellicose statements that the time had finally come to rid India of these people; indeed, Mabbut had heard

155

that military action was imminent. No wonder they were touchy.

'What is their problem?'

'You.'

'Me?'

At that moment he felt a welcome breath of air as the door was pushed open. More orders were issued and his blindfold was removed. A young man in army fatigues stooped to enter the room. His complexion was lighter than that of most of his colleagues, his oval face severe and unsmiling. In the top pocket of his combat jacket was a neatly clipped row of pens and in his hand was a steaming bowl of freshly cooked rice and meat. He gave instructions, without shouting, and two men, one of them quite severely astigmatic, came forward, dragged Farud and Nirwan to their feet and bundled them out of the room.

The man smoothly lowered himself into the lotus position and set the food in front of him. Whatever it was, it seemed like the best thing Mabbut had ever seen. Pushing back the sleeves of his fatigues the man reached out and took a large forkful, which he ate slowly and with pleasure.

The man had seemed almost like a friend when he came in, not rough or bemused like the rest. A man with some style. A man he could talk to. So the fact that this person was not only not talking to him but was blatantly ignoring the most elementary rule of hospitality, the sharing of food, caused Mabbut to experience a sudden, and quite profound, sense of his own vulnerability.

It must have taken the man the best part of ten minutes to clear his bowl. Then he called out, not loudly, but with authority, and within a moment a jug of water and a single cup was produced. He drank deeply and appreciatively, again ignoring Mabbut.

Finally, pushing the empty bowl to one side, he reached into a breast pocket and extracted a cigarette. He lit it, and looking Mabbut in the eye, he exhaled slowly. When he spoke his English was nearly perfect.

'You have eaten well for many years. We have a long way to go before we catch up.'

'I don't know what's going on here, but . . . '

'You don't know what's going on here? Isn't it obvious?'

'Obvious?'

'You read the newspapers. People like you always read the newspapers. And you watch the television, listen to your radio. Don't tell me you don't know what's going on here.'

'I'm sorry, but I . . . '

'It's a war. A war between those who have eaten well for many years and the rest of us. You come here with your cranes and your bulldozers and you take our land, our culture and our way of life, so we come here to fight you. You are my enemy.'

All this was delivered in a soft, beguiling voice. There was no aggression or threat in his tone. The man drew another deep breath and exhaled. When he spoke again his voice was flat and matter-of-fact.

'The two Indians you are with will be taken into the jungle. You will not see them again.'

Mabbut, sweating profusely a second ago, felt a cold wave chase up his back.

'Don't harm them, they've done nothing.'

'They've done nothing, that's true. When they could have done something they've done nothing. They would rather help you than help their own people. What do you call them in your country? Traitors?'

Outside there were cries and shouts, then silence.

'Look, they gave me a ride here, that's all.'

The man rose and walked close to Mabbut, staring down at him, contemptuously.

'The car is licensed to one of the most expensive hotels in Bhubaneswar. We know them well. They provide all the cars for Astramex. Are you telling me you just happened to hitch a ride?'

Mabbut wished with all his being that he'd never let Ron Latham near this thing. He'd wanted to come to India under cover, move as and when he wanted, but Latham had insisted on the car and the hotel. 'It's our money, Keith, remember that.' Well, now look where that money had got him. Quite possibly facing execution. And only three days into the trip.

'I'm not with any company,' he began.

'You're lying.'

'Why should I lie?'

'You have maps marked with the route to the refinery. You have a camera.' He reached into a pocket on the side of his trousers and held up a thick wad of thousand-rupee notes. 'You have money.'

Mabbut realised with a growing sense of helplessness that they must have searched the car thoroughly, his bag included.

'Yes, Mr Keith Mabbut, I know where you are going, and your men will confirm this when we take them into the jungle.'

'Look, I'm just a tourist. I have no links with any company.'

'If you were a tourist you wouldn't be here. Tourists go to the temples.'

Try as he might, Mabbut could not keep the desperation from his voice.

'I wanted to see the interior. I wanted to see the local people. I don't like going where everyone else goes. I hate crowds.'

He saw a momentary flicker in the other man's eyes. For the first time in this chilling encounter he sensed a hint of an advantage. It was his only chance. He must lie, and lie well.

'I'm an independent traveller. I like to see what I want to see. Nobody is telling me what to do. I am not working on anyone else's account, believe me.'

He would never know whether his interrogator was on the point of believing him or not, for at that moment the first four bars of Beethoven's Fifth emanated from Mabbut's trouser pocket. His mobile phone was the one thing they hadn't found. As the chords jangled out again, Mabbut opened and closed his mouth soundlessly.

His captor came up close behind him and pulled off the strap around his wrists.

159

'Answer that.'

Mabbut slowly withdrew his phone. As he raised it to his ear, the man reached down and snatched it away from him. Eyes fixed on Mabbut, he put the phone to his ear.

'Yes?'

Someone went by the door. A child laughed and was quickly silenced.

'Yes, Mr Mabbut is here. Who shall I say is calling?'

There was a short pause and then an extraordinary transformation came over his face. He straightened up and the air of menace was replaced by one of concern. He ran a tongue across his lips and nodded.

'Yes. OK.'

Glowering, he lowered the phone and handed it back to Mabbut.

Mabbut tried to keep his voice under control.

'Hallo?'

The reply was not at all what he expected. A slow, rolling, half-amused drawl, almost a chuckle. And just a hint of a Scottish accent.

'So you've found the real people?'

Never had a voice been more welcome. Even if it was taunting him.

'Yes, I have. I have indeed.'

'I hope they're treating you well.'

'They think I'm with the mineral company.'

'Most of you are.'

Mabbut was seized, very briefly, with a renewed sense of panic.

'I have nothing to do with them!'

'Well, you seem to have fooled my people at

the guest house, so I'll give you the benefit of the doubt. Until I see for myself, that is. Hand me back to Romera.'

Mabbut must have betrayed a moment's confusion.

'Romera,' Melville repeated. 'The man who wants to kill you.'

5

It was two in the afternoon when he awoke. The inside of the tent was womb-like and powerfully hot. He looked twice at his travel clock, then lay back staring for a while at the peak of the tent. The first thing that struck him was that there was a peak at all, making the tent feel more like a tepee. And no polyester or aluminium ribbing here — this was a proper canvas tent, awakening childhood memories of campsites and fruit gums.

It had been almost light when he finally got to sleep, after Melville's men had come to the village and extracted him. Nirwan and Farud, who had been taken into the forest, had already left. So terrified had they been that as soon as they were freed they'd headed hell for leather back to their homes and wives and children, leaving Mabbut no option but to go wherever he was taken. The two very dark-skinned, wide-eyed boys Melville had sent to collect him had smiled a lot but spoke no English, so Mabbut could glean no information about where they were or where he was being taken. They had arrived with a flourish an hour or so after Melville's call, their battered jeep racing into the village ahead of a cloud of rising dust. They looked as though they were enjoying what they were doing, and were received with envious admiration by the younger villagers. The older men and women had remained aloof, clearly still intimidated by the insurgents in their midst.

Mabbut pulled aside the tent flap and looked around him. He was in a circular encampment outside a small village of mud and wattle huts. Majestic trees stood in isolation among wispy brown grassland, giving the impression of some great estate gone to seed. Mabbut could see no one else around, but then his eye was caught by movement in the village, and the sound of a voice. He looked again and saw a young child leaning out from the corner of a hut, staring towards him. He waved. The child disappeared.

Mabbut felt an urgent need to relieve himself. There was a stout tree near by so he walked over and stood behind it, making sure he was hidden from the village. As his pee hissed copiously on to the dry grass, he luxuriated in the pleasant sense of relief on all fronts. Then he heard a noise and, peering warily out from behind the trunk, he found three small boys standing in a line, watching him curiously.

The tallest of the three seemed to be the spokesman.

'Toilet,' he said, leading Mabbut to one of the farthest tents. He solemnly pulled aside the flap to reveal a privy, towel rail and canvas basin with water beside it.

'*Shukriya!* Thank you,' said Mabbut, hoping that a wide, self-deprecating smile would encourage them to laugh at his foolishness. If anything, it merely added a hint of pity to their serious, uncomprehending gaze. On an impulse, he returned to his tent, rummaged around in his things and retrieved a quarter-pound bag of Glacier Mints. He took out three and turned back to the children, only to find that another three had joined them. He went back to the bag and took out more sweets, by which time six more expectant faces had gathered. This time he brought out the bag. There were just enough to go round. The smaller boys clutched the tiny white polar bears warily until the ringleader popped one in his mouth. Soon there were more than a dozen little jaws at work. In the distance Mabbut could see a row of veiled heads peering curiously over the scrub-and-stick fence at the edge of the village. There were shouts and the children turned and ran home.

Mabbut gratefully took the last mint in the bag, aware that he was not only hungry but hot. Seeking the shade of the tent, he took out his notebook and pen. The last twenty-four hours had been so extraordinary he scarcely knew where to begin. In fact he couldn't begin. Writing things down had been his life, but at this moment, words felt superfluous. He was in the grip of events. He sat cross-legged on his low bed and, a little nervously at first, he listened to the silence around him.

After what seemed a very long time he heard whispers and a small hand reached in and cautiously pulled aside his tent flap. It was the same boy who'd spoken to him earlier.

'Food,' he said, beckoning Mabbut outside.

The boy had not come alone and a much emboldened little group greeted Mabbut's emergence from the tent with a puckering of lips and a raising of fingers to mouths. Their ringleader pushed them aside and, taking Mabbut by the hand, led him towards the village.

★ ★ ★

Mabbut wasn't sure what he'd been given to eat. It was some kind of corn mash, sticky and substantial but not particularly tasty. It was served with rice and chillies, in a bowl made from a large leaf that had been folded and pierced at either end with sharpened sticks. He ate in the cool semi-darkness of a room in one of the huts. In shape and size the room was almost identical to the one in which he'd been interrogated the night before. Two young women and an older man sat with him, while some of the bigger children watched from the doorway, silhouetted against the sunlight. They were not short of entertainment as Mabbut struggled both with the lotus position and with the unfamiliar technique of eating with his fingers. The older man, it seemed, couldn't bear to watch such incompetence and, bending low, he disappeared into the recesses of the house. The women, elaborately ornamented, gazed impassively at Mabbut. As his eyes adjusted to the gloom, he could see that the doorways on both sides were bordered with ornate patterns in what looked like pen and wash. After a while the older man reappeared with half a coconut shell full of a sharp-smelling milky juice. Mabbut took it, bowed, and sipped gratefully. Whatever it was, it wasn't milk. After another more cautious draught he handed it back. The man smiled broadly and insisted he drink again. After which he could remember very little.

* * *

'Are you all right in there, Mr Mabbut?'

Mabbut pulled himself up with an involuntary groan. He was lying stretched out on his bed and darkness had fallen.

Hamish Melville's head appeared through the tent flap. His eyes sparkled and his face was creased into a smile. He held out a water bottle.

'You might need this.'

He watched as Mabbut drank deeply.

'How's the accommodation?'

'It's comfortable, thank you very much.'

'These came from a disbanded Boy Scout group in Peshawar. Headmaster of the school thought them a little too Baden-Powell, you know, not quite in keeping with the times.'

Mabbut finished the water.

'Anyway, when you're ready, come and join us.'

Mabbut felt distinctly groggy. The water had helped, but his mouth still tasted foul and he realised he'd not cleaned his teeth for at least twenty-four hours. He found his toilet bag and toothbrush and did the best job he could. When he stepped outside he found that the campsite had been transformed. Lamps had been lit and beneath the tree where he'd relieved himself a generator thrummed. A trestle table had been set

166

up, to one side of which was a fire over which a blackened pot was being stirred. Melville was at the table staring into a laptop. Three Indians, all young and neatly dressed in tight cotton shirts or T-shirts, sat around him. One was on a mobile, the other two were studying a map. Hearing Mabbut clear his throat, they looked up. Melville turned and called him forward with a wide introductory sweep of his arm.

'Gentlemen, meet Keith Prynne Mabbut, citizen of the UK, born twenty-ninth March 1953. The year of the coronation,' he noted with mock gravitas. 'Passport number 276394702. Occupation? Well, I'm sure we'll find that out in due course.'

He indicated the one unoccupied chair at the table.

'Mr Mabbut, welcome to the University of Life. This is Kumar, this is Mahesh, Kinesh next to him and I'm Monsieur Steiner. From Antwerp.'

There was appreciative laughter around the table.

'Sit down and we'll get you a beer. Not Belgian, I'm afraid.'

Mabbut knew he was being teased but guessed that this was all part of the process, a bluff but necessary way of flushing him out. After all the game-playing of the last few days it was almost a relief, but he was aware that, now more than ever, he needed to keep his wits about him.

One of the young men poured a beer and put the glass in front of him.

Melville tapped at his keyboard with an air of

167

finality, closed his laptop and took in Mabbut's beer appreciatively.

'I'll have one of those too, Kumar, if you don't mind. As we have a guest.'

*　*　*

Food was laid on the table in a cluster of small stainless-steel bowls. Deep-fried aubergine, spinach, spiced okra, beans, lentils, pickles, yogurt and tamarind juice — 'good for a hangover', Melville assured him. Rice was ladled on to individual plates. Mabbut was discreetly handed a spoon, but the others, including Melville, tucked in with their fingers, moulding the rice into a ball which was then dipped in the various dishes before being popped into the mouth with a neat flick of the thumb. Melville's long and elegant hands were well suited to this dipping and rolling and he seemed as deft at the technique as any of his Indian companions.

Mabbut decided it was time to express his gratitude to Melville, for rescuing him.

The big man shrugged.

'There are a lot of people round here who don't like white folks, period. And why should they? They see them arrive in their big cars with their World Bank briefcases and they know that they're not here for a walk in the woods. They're off to the refinery. The refinery that was built on twenty-three local villages, and surrounded by a ten-mile barbed-wire fence. The refinery that makes people's eyes burn and their skin itch and their water taste bad.'

He threw out an arm in the general direction of the village.

'Give or take the odd ritual sacrifice, the Kidonga are basically friendly people, Keith. They look after each other, and they look after the place where they live. They don't want much more than to be left alone. But as they live on some of the most mineral-rich land in India that's getting to be a little more difficult. But they know I'm on their side. They trust me. That's why they gave you afternoon tea.'

He broke into a wheezy laugh.

'And a cocktail, I hear.'

At this, the laughter echoed round the table.

'A sago-palm special on your first day here. Now that *is* an honour, Keith.'

Melville's wide shoulders shook and eventually Mabbut joined in.

'Then there are those who pretend to be on their side,' Melville continued, 'while basically using them to fight their own war. Eh, Kumar?'

The stockiest of the three Indians angled his head in agreement, puffing his cheeks out as he did so.

'You mean the Maoists?' asked Mabbut.

Melville chewed and swallowed. Then he stood, picked up a cup and walked to a plastic bucket from which he drew water. He splashed it on his hands then nodded at Mabbut.

'Naxalites, Maoists. Naxals. Mostly well educated, committed to the overthrow of the government, the state and pretty much everything else they don't like. They attach themselves

169

to the tribals, appropriate their suffering and turn it into anger. Then they turn the anger into control. And they *do* kill people. Mostly policemen, but they can be unpredictable. You just happened to wander into a village that's one of their recent acquisitions.'

'Farud was right, then.'

'Farud?'

'My guide.'

'Some guide.'

'He didn't want to come up here.'

'He didn't have to.'

This remark hung in the air, and Mabbut was aware that the mood around the table had changed imperceptibly. He took a sideways glance at Melville and found the craggy face turned towards him, the deep blue eyes appraising him as they had done when they first met in the street in Bhubaneswar.

'Most 'lone travellers' can't afford to hire a Toyota, Mr Mabbut.'

For a few moments only the sound of the generator broke the silence. Mabbut knew he mustn't be stared down.

'Well, thank you for saving our lives,' he said quietly.

Melville's eyes flicked across the table.

'Thanks to Kumar, I know most of those Maoist boys.'

He pushed his plate to one side. As if at a signal, one of those who'd driven Mabbut back the previous night materialised from the darkness and began to clear the table.

'They're not all bad,' Melville added. 'We may

disagree on motivation but we agree on fundamentals.'

There was a pause. Once again Mabbut felt that he was being given space to explain himself, but the moment passed. There was general movement as people got up from the table and Melville accepted a cigarette from one of the men. He squatted down and lit it using a stick at the edge of the fire, straightened up and took a deep pull. He coughed lightly but involuntarily.

'Parval, sorry, Mr Singh, told me you were interested in the Astramex refinery.'

Mabbut flinched. What else had he told him?

'He . . . Yes. He thought that I might be more interested in that than another day of temples.'

'The temples here are world class.'

'I agree. But there are maybe a little too many of them.'

Melville pushed back his hair and flicked his cigarette ash to one side.

'Parval is quite political, you know. He has an agenda. I'm sorry if he forced it on you.'

'Well, he was only trying to help.'

'He must have thought you'd be interested.'

'Yes.'

'Because most tourists aren't. Interested.'

Melville returned to the table, pulled a lamp up close to him and bent over the map. With his long hair, round glasses and his long beak of a nose, he looked like some ancient alchemist.

'Maybe he thought you were a kindred spirit?'

Mabbut looked back into the darkness beyond the camp.

Singh and Melville were formidable. They

171

both had the same incisive way of cutting through bullshit. Manoeuvring him towards the truth. There was no way back. From now on it would have to be damage limitation.

'I was once an environmental journalist. We sort of hit it off.'

'A journalist?'

'Long time ago. I wrote for local papers mainly. Some nationals. Occasionally. I did a series of stories on pollution. Chemical spills from old-fashioned plants, that sort of thing.'

'And?'

'And I stopped doing it. I didn't make myself very popular.'

Melville nodded. 'I can imagine.'

'And my wife was more interested in a secure income than environmental glory.'

Melville leant back and began to roll himself another cigarette.

'Family?'

'Two children. Well, not children, young adults, I think they call them.'

'A happy family. I envy you.'

'That's what I thought, but my wife thought otherwise. She's not living with me any more.'

Melville raised an eyebrow.

'So what are you doing now?'

Mabbut came very close to an admission, but some instinct told him to hold back.

'Well, I've just finished a vanity project for an oil company. Nothing I was proud of. So yes, I thought I'd look around the world for a bit.'

Melville drew his head back in mock disapproval.

'A vanity project for an oil company? What sort of thing's that?'

Mabbut smiled cautiously. This was a delicate game.

'*A History of the Sullom Voe Oil Terminal.*'

Much to Mabbut's relief, Melville greeted this with a rich chuckle.

'No threat to Harry Potter, then.'

'I don't know about that. It's another tale of Scottish wizardry.'

Melville nodded in agreement. He took a pull on his cigarette, and as he exhaled, he frowned, as if recalling something.

'From what I know, the Shetlanders did pretty well out of Sullom Voe.'

'That's true.'

'There are plenty of people here who think that aluminium will be the saving of this place,' Melville went on. 'It's a poor area, after all.'

He looked across the table. Again Mabbut had that disconcerting feeling of being mentally frisked. But he had told enough of the truth to be able to return Melville's steady gaze.

'So what do *you* think?'

Mabbut shrugged. 'I've no idea, I'm just looking and learning.'

This seemed to amuse Melville.

'And who's going to look after you, now that your guide's gone home?'

Funnily enough, this was something Mabbut hadn't really thought about.

'Well, I shall look after myself. There must be a tourist office in the town.'

There was a grunt of laughter from Melville.

'This isn't Paris.'

'No, I suppose not.'

Melville folded up the map, took off his glasses and rubbed his eyes. Then, as if he had taken a decision, he briskly stood up.

'We can get you back to Bhubaneswar, but we've a little business to do on the way.'

Mabbut realised there was only one possible answer.

'That's great. Thanks.'

'We start early. But then everyone does round here.'

'I'll be ready. And, well . . . '

It was time to take the first step towards full disclosure.

'Yes?'

'I just wanted to say what anyone who's ever cared about the environment would say. It's an honour to meet you.'

Melville's expression hardly flickered. A hint of a smile, then he reached across the table for a pile of papers.

'You'll find some water in your tent.'

Mabbut nodded.

'Thank you. And goodnight.'

He was on his way to his tent when Melville called out to him.

'Mr Mabbut. There is one important rule. What happens here, stays here. I'm sure you understand.'

'Of course.'

He held Melville's eye for a beat longer than was comfortable.

'Sleep well.'

6

The call came before dawn.

Mabbut drank in the sweet, cool smell of the morning and downed his cup of black tea. Village life was already in full swing. Smoke rose from fires, cockerels were crowing, chickens clucking, and dogs barking. Figures could be seen beyond the village limits, squatting out in the countryside, adding their contribution to the night soil. With a tinkling of bells, a line of goats was being led out of the compound by two small children. Breakfast was modest and by the time the first light had risen on the eastern horizon, the tents had been struck and the two vehicles packed up and made ready.

Melville was businesslike. The banter had gone and he communicated through a series of barked orders. Once he was satisfied, he waved Mabbut towards a jeep. It was the one in which he'd been rescued two nights earlier.

'You ride up front with Kinesh.'

Melville, dressed in a cotton shirt and a billowing shalwar, slung his backpack into the vehicle in front, and jumped aboard. Kumar revved his engine, hooted the horn and the two 4x4s turned away from the camp, circled the village and bounced away to the west.

Kinesh was the youngest of the three who'd been at the table last night; he sat tall and very upright, as if he might have been in the army at some point. He kept his eyes firmly on the road ahead.

The jeep tipped forward as it followed Kumar's into a red earth ravine. Mabbut clung on to the handle above the window as they accelerated up the bank on the far side. He was painfully aware that his presence among the group was not likely to last long. Last night he was a new arrival, an amusing diversion at the end of a busy day. This morning he was a burden. He could sense this coming off Kinesh as the car swung along the track and the young man stared silently ahead. Mabbut knew that there was a distinct possibility that his pursuit of Melville could be over in the next few hours. He had to start work. With whatever material he had.

Mabbut looked across at his driver. He was light skinned, with a strong, angular profile and a large jutting nose.

'Have you worked for Mr Melville long?' asked Mabbut.

Kinesh nodded. He was adjusting the mirror.

'When he comes here.'

'Which is how often?'

'Two, maybe three times a year, sir.'

Kinesh threw the vehicle into four-wheel drive as they dived down into an old river channel, empty of water but thick with freshly dried mud.

'It must be a privilege to work with him.'

'Yes, sir.'

The 'sirs' rang with contempt. Mabbut waited a while before he spoke again, partly to see whether Kinesh might volunteer something,

176

partly because he didn't want it to sound like an interrogation. At that moment, two vividly coloured birds flew out of the bushes ahead of them and disappeared into the trees in a flash of scarlet and grey.

Mabbut grunted with surprise.

'Red-whiskered bulbul. *Pycnonotus jocosus*,' said Kinesh matter-of-factly.

'Thank you.'

'Mountain birds.'

'Are we high up?'

'Eight hundred metres.'

The plain had levelled out by now and Kinesh hung back as the dust cloud from Kumar's car billowed out ahead of them.

'Were you born here?'

Kinesh shook his head. 'Only Kumar is from here, sir.'

'And you?'

'I am from Delhi.'

'So how come you hooked up with Mr Melville?'

'I was at university. I'm studying biology and environmental science and he came to talk to us. About the damage we are doing to our environment. Here in India.'

Mabbut looked around him. The trees were more abundant here than at the camp, and there were bright yellow bushes and smooth grey boulders rising behind them.

'Looks pretty good to me.'

Kinesh smiled grimly. 'Wait and see. Sir.'

★ ★ ★

The sun was high and hot by the time they reached a metalled road. After the jolting of the past hour Mabbut breathed an audible sigh of relief. Kinesh pointed to an incongruous line of grey electricity pylons, hoisting swags of cable across the road and into the bush.

'On their way to Kowprah, sir.'

'Kowprah?'

Kinesh sounded almost scornful.

'The biggest aluminium refinery in the state.'

'But more electricity's a good thing for everyone, isn't it?'

'If everyone had it, yes, sir. Seventy per cent of this supply is for the private mining companies. One ton of alumina needs 250 megawatts of electricity. Kowprah will produce six million tons of aluminium, so they need 1,500 million megawatts a year. Which is sixty million tons of CO^2. And they want more plant, so that means moving more people off the land they have lived on for two thousand years.'

Kinesh blared his horn as a packed bus hurtled past, pushing them close to the serrated rim of the road.

'And now they want the sacred hills too, in order to make them even more rich!'

There was something about Kinesh's delivery that raised Mabbut's critical hackles. He'd heard the same thing said at Sullom Voe. If anyone gets rich it's bad for everyone else. He had sympathy for the view but basically it was dishonest.

'We all use aluminium. Your car. Your mobile phone. Your cooking pots and aeroplanes.'

'And we pay a lot of money to the company,

178

sir. They make big profits from us. But the people who live in the way of Kowprah pay with their livelihood. Five thousand hectares of farmland cleared for the refinery.'

'But you are an educated man, Kinesh. Do you not think people have to change, learn new things, to be given the chance to be as educated as you are?'

'Sir, my father once told me, 'You carry too much in your head, you should learn to carry more *on* your head'. That was what my father told me, sir. To respect the old ways.'

For the first time his passion sounded personal. And for the first time, the merest flicker of a smile crossed this serious young man's face.

The road flattened out and Mabbut felt his eyes closing as the steady hum of the engine and the monotony of the landscape lulled him to sleep. He woke suddenly, thrown forward by an abrupt halt and the sound of a deep-throated horn. A truck was hurtling straight towards them, veering away from head-on collision by a matter of inches.

'Bulk carriers from Kowprah, up and down this road all the time!'

Kinesh reached for a cloth and wiped his hands, before slowly moving off again. Mabbut could now see what the problem was. Half the road was being relaid and traffic had been diverted into one lane.

Kinesh gestured ahead.

'They want a bigger road to take all the trucks. That's what is happening here.'

Mabbut looked out curiously as they passed the roadworks. It seemed as if all the work was being done by women. Some wielded pickaxes and were opening up holes in the road, while others filled their baskets with granite chippings and carried them on their heads to the holes. The women were of all ages, from young girls to grandmothers, and all wore dusty saris, which drifted in the breeze. None had protective clothing of any kind.

'They're women. The road builders are all women!'

'You'll see them all over India, sir.' Kinesh nodded grimly as they bumped over the freshly laid road. 'They're Dalits.'

'Bottom of the caste system?'

'They are outside the caste system, sir. They are untouchables.'

'But they must have rights. To be dressed properly, at least.'

'They have no rights, sir,' Kinesh replied quietly.

Two women stepped back to let them pass. Both were tall and fine featured but the work had left them gaunt and lifeless. Their eyes met Mabbut's as the car drove past, but there was no change in their expression. For a long time Mabbut stared into the wing mirror, unable to take his eyes off them as they slowly went back to work, like phantoms.

A few miles farther on Melville's car signalled a left turn and they followed a road which led up through the forest for an hour or more, before pulling to a halt on a rock-strewn track. Melville was first out of his vehicle, camera slung over his shoulder, directing the others with brisk hand movements. His wayward hair was tucked beneath a felt cap, and his white kameez flew up as he ran. Mabbut was impressed. Here was a seventy-five-year-old ex-banker looking for all the world like a mujahed taking on the Russians. Putting his finger to his lips, Melville beckoned Kinesh to kill his engine. He came across to the car, and they spoke briefly in Hindi. A small yellow bird skittered across the glade and Mabbut noticed Kinesh's sudden upward glance. Kumar and Mahesh didn't seem interested. They stood by their jeep, loading backpacks.

Melville came across and whispered into Mabbut's window.

'We're stopping for a while. To take some photographs. A bit of fieldwork, you know.'

'Can I come with you?'

'No.'

Melville nodded at Kinesh.

'If you want to help you can stay with Kinesh and keep an eye on the vehicles.'

With that, he motioned to Kumar and Mahesh and the three of them moved quickly away, over a fallen tree, down a narrow water-course and out of sight.

A radio crackled, and Kinesh leant into the cab. There was a brief discussion then the receiver was clicked off.

⋆ ⋆ ⋆

181

'Water, sir?'

'After you.'

'There's one for each of us.'

The water was cool and Mabbut drank greedily. A sudden, very loud crash came from the trees above him, and he jumped, spilling the water as he did so. Kinesh reached into the glove compartment and took out a pair of binoculars.

'What was *that?*' Mabbut asked.

'Malabar pied hornbill. *Anthracoceros coronatus*,' Kinesh replied, scanning the trees. 'Yellow beak. Blue, black and white tail. Powdered hornbill beak is very much sought after. It is good for vigour.'

He followed the bird with the binoculars as it flapped off noisily into the forest, then turned back to Mabbut.

'You like birds, sir?' he asked as they wandered a short distance along the track.

'My father did. He was brought up in the country.'

'And you were not, sir?'

'No, I'm a city boy. Leeds. Yorkshire. I live in London now.'

'I should like to see London,' Kinesh said with feeling. He glanced up into the trees again, as if searching for something.

'I hate it here.'

'You hate it? Why do you hate it?'

'I don't like what India is becoming, sir. It is a country of the very rich and the very poor. And because so many are very poor, the rich can get richer even quicker. And they don't care, you

182

know. They don't even live in this country, most of them.'

'It's progress, Kinesh.'

'That's what I used to think, but Mr Melville has changed my mind. He says we have to be true to each other. We have to recognise that we are all similar. No one is inferior. That's what he says, sir, and believe me — '

'Ssh!'

Kinesh turned at the same time as Mabbut. They watched as a black SUV approached along the road below them and drew to a halt. Two men got out. They were wearing dark glasses, identical white shirts and chinos. Kinesh's eyes widened.

'Security!' he whispered.

One of the men was staring up at their cars. The other had lit a cigarette. He took a leisurely drag, then the two of them began to advance up the track.

'I must warn the others,' said Kinesh. 'You stay here. Keep them talking.'

'About what?'

'Anything.'

Kinesh, bent double, snaked his way back to the vehicles.

Mabbut walked towards the men, trying to look assured, innocent even. He was aware that his heart was beating fast and his legs felt oddly unsteady. He gave them a broad smile.

'Beautiful spot.'

The two men stopped.

'Where you from?'

'England.'

183

'UK?'

'If you'd rather.'

'Why do you stop here?'

'Er . . . I'm birdwatching.'

The taller of the two men took off his imitation Ray-Bans and appraised Mabbut.

'The birds round here are fantastic, don't you think?'

He could hear the crackle of the radio from their car. Mabbut knew he had to press home the advantage.

'I've come all the way from London to see them.'

'See what?'

'The Malabar pied hornbill. *Anocatheros corona*. The Red-whiskered bulbul. *Picolotus jocotus*. And so many others. There's one now!' Mabbut shouted and pointed into the forest behind them. As they wheeled round, he stole a quick look back at the vehicles. Kinesh couldn't be seen. Mabbut smiled what he hoped was a suitably deranged and obsessive smile as the men turned back to him.

'Did you catch that? Tiny bird. Blue upper parts, tan breast. Native of Nepal. Lovely.'

His act certainly worked on one of them, who shook his head, muttered to his companion and began to back away, but the other man lingered, looking behind Mabbut towards the two vehicles.

'Why two?'

'Why two what?'

'Why you have two vehicles?'

'There are a group of us.'

'Where are the others?'

'In the forest. Spotting.'

Then Mabbut made his first mistake. As the younger man moved up the slope towards him, Mabbut instinctively went to block his path. It was a clumsy move and the man, now close enough to Mabbut to see the sweat on his face, tensed up and shouted to his colleague. He in turn headed back up the hill.

'This is a high-security area,' said the first one. 'We should like to examine your cars.'

'Are you police?'

'It would be in your interest to let us see them.'

They pushed past him, and Mabbut turned, stricken. There was nothing more he could do.

Then, quite suddenly, from deep within the forest, came a growing, surging roar. The tree canopy sprang into life, and the air was split by shrieks and screams and the beating of wings. The massive roar came again, much nearer now, and the squawks intensified. Trees and branches began to sway and all heads turned towards the road. There, where once had been a dense and leafy vista of sal and tamarind, stood a wall of steel. Mabbut recognised it instantly. It was the convoy. The huge haulage unit at the front, its cab as high as the young trees around it, steamed and hissed with anger as it towered over the white Subaru that stood in its path. A third and prolonged blast of the horn sounded. The two security men raced down to the road as the sound filled the forest, amplified by others behind it in a syncopated bellow of rage. Mabbut

185

watched open mouthed as the SUV skidded round, and like a mouse before an elephant, shot off down the road. With a squeal of releasing air brakes the truck lumbered into motion, drawing its massive load behind it. Then the next in line began to haul itself up the hill, boughs snapping in its wake. The third transporter, which had been halted on a steeper slope, took longer to get going. The cab reared and bounced like a horse at a jump, and it seemed an age before the gears engaged and the last of the immense loads thundered by, leaving behind it something equally unnatural: a forest devoid of any sound at all.

Mabbut remained standing there for some time, shaken, almost literally, by what he had seen. He turned only when he heard voices behind him. Kumar and Mahesh were zigzagging back through the trees with Melville a little farther behind. Kinesh was already at the cars, stowing equipment, fitting cameras back into boxes. Melville grinned at Mabbut as he emerged into the glade.

'Good work, guys!'

He called out to Kinesh. 'Map?'

He looked at the map briefly, then, calling out co-ordinates to Kumar, jumped into the first jeep.

'Let's get out of here!'

It was a difficult half-hour as the vehicles skirted the main road and weaved along forest tracks. Kinesh said little as he concentrated on squeezing the jeep between trees, crossing streams and negotiating tricky gradients, and it wasn't until they reached the outskirts of a sprawling village that Mabbut realised how much his companion's attitude had changed in the course of a morning. Elation had tempered caution, and youthful exuberance had softened his seriousness. As they sat round a table in the anonymous main street he realised that this mood had filtered down from the top. Melville's eyes shone as he spoke.

'That was something! I tell you, if we wanted proof that they're stepping up capacity, we have it now. Those new smelters are so important they'll be moving the parts in twenty-four hours a day. That's why their goons are driving around the forest like they own the place.'

He looked at Mabbut, and his smile finally seemed devoid of suspicion.

'I'm sorry you had to meet them face to face. If they'd looked inside our vehicles we'd have been in real trouble, so thanks for helping out.'

Bhindi bhajis arrived at the table, freshly fried from the pan.

'Why are they all so jumpy?' asked Mabbut as he ate.

'The Kowprah refinery was built five years ago after a whole series of dodgy planning permissions. A lot of money went into a lot of pockets. Astramex got what they wanted and the state lost six hundred hectares of good farmland.'

Melville seemed to be in his element. There was none of the caution he'd displayed back at the camp. This was Melville unplugged and all Mabbut had to do now was listen, and try to

187

remember what he said.

'These guys can never get enough. Once they've sniffed the ground then it's only the dollar signs that matter. Astramex want to double the amount of aluminium coming out of Kowprah. And what we found proof of this morning is that they're not bothering to wait for permission. The new equipment's being shipped in fast. A fait accompli. That's the way these people operate. Do what you want and don't let the other side stop you.'

Melville paused, took some more food and passed the plate around.

'The trouble is that the Kowprah refinery is limited at the moment by having to bring the basic raw material, the bauxite, in from outside. If they can find it somewhere closer then things will be a lot easier for them, and a lot more profitable. And, surprise, surprise, they have found bauxite deposits a *lot* nearer — in the hills right next to the plant! What could be better than that? Except that there are people living in those hills, thousands of them, and they've been living there for as long as anyone knows. They worship the Masoka Hills as the reason for their survival. And not without good reason. Bauxite holds and distributes water, so two or three rivers and a whole network of streams rise on those hills. Strip the crown and the rain will just run away down the flanks. That will mean the end of a way of life and an irrigation system that provides cultivable land right down to the sea.'

He gestured to Kumar, who reached into his bag and produced a bottle of water, loosening

188

the cap as he passed it over. Melville drank deeply and passed it across to Mabbut.

'Thanks to this morning's nature ramble we now have incontrovertible evidence that Astramex is bringing in heavy plant that can only be justified by the extraction of bauxite from the local hills.'

'So, what can you do about it?'

Melville exchanged glances with the three others. He looked at Mabbut carefully, but not unkindly.

'We shall see . . . '

7

Mabbut was happy. Not just with the events of the day, but also because there had been no more mention of putting him on a train back to Bhubaneswar — at least, not yet. For a second night he found himself in Melville's camp. It was set up at the base of a smoothly eroded granite outcrop whose quartz crystals sparkled in the glow of the setting sun.

Kumar and the boys busied themselves with a generator which coughed and spluttered into life. In his tent Mabbut took out his phone and found two text messages from Ron Latham, which he ignored, and one from Krystyna, leaving only her name. There was just enough battery left for a single call. He checked the coast was clear, then tapped in her number. There was a long pause. He was about to hang up when the connection clicked in.

'It's me.'

She seemed to be expecting him.

'Where are you?'

'I'm in India.'

'Are you safe?'

'Yes, of course I am. Why shouldn't I be?'

'Your agent rang me. Then a man who spoke like a recorded message.'

'Ron Latham? He rang you?'

'He kept asking if you'd called. Why is he chasing you?'

'He's paying me, that's why.'

He could almost hear the sound of her ears pricking up.

'Should I tell him you called?'

'No, Krys. Don't have anything to do with him, he'll never leave you alone.'

'Is he going to make you rich?'

'Would that make a difference?'

'It would make a difference to you.'

It wasn't the answer he'd hoped for.

'Where's Rex?'

But the phone went dead. No more charge.

'Fuck!'

'Everything all right?'

A shaggy grey head peered round the flap. It was Melville.

'We're eating soon.'

'Oh, thanks. I'll join you.'

Melville pointed at the phone.

'You want that thing charged?'

'Sometimes I think I prefer it this way,' said Mabbut, trying to make light of the situation.

'Couldn't agree more. Only use mine for working.'

Mabbut handed the phone to Melville.

'When you're ready, then. Kumar's cooking. Not to be missed.'

Outside a fire had been lit and Mahesh and Kinesh were hunkered down around the portable table. Cobra beers were opened and laptops and mobiles set up. All three men were engrossed in their work, which consisted mainly of long phone conversations, almost entirely in Hindi. Occasionally Kumar would be called away from the fire and another language was spoken.

Feeling rather like a spare part in the midst of all this activity, Mabbut wandered to the edge of the camp. The sun dipped below the horizon and night came almost instantly. He walked a little farther, outside the ring of light around the camp, and sniffed the air. It was very dry here and the smells he picked up were reminiscent of fire, of burnt things. A breeze blew up and he could hear the creaking of a tree branch. He squatted down, ferreting around in the dust until he found a stone whose weight and smoothness pleased him. Turning it over in his hand, he tried to concentrate his mind on what had once been his life. Krystyna sitting with him at the kitchen table, shaking her head at his outrage over something he'd read in the newspaper. Or Sam, before the theatre had seduced him, chasing a ball on a Suffolk beach, and Jay, before the complications of Shiraj, lying on her tummy in front of the fire, twisting a lock of hair as she devoured a book.

★ ★ ★

'Keith!'

It was Melville's voice.

'Grub up!'

Mabbut checked his watch. Almost half an hour had gone by and he was still holding the stone he had picked up. He stood and hurled it as far as he could into the bush then turned back to the camp.

They ate simple but tasty food — tandoori chicken with lentils and potatoes and a small but spicy curry. A lamp in the centre of the table flickered in what was now a deliciously cooling breeze. They reminisced about the day and there were many jokes about Mabbut's sudden conversion to birdwatching. Melville lit a cigarette and took another beer and embarked on a long and elaborate account of the mating habits of the hornbill. Kumar picked up one of the clay pots in which the food had been prepared and described in detail how a nearby tribe had devised a similar pot for the collection of sago palm juice. The young boys would carry these pots to the top of the trees and hang them there to collect the sticky white sap, which was converted into the indispensable village brew. This led to a spirited argument about how much could be collected from each tree. Mahesh had heard that it was a litre a night. Kumar swore that a good tree would give as much as five litres a night, and another five during the day. This led on to a discussion of how best to climb trees. And, almost inevitably, to a late night race up a nearby mahua tree, won, impressively, by Kumar. A triumph of technique over physique.

Sometimes Melville joined in and sometimes he sat back and regarded his protégés like an indulgent father. Far from playing the role of guru, he seemed happiest indulging in jest and banter. At one point, Kumar chided the great man over his inability to master *toi*, the dialect of the Masira peoples. Melville protested, and after a few misplaced attempts he brought Kumar to

193

his knees with laughter, then saved the day by faultlessly reciting the local names of all the village chiefs.

It was one of those rare evenings that could never be planned. When everyone present — Kinesh, the thoughtful idealist from Delhi, Mahesh, the high-tech wizard with three children in Kolkata, Kumar, the educated tribal, Melville the living legend and Mabbut, his secret biographer — ceased for a few hours to be anything other than fellow human beings. This was certainly Mabbut's view as he walked some distance away and stood, a little unsteadily, relieving himself beneath the tree up which Kumar had so recently scampered.

When he turned back to the camp the boys had gone to their tents and only Melville was left, sitting at the flimsy table, map open in the lamplight, his profile throwing shadows over a nearby tent.

He looked up as Mabbut approached, and laid something on the table.

'Your phone. All charged up.'

'Thanks. And thanks for including me. That was a good night.'

He went to take the phone but as he did so, Melville withdrew it.

There was a moment's pause. Something had changed. Melville was examining him with that uncomfortable inquisitorial stare again. Mabbut was aware that the beers had loosened his tongue. Maybe he'd said too much.

'We'll be moving early tomorrow. Kumar'll call you at four.'

Mabbut gave a grimace.

'Fine. Early bird . . . '

'We'll drop you at Kindara Junction by six. There's a train to Bhubaneswar at seven thirty. Sleep well.'

Melville returned to his map, one hand still resting on the phone. Mabbut stood there, feeling foolish. He had deluded himself that what had happened that day was confirmation that he was now a part of it all, whatever 'it' was. Now he was quietly and firmly being reminded of reality; that, as far as Melville was concerned, he was in the way and would remain so. But something, some sprig of indignation, stirred inside him. Mabbut reminded himself that he was fifty-six years old and had at one time been a journalist whom many had envied. He had come so close to his story, and he was not going to lose it without a fight.

'I'd like to stay with you, if that's possible.'

'I'm sure you would.' Melville didn't look up.

'I can pay my way. Put some money in the kitty.'

Melville dropped his pencil and it slowly rolled across the map, stopping, as if he'd always intended it to, just before the edge of the table. He looked up. His eyes were flat and hard.

'I can't do that, Keith.'

Mabbut felt a chill and at the same time a realisation that, for better or worse, cards must be put on the table.

'I can't do that,' Melville repeated. 'Not without knowing a little more about you.'

195

Mabbut shrugged. 'There isn't much to know. I'm just . . . '

Melville held up the phone.

'Like why you're working for Urgent Books.'

★ ★ ★

Which is how it happened. Instead of telling Melville why he was here, Melville told *him* why he was here. Ron Latham's name and number were all over his mobile, a string of Latham's messages awaiting replies. And Melville's tentacles seemed to stretch far and wide. By the time the short, sharp grilling was over, it was clear that Melville had most of the information about him. He knew about the car hire, he knew about the hotel bookings. There was nothing left to deny.

'So, why *are* you here?'

'To write a book about you.'

Melville betrayed just the trace of a smile.

'Now we're talking. You mean *they* want a book about me, and they're paying *you* to do it.'

'Is that such a bad thing?'

Melville leant back.

'I can save you a lot of time and effort right now. I'm not interested in talking about myself. I'm interested in what I can do, in the time left to me, to prevent a little of the damage we seem hell bent on inflicting on this long-suffering planet. I'm not the story.' He gestured towards the horizon. 'These people are the story. The Masira Kidonga, the Musa, the Gyara. The way things are going they have even less time than I do. And that's just here in India. There are people all over the world who are being rolled over. I don't have time, Keith, for newspaper puffs and glossy profiles. That's another world. The world that wants us all to keep buying and consuming and stuffing ourselves, whatever the cost to those around us.'

Mabbut felt invigorated by finally being able to talk openly. And he felt a vehemence too.

'With respect, Mr Melville, you could just have handed me the opening paragraph. That's why, like it or not, you are admired by every generation. You've earned it by following your own path, by not taking anyone else's shilling and that gives you the immense privilege of being listened to. Your story is the story of all the causes you've championed. Through your story, their story is told. It's what you've dedicated your life to — giving a voice to the anonymous and powerless. I just want to help that voice be heard.'

Melville's pole-like frame had bent lower and lower over the table. His long, thin hands had come up over his face, and it was clear he was shaking. Mabbut wondered, just for a moment, if he might have moved the man, but when Melville finally straightened up, it was somewhat humiliating to see that the tears were tears of laughter.

'Oh dear!'

Melville took a deep breath and gestured at the table.

'Sit yourself down, before you have a heart attack.'

Mabbut, by now deeply confused, pulled out a chair.

'I'm sorry. I didn't mean to mock, but I had you down for an old hack.'

Melville held up his hand to forestall any protest.

'A decent old hack, but suddenly . . . '

He shook his head, still gurgling with laughter.

'You're Martin Luther King, for fuck's sake!'

There was a sudden gust of wind and a hiss as dust scattered. Melville wiped his eyes and spread his hands apologetically.

'I'm sorry. We've all been working too hard.'

He reached for a tin and picked out a hand-rolled cigarette.

'So, Keith, before I kick you out for spying, I feel I at least owe you an explanation. Smoke?'

Mabbut shook his head.

'Bad habit.' A flame sprang from the match. 'One of many.'

Melville drew on the cigarette and looked up at the night sky.

'What you have to realise is that I'm not a god figure. I'm not even a good figure. I'm someone who wasn't great at school, who flunked university, who chased women until he found the wrong one, and then married her. I travelled to get away from the mess I'd left at home, found that I could get on better with people abroad than I could get on with people at home, and that's pretty much all there is to it. I'm not an admirable man, Keith. I like these people. I stay out here because I like them much more than the idiots I have to deal with back home. If the

198

media has me down as some kind of recluse, that's because I have three million better things to do than accept awards and give press conferences. I work at my own pace, in my own way, with people I respect. If that's being 'a wild card' or 'a man of mystery', so be it. You people love labels, you love to have everyone pinned down like butterflies on a board. It is one of the great illusions that a free press makes us all free spirits. What they really want is for us all to come out alike. Quantifiable, accessible, programmable. Die-stamped off the same production line.'

He took one more drag on his cigarette then flicked the stub past Mabbut into the darkness.

'So, forgive me, Keith, if I'm not quite ready for the file marked 'Hamish Melville, Living Legend'.'

He half rose, as if to bring the evening to a conclusion, but Mabbut held up his hand. Melville had set out his case. Now it was his turn. And perhaps his last chance.

'Look, I apologise for being devious and secretive, but the really important thing is that I took on this book because I believe in the same things as you do. I always have. I fought big companies because I knew they were lying, and that in some cases people were dying because of those lies. I like to think that, in a very tiny and marginal way, I was fighting the same battles as you. The difference between us is that I'm that lowest form of human life, a journalist. But we need the public eye to help us fight our battles. Being heard by as large an audience as possible is what we have to do. You have been very successful at what you do — getting projects cancelled, saving lives and livelihoods — but you never have to explain yourself to anyone.'

Melville made to speak.

'With respect, Mr Melville, I know what you're going to say. 'So what? Why should I?' That you couldn't do what you do without privacy. But what you can't expect is that people such as myself, and others who see you as a role model for getting good things done in a shitty old world, should be incurious about how you do it. You may think of me as a spy, but all I can say is that I'm spying for the best possible reason, which is that I think the world is a better place because of you, and I want more people to follow your example.'

Melville stood. He sniffed the air and looked up into the sky.

'Weather's due for a change,' he said, not altogether happily. Then he checked his watch.

'We've an early start.'

Mabbut nodded and reached for his phone, but Melville kept his hand on it.

'I'll hang on to this if you don't mind.' He smiled. 'Security precaution.'

8

Kumar's shouts woke him from a very deep sleep. Mabbut felt desperately tired. His bag, full of dirty laundry, lay beside him. He felt sticky and grubby and he was sure he was beginning to smell.

As soon as he'd emerged from his tent, Kumar and the younger boys moved in to dismantle it. Melville, who had found a freshly pressed kurta from somewhere, seemed positively energised by the lack of sleep. If he'd been discursive the previous night, there was no sign of it this morning. He was deep in discussion with Kinesh and Mahesh. Mabbut went over behind the tree, peed and cleaned his teeth. Anything more elaborate would have to wait till later. When he came back, Melville was at the table holding a flask.

'Coffee?'

'Please.'

He poured Mabbut a cup.

'I apologise for last night,' he said briskly. 'I was defending my territory.'

He held the cup out to Mabbut.

'Maybe I've just grown cynical over the years. I assume everyone who wants to know more about me is out to stop me doing what I do. But you helped us yesterday, and the boys like you, so here's the deal. Instead of taking you to the station, I will give you Kumar and a car. He

201

knows these tribal areas, he's Masira himself. Go with him and you will at least have a chance to see the people we're fighting for, and what they're fighting against. Then, maybe, we'll have something to talk about.'

He drained his cup and indicated the stocky figure of Kumar, who was loading Mabbut's bag into the back of an old Land Cruiser.

'Are you sure you can spare him?'

Melville held out his hand.

'Think of it as the first and last day of our new public relations department.'

He laughed loudly, and walked off to confer with a group of village elders. There was much grasping of hands and clasping of arms. It was as if something was in the wind.

Mabbut climbed into the Land Cruiser and settled himself beside Kumar, who was checking his rear-view mirror. Kumar was a local, with thick long hair, a square and homely face and broad features.

Ahead of them, Melville climbed into another car with Mahesh and Kinesh. The headlight beams stabbed out and they started to move, rumbling over the hard red clay past spectral groves of eucalyptus and mahua. As the first hint of light crept into the eastern sky, Mabbut wondered how he could have done things differently, and if he had, whether he would now be travelling with Melville.

After a half-hour or so, Mabbut was woken by the crackle of a radio. Kumar pulled a receiver towards him and words were exchanged. Kumar nodded approvingly, replaced the receiver, and accelerated along a partly tarmacked road. Mabbut looked to his left just in time to see Melville's vehicle peel off, bounce up a dirt track and disappear into the forest. He thought he saw Melville wave goodbye.

'Where are they going?'

Kumar ignored the question. 'Mr Melville says I am your guide now. There are many things he wants me to show you.'

They made their way north-west, on gently rising ground which led deeper into the interior than Mabbut had been before. This was a largely empty land. Weathered rocks and scrubby bush with the shadow of the hills away to the west. It was a landscape both serene and sinister. At the top of an incline Kumar pointed out the remains of a mobile-phone mast, destroyed by the Maoists a month before. They passed a police post, so heavily fortified it looked like something from a war zone. A few miles beyond that, stacks of concrete sleepers marked a wide strip of land from which the trees had been cleared, awaiting, Kumar explained, the go-ahead for a railway to the refinery. Then suddenly the car slowed and he pointed excitedly into the distance.

'That is my home.'

Mabbut could make out a misty, russet-brown ridge a few miles ahead. It looked much like any of the other low, wooded ranges that ran one after the other as far as the eye could see. After a few miles the road narrowed and the scrubby trees turned into woodland, which then turned into forest. Then they were out of the trees and on to a flat, cleared plain. They entered a small town at the junction of a road and a railway. At the far end of a crowded main street they came to a long, high wall topped by coils of razor wire. Mabbut glimpsed through the gates a well-kept campus and a sign proclaiming the Masoka Hills Agricultural College.

Why would anyone put razor wire round an agricultural college, Mabbut asked. Because Astramex paid for it, Kumar replied, and they have many enemies. On the far side of the town, with the walls of the agricultural college still visible, they came to a small settlement of traditional low thatched houses surrounded by smaller brick and concrete units with tin roofs. Kumar's family lived here, and Mabbut met his thin but sharp-eyed father, his quiet, shy sisters and two or three children who followed his every move with increasing amusement. His mother, he said, had died in childbirth many years ago and now his father had another wife. She was in the fields that day gathering rice for winnowing. They were a happy group, and Kumar proudly showed off his new friend.

'I tell them you love our land,' he said with a grin. His parents had lived up in the hills, but when the road was built and the interior opened up to industry the missionaries came and converted his people from animism to Catholicism. In return for saying their Hail Marys they now had a school, electricity and new houses. They were the lucky ones, according to Kumar. Their land was safe from the mining. For the moment.

It was the hottest time of the day, and Kumar

suggested they stay overnight with his family. The next day he would take Mabbut to the hills. They would visit the villages of the remotest tribes, the ones most threatened by the mining. Kumar explained it would involve a long walk, so they would start early.

The rest of the day was spent meeting relatives, a steady trickle of whom passed by to see the foreigner. In the late afternoon they walked round the village. Mabbut was shown a freshly painted, tin-roofed building that doubled as a school and church. He met the man who owned the only television set in the village, which he generously set up in the middle of the main street every night. He inspected the new concrete buildings and had his shirts washed for him in the pond at the back of the houses. The people couldn't have been more friendly, but there was something sad about Kumar's village, Mabbut thought. Some spirit seemed to have gone out of it. The embarrassed giggling of the young when his father sang traditional songs, the T-shirts and jeans that the children wore, all gave the impression that an old way of life had lost its relevance. But Kumar clearly regarded what had happened to his village as a good thing, the perfect third way between assimilation and extinction. To him, contact with the outside world was acceptable as long as religion, rather than commerce, was the driver. In one generation it had enabled him to realise opportunities he'd never have dreamt of.

As they finished their evening meal and talked of the day, Kumar chided Mabbut.

'Why aren't you writing all these things down, Mr Journalist?'

Mabbut felt guilty. He wasn't writing because he was far less certain about everything now. If Astramex represented the wrong way, then what was the right way? To leave people who didn't want to change alone? To offer them some change but not too much? Could — should — the modern world tolerate ignorance, even if it was blissful ignorance?

Mabbut promised Kumar that he was taking it all in and would write up his notes later. So, after the meal was cleared away, and with Kumar's family and friends gathered around him in the glow of the lamp, Mabbut reached into his bag, pulled out his notebook and began to write.

A look of deep disappointment crossed Kumar's face.

'You have no laptop?'

★   ★   ★

Early the next morning they went into the town, parking the car up by the station.

'Now we walk.'

Kumar had made it clear to Mabbut that white men in vehicles, indeed vehicles of any kind, would not be welcome in the village they were going to see. The Gyara tribe who lived in the hills were the most cut off from the outside world and also the most threatened by the mining company's plans. If Mabbut and Kumar were to get access they would have to approach, as equals, on foot. The village was ten kilometres away.

As they crossed the railway line and began the climb across scrubby grassland small groups of men and women came down the path towards them. Some of the women were young, still girls, with coarse dark hair arranged in waves and combed outwards so that it resembled small black bonnets. Decorations abounded; clips, pins, combs and small knives for cutting fruit were tucked into their hair, with small brass rings through ears and nostrils and heavier, wider rings through pierced, stretched earlobes. Their arms bore fine-patterned tattoos and they were swathed in multicoloured saris and cotton wraps. Most carried goods in large woven baskets on their heads. Two of the women, Mabbut noticed, were carrying babies as well. The women walked together, chatting as they went. The men, dressed in shorts and cheap shirts, carried axes and bundles of wood on their heads. They were all on their way to the market in town, Kumar told him, to sell things like fruit and firewood in exchange for dried fish, salt, oil, spices, wine and tobacco.

Kumar greeted these people in their dialect and passed on to Mabbut any information he'd gleaned; the pineapple harvest was good; they were sacrificing a buffalo in a nearby village and much sago palm would be drunk; three babies had been born in the last week.

After a while there were fewer people passing and Mabbut and Kumar spoke less as the track began to climb steeply and the forest grew closer and thicker around them. The heat was building too, despite the cooling shade of the trees, and Mabbut frequently had to stop to get his breath back. There were rewards to be had. No noise, no cars, no electricity pylons or security fences. A pristine, sylvan world, with shafts of sunlight piercing the forest canopy, highlighting the yellow butterflies as they fluttered above the shallow streams. In occasional clearings banana, pineapple and jackfruit trees grew, and sometimes there was pasture for goats and cows.

They had been moving for almost two hours when they turned a corner. Ahead of them, where the slope flattened out, was the village they had been looking for. It wasn't fundamentally different from the tribal villages Mabbut had already seen — a rectangular layout, long low houses on either side of a central open area — but here, deep in the forest and high up the hill, there was a much greater feeling of isolation. Unlike the town, where they were outsiders to be exploited, this was very much the Gyaras' land. This was their world, and theirs alone. Here, Mabbut had to adapt to their way of life, rather than the other way round.

Kumar, too, seemed a little in awe. For quite some time he stood respectfully at the edge of the woods. Then, beckoning Mabbut to stay close to him, he walked slowly towards the houses. No sooner had they moved than a terrific din broke the silence. Half a dozen excitable khaki-brown mongrels raced through the village and ranged themselves between the buildings and the two men, blocking their approach.

Mabbut, who'd never been comfortable in any sort of dog-versus-man situation, hung back. Their arrival seemed to have the opposite effect on Kumar, who beamed at the line of panting jaws and thrashing tails as if this were the invitation he needed.

The dogs continued to bark, more for the sake of it than from any great sense of conviction, but they soon grew bored and scattered back to the other end of the village. An imperious black hen appeared from between the houses, her chicks scuttling along behind. A dusty bicycle leant against a pile of wood. At the centre of the open area was a neatly arranged group of stones. Mabbut pointed to it. Kumar nodded.

'That is the place for sacrifices. The old villages still have them. They sacrifice a cow or a goat and scatter the blood to make the fields more fertile.'

'Do you have sacrifices in your village?'

Kumar smiled, almost shyly, and shook his head.

'No. We don't have them any more.'

There was little or no movement from the houses, but as they walked by them Kumar called out softly and Mabbut could hear the odd, shy greeting in return. He became increasingly aware of faces peering back at him from beneath the beetle-browed roofs; mostly women and children, crouched together away from the heat of the day. Across the entrance to one house two young girls lay stretched out, propped languidly on their elbows like odalisques. They were dressed in all sorts of finery and returned

209

Mabbut's gaze quite unselfconsciously. There were few men to be seen, apart from one old man who lay alone at the entrance of a house, his lean frame shaken every now and then by a hard, bronchial cough.

There was an atmosphere of inertia, though even as the thought occurred to him, Mabbut realised this was his own interpretation, based on little more than the fact that they weren't getting up to shake hands or offer him tea and biscuits. They were certainly not listless. When Kumar talked to them the children looked as bright and mischievous as children should be. A little girl, sitting on her mother's knee with three gold rings through each of her ears and a pin through her nose, examined Mabbut curiously. An older girl, her neck draped with strings of beads and metal necklaces, watched him warily out of the corner of her eye as she leant forward to shoo away the dogs.

While Kumar was busy dispensing sweets to the children, Mabbut peered into one of the front rooms. The ochre walls were delicately inscribed with dots and triangles and stick figures. There were similar markings around the smoothly carved doorways and on the beamed ceiling. He crawled inside. It was cool and dark and soothing and Mabbut felt comfortably enclosed as he squatted on the hard earth floor. Outside, the barking became more sporadic but the coughing more persistent. He must have stayed in the room for some time because when he emerged, blinking against the light, he found Kumar talking to a man he hadn't seen before.

The latter was young and desperately thin, with a small round face and intense close-set eyes.

'Mr Keith!' Kumar exclaimed. 'This man will take us to the top of the hill. The sacred hill.'

Mabbut thought ahead, to the ten kilometres already separating them from the vehicle. He was hot and hungry and every muscle ached, but there was a look in Kumar's eye that brooked no refusal. He nodded, reached for his water bottle and took a long drink. By the time he'd screwed the top back on, the other two had already set off. Mabbut heaved on his backpack and, catching the eye of one woman, he raised his glance heavenwards. To his surprise she laughed.

They proceeded out of the village past orange and banana trees and a weathered timber frame on which strips of meat had been hung out to dry. The dogs summoned up enough energy to yap and bound about at their departure, but once they were in among the trees the silence of the forest returned, and with it the feeling that they were in an ageless world, free of any human context. There was only the faintest of tracks to follow, and as the cover thickened around them it was clear that without their guide they would have quickly become lost.

They must have climbed for a half-hour before the guide stopped and pointed ahead. Kumar stopped too and pointed to the last few metres of the hill, which rose steeply to its crest. He turned and shouted back to Mabbut, whose heart was thudding alarmingly.

'From here is where they mine!'

His indignation rang round the forest.

'All this,' he raised his arms above his head and pulled them apart violently, as if tearing open a curtain, 'gone!'

It was then that Mabbut finally understood the magnitude of what would happen when Astramex came for their bauxite. Deliberately ripping forty feet from the top of these secluded hills was almost unimaginable. From here, looking back the way they had come, down to the sleepy village two hours' walk away from the rest of the world, with its barking dogs and coughing man and smoke rising lazily from the fires, the scale of the potential destruction induced a sort of giddiness.

Kumar set off after the guide, pushing towards the crest of the hill. Mabbut looked up. Beyond him more trees and then the open sky. He took a deep breath and started to scramble after them.

When at last he reached the top he found himself on a wide flat plateau. The air was cooler here and a breeze was blowing. Behind him, as far as the eye could see, the hills rolled away in waves of brown and green. Apart from the odd plumes of smoke there was nothing in the broad landscape to suggest human habitation. Then he heard Kumar calling and reluctantly he set off, picking his way through the spiky bushes towards the other side of the hill. As he reached his two companions he found Kumar looking intently out to the west through a pair of binoculars. He offered them to Mabbut. But Mabbut didn't need the glasses to see what lay on the far side of the mountain.

The vast agglomeration of the Kowprah

refinery sprawled across the valley floor. Whereas the prevalent natural geometry of the Masoka Hills was smooth and rounded, the refinery was all hard angles and straight lines. With its cluster of grey funnel-like smelters and gun-barrel chimney stacks, it resembled some hulking battleship, the power cables its moorings, and the sinuous outlines of the paddy fields the water swirling around it. Kumar, voice raised against the wind, was pointing to one end of the complex, where the late afternoon sun glinted on two strips of water.

'This small one, see! That is ash pond. Ash flurry from power plant. Big one is red mud pond. Sodium hydroxide. Mr Keith, company say no leaks, Mr Melville say many leaks. Into the streams and rivers. We say 'You have poisoned us'. They say, 'Look, no one want to farm here, so we can take more land for our refinery'.'

The plant gave off a menacing sense of purpose, of ramped-up energy. Mabbut knew about the terrific heat required to refine alumina, and the need to keep smelters such as these running twenty-four hours a day. What was the formula? Fourteen thousand kilowatt hours and 1,400 tons of water for one ton of aluminium? And he counted twelve smelters down there.

'Mr Keith, look there. Please!'

Mabbut followed Kumar's outstretched arm to a forest of cranes and the half-finished smelter pods rising at the point nearest to the hill.

'They are building more, you see. You know why? Because they believe they will soon take

213

these hills. See that?'

Mabbut could see it very well. Snaking away from the nearside of the refinery was a steel-framed conveyor belt, as yet unused, heading up through the forest towards them, aimed straight at the Masoka Hills like a serpent's tongue.

'Can they be stopped?' he shouted back to Kumar.

'Everyone talk, everyone cry. Then everyone get given school or house or telephone. So everyone do nothing. Only one man on our side, Mr Keith! Only one man Astramex scared of now. You see.'

9

The night train to Bhubaneswar slowly gathered speed as it eased its way across the tracks at Kindara Junction and on to the line that led south. It was comprised of twenty dull green railway carriages, all of which had identical rows of open bunks running through them, stacked in threes on either side of a narrow gangway. Most passengers were already either asleep or preparing for bed. Occasionally there was the cry of a child or a low muttering between relatives as the last portions of food were shared out. At an open window at one end of the last coach but one, two people were very much awake. Keith Mabbut and Hamish Melville stood side by side, taking in the night air. Melville held an elegant leather-covered hip flask, filled, he said proudly, with the very best Indian whisky. Every now and then they had to flatten themselves against the door as large ladies in voluminous saris wafted by on the last toilet break before bed.

Two days had passed since Mabbut and Kumar had stood on the top of the Masoka Hills and seen the titanic industrial complex extending towards them. After the long, profoundly sad walk back down the hill and through the village, Mabbut had returned to Kumar's family home, and, being barely able to move the next day, had sat beneath a spreading cassia tree feeling like an ancient scribe as he filled his notebook while

215

Kumar, the modern tribesman, made repeated calls on his mobile phone. Which was how Mabbut had first learnt of what came to be known as the Kowprah Blockade. Apparently, on the night after they had returned from the sacred hill, a well-marshalled crowd of Masira Kidonga, Musa and Gyara people had emerged from the forest in the dead of night and occupied the road in front of the Astramex plant at the precise moment when three vast turbines intended to double production at the refinery had arrived at the main gates. As the trailers approached, a thousand people had sat down in front of them, blocking the road and forcing the vehicles to pull up. At which point lights had flooded the area and cameras had begun to record the scene. Astramex's security had been taken completely by surprise and their accusations of violent and illegal protest were contradicted by the highly skilful, professionally shot footage that appeared on the Internet within minutes. It was the largest mobilisation of indigenous people ever seen in India.

'And no one knows it was you?'

Melville shrugged and smiled.

'Only those who need to know.'

'But it was your idea?'

'It was Gandhi's idea originally. We just brought it up to date.'

Mabbut and Melville had met at Kindara Junction, Mabbut brought by Kumar and Melville by Kinesh. There had been emotional reunions followed by equally emotional leave-takings. Melville hugged the boys like some

216

demented grandfather and even Mabbut was given a warm embrace by Kumar as they climbed aboard.

As the train pulled out of a long curve and began to gather speed, a rush of cool air flung Melville's thatch of grey hair this way and that, making him look like Moses about to part the Red Sea. He handed the flask to Mabbut.

'Try it.'

Mabbut grimaced as he took a sip. 'Not bad.'

'Amrut whisky. Distilled in Bangalore. You can get it in New York now.'

He laughed.

'It will help you sleep. And believe me, on this train you'll need all the help you can get.'

Mabbut took another sip and handed the flask back to Melville. There were so many questions he wanted to ask.

'All those people you organised. Tribes that don't even engage with each other, let alone the rest of the world . . . '

'Look, Kumar is a Masira. His family came from the hills. They used to chop wood and walk ten Ks to sell it for charcoal. They'd never seen a white man till the missionaries arrived. He was brought up at the bottom of the food chain. Well, tell me, you've spent time with him, is there anything you can do that he can't? Given the right opportunities, those who want to can achieve anything.'

The train was racing now, swinging alarmingly. From somewhere beneath them sparks flew off into the night. Melville pushed up the window until it was merely ajar.

217

'So they do *have* to change?' asked Mabbut, grabbing at the door handle. 'The Masira and the Gyara, and all the others who live in those hills. Even if it's just to help them fight change?'

Melville took a long drink then paused for a moment's appreciation.

'Put it this way. It's not their fault that they live on top of all these resources, but they do, and those who want to get at the resources are never going to give up. Not while you and I need our phones and computers and cars and trains and aeroplanes. So, yes, they need to change, even if it's only to become aware of what's going on and find ways of dealing with it.'

'That village Kumar showed me . . . Below the sacred hill.'

Melville nodded. 'Nakya Marund.'

'It was like a different world. A different pace of life. Completely different values from our own. I couldn't say if the people were happy or unhappy, but they seemed to be content. They've lived with the forest for a thousand years, not, as far as I could see, oppressing anyone or destroying the planet. Shouldn't we be learning something from them, rather than wanting to change them?'

'Forgive me, Keith, but you sound like someone who's just woken up from a very long sleep. I've been working in these places, with people like the Gyara, since I left the City. That's thirty-five years ago now. And everywhere the problem is the same. The modern world is closing in, it's inescapable and very hard to

218

resist. Now, in Kumar's case — that's not his real name, of course.'

'No?'

Melville shook his head. 'He's been in quite a lot of trouble. A bit of a hothead until I got hold of him. But in Kumar's case the missionaries got to his village before the bulldozers did, so — now they have more options. The people you saw living below the hill don't have to say their Hail Marys or live with trucks rolling by on a brand-new road but they have very few other options. If some minister in Delhi allows Astramex to strip-mine there's not a great deal they can do about it. They can either move out to government accommodation or wake one morning to the sound of men shouting, trees falling, children yelling and bulldozers tearing their sacred hill to pieces.'

Mabbut opened his mouth but Melville raised a hand.

'Don't say it. It's obscene. Everyone who comes here, everyone who hears about it for the first time, says it's obscene. Unfortunately that doesn't help the Gyara. They don't have a word for obscene. Nor do they have a blog or a Facebook page. If the worst comes to the worst they will simply have to do as they're told. They are powerless.'

He handed the flask to Mabbut, who held it, without drinking.

'I thought that was why you were here. To save people like that.'

'Keith, you're the same as everyone who 'cares' about these things. You go from indignation to despair in one bound. There *is* a way to help the powerless, and that is give them power. That's what we do. That's what last night was all about. Astramex has huge resources, massive funds, and an international PR machine. What they don't have is the culture of the hill tribes. They've forgotten that the ancestors of these people have fought against bastards like them many times before. They fought off the British Raj, and they fought off the Indian rajahs. Independence is in their genes.'

Mabbut was thrown forward as the train gave a violent lurch. The lights went off and came on again. Melville hardly seemed to notice.

'So, that's the first thing we can use to our advantage. The Gyara and the Masira may not want to live together but neither wants anyone else moving into these hills. That's a force we can use, something my guys, people like Kinesh and Mahesh, instinctively understand and can use to mobilise people. The other thing to remember is that to survive the way they have done, the *adivasi* have had to be resourceful. These are not stupid people. Like Kumar, they learn fast. This gives them the advantage of surprise when dealing with people who dismiss them because they didn't go to college. So let outsiders think they're stupid. We can use that too.'

The train braked sharply, shuddering as wheels ground against rail. Mabbut lost his balance again and found himself clinging to his companion.

'D'you think they can still win?' Mabbut asked, recovering his balance.

'In this scenario nobody wins. But I think there's a real chance they could limit the damage. And a real chance that their land might be saved. And don't forget, one success gives heart to a hell of a lot of people. The ripple effect. But do I think they can live cut off from the modern world? Sad to say, Keith, I don't.'

The train had come to a halt. Mabbut could see a red light and the hear the hum of the engines up ahead. Melville straightened up, stretching his arms above his head until they touched the roof of the carriage. He yawned mightily, and shook his head from side to side. For some reason Mabbut was reminded of a lion after a kill.

'And now, I think, time for bed.'

Mabbut wasn't tired. There was too much going through his mind. India. The children in the threatened village. The girls who had stared at him. Kumar's father singing. The fires in the forest, the dogs, the goons in their SUVs. He hadn't expected it all to affect him quite as much. His reflections were interrupted by a shout from the track. The signal changed to amber and the train began to move arthritically. As it gathered pace, the squeaking and squealing resolved themselves into a series of soothing rhythmic clicks. Lowering the window, Mabbut could see that they were crossing a bridge. Below them a broad river shone brightly in the moonlight.

He was elated that he'd found Melville, and was aware that he had enjoyed extraordinarily privileged access, but the journalist in him recognised that he still needed to find out more about the man. About his future plans. About his supporters and his seemingly unlimited funds. About his ability to move so swiftly and silently across the world. As the train clattered on through the night he realised that if the fine details about his subject were still opaque one thing was clear and unequivocal. What he'd seen in the Masoka Hills had aroused an indignation that Mabbut thought he'd grown out of long ago. The hack work he'd been involved in recently had made him immune to shock or surprise. He'd fallen for the spirit of consensus. Well, this was his chance to retrieve some of the anger that had once motivated him. Whatever Melville's decision about the book, Mabbut felt it was his duty to record everything he'd seen. He took out his notebook, balanced himself against the door and began to scribble down as much as he could remember.

It was an hour or more before he at last made his way to bed. On the bunk below him Hamish Melville was spread out, the heavy, dark grey railway blanket barely covering half of his long, rangy body. He was fast asleep.

★ ★ ★

By the morning, the train was over an hour behind schedule, and the passengers, many of them families with young children, having washed, tidied away their bedding and drunk tea from the urn that passed for on-board catering,

seemed resigned to another day that wasn't
going to plan.

Melville had risen early. He'd managed to find
the only food on the train, two packets of salty
biscuits, one of which he'd lobbed up to
Mabbut's bunk, before retreating to the end of
the carriage 'to make some calls'. Mabbut had
got used to this pattern: the convivial companion
by night, the man of action in the morning. He
would just have to be patient and hope that
they'd have a few more nights together before he
had to leave India.

It was only when he and Melville were in the
neutral territory of a crowded Bhubaneswar
station that Mabbut realised he was going to
have to be the one to raise the question of their
meeting again.

'Will you be going back to the Farhan?' he
asked, as they marched in step up the long
platform.

Melville threw Mabbut a sideways look.

'You're not going to give up, are you?'

It was now or never.

'That's up to you. I feel privileged to have
seen what I've seen. I've enough material to
write a book about you, though I'd never
make a move without your say-so. And yes, if
I'm honest, I think it could be a great book.
Especially if you wouldn't mind talking to me
again.'

Melville said nothing. He was looking ahead,
scanning the crowd at the end of the platform.

Finally he turned to Mabbut.

'Look, I've some people to see. Why don't we

meet for dinner? Then you can ask me whatever you like.'

Mabbut restrained an urge to hug the man.

'Seven thirty at the Pearl Room? Everyone knows it.'

They shook hands.

'See you then.'

Mabbut thought he saw an arm raised somewhere ahead of them and Melville moved, surprisingly nimbly, past the oncoming crowd and disappeared through a side door into the shimmering sunshine.

★ ★ ★

Mabbut had called ahead from the train and re-established contact with Farud, who sounded immensely relieved, having last seen his client in a village run by the Maoists. He had booked Mabbut back into the Garden Hotel, and here Mabbut ordered a late breakfast, took a long shower and a leisurely shave, bundled up his filthy clothes and sent them to the hotel laundry. Slowly, during the course of a long and lazy afternoon, he reoriented himself to the world he'd left behind the day he took the decision to visit the Hotel Farhan. He talked to Jay, left messages for Sam and Krystyna and promised to accompany Farud to a half-dozen 'unmissable' temples over the next few days. It was with a distinct hint of smugness that he picked up the phone to Ron Latham. Without giving away everything that had happened, he could sense that Latham was just the tiniest bit impressed.

The initiative was no longer just with Urgent Books.

Mabbut wrote up his notes, slept a little, and then, as if to complete his return to the modern world, he switched on CNN News. He was only half watching when his eye was caught by a 'breaking news' strapline rolling along the bottom of the screen. He didn't catch it all the first time so had to wait for unemployment figures, bank profits, a small earthquake and a shock Test match result to roll by before it scrolled round again. But there it was, large as life, in one side, out the other: 'Kowprah Sit-In: Judge puts restraining order on bauxite mine'.

Selecting a crisp, clean shirt from those newly hung in his wardrobe, Mabbut dressed, slipped a voice recorder into his trouser pocket, and, checking the clock one last time, made his way to the lift and down to reception.

'The Pearl Room?'

A slim, immaculately dressed young man looked up from his screen.

'Good choice, sir. Shall I make a reservation?'

Mabbut smiled politely.

'It's all right. I'm expected.'

10

'I'm so sorry, Mr Mabbut, but Mr Melville has had to fly to Delhi. He sends you his apologies.'

Even as he'd approached the restaurant something hadn't felt quite right. For a start the Pearl Room looked to be the sort of place from which Melville would normally run a mile. It was glamorous and high profile, part of a luxury hotel chain. There had been elaborate security checks of his taxi's engine and interior even before they'd reached the entrance. Ahead of him, a large white Mercedes had disgorged a group of silk-clad, sari-swirling women who had chattered their way through a door held open for them by a tall, dignified Sikh complete with turban and waxed moustache. This was corporate India. Jackets and ties were in evidence. Mabbut was shown to a table for two where a homely, attractive, slightly plump Malaysian lady greeted him warmly.

'My name is Wendy Lu. I work for Hamish. He asked me to make sure that you have everything you want.'

She was small, middle aged and had an easy, maternal manner, but Mabbut had been unable to conceal his disappointment and she seemed to pick up on this. She gestured to the place opposite her.

'He said that you have worked hard and you deserve the best meal in Bhubaneswar.'

She looked around the room.

'And this is the best, believe me. Some say it is the best cuisine on the entire east coast.'

Mabbut opened his mouth to say something, but she chattered on.

'Their speciality is seafood. I hope you like seafood, Mr Mabbut. A drink first? Maybe you like gin and tonic?'

She giggled rather endearingly and indicated a half-full glass in front of her.

'My poison, I'm afraid.'

'When will he be back?'

She summoned the wine waiter.

'I shall have one more, please, Minoo, and then that's it, and you must tell me that's it.' She wagged her finger coquettishly. 'And for my companion . . . ?'

'I'll have, um . . . a glass of champagne, please. Bangalore?'

The elderly waiter bowed politely. 'We don't serve Indian champagne here, sir.'

Wendy Lu intervened.

'A glass of your best French, Minoo.'

'Certainly, Miss Lu. My pleasure.'

Mabbut wanted to show that he was a bit put out about Melville but Wendy Lu's almond eyes and playful smile soon dissolved any resentment.

'You like your Indian wines, then, Mr Mabbut?'

'Mr Melville gave me some tips.'

'Ah, of course. A week on the road with Hamish is an education. In many ways.'

'He must be a very happy man tonight.'

'We are all over the moon,' she enthused,

before looking around the room and lowering her voice. 'This is a major setback for Astramex, Mr Mabbut. The first they have suffered.'

Mabbut followed her eyes round the other tables. Their fellow diners didn't look like the sort of people who would be celebrating the Kowprah blockade. Most were rich Indians, though there was a sprinkling of white and pink faces. An Australian voice carried across the room and at a nearby table two very large Americans, both with black bootlace ties, loomed over their Indian companions. What brought them here, to Bhubaneswar? Mabbut wondered. And hadn't he seen them before?

Miss Lu leant across the table, spoke sotto voce.

'Private security companies.'

'Ah.'

'They'll try to blame Kowprah on the Maoists, but they won't be able to. The Maoists could never have organised anything on this scale.'

A glass of champagne arrived and was set down beside him. Mabbut felt better. This might be the enemy camp, but that made victory all the sweeter. He raised his glass.

'I feel we should drink to Hamish.'

'Yes, indeed.'

They clinked glasses and smiled at each other. How easily they seemed to get on together, Mabbut thought. As if they were old friends. Was this another example of Melville's people skills?

'So. When will he be back?' he asked.

Wendy Lu rolled the ice around her gin and tonic before returning his gaze.

'He won't be coming back, Mr Mabbut.' She reached into a bag on the seat beside her. 'But he told me to give you this.'

★ ★ ★

A sliver of pale grey light crept under the rim of his window shutter. Mabbut raised it gently and peered out. There was nothing much to see, just the merest intimation of morning. He lowered it again and checked the screen. Time to Destination: 3 hrs 10 mins. The nearest city was showing as Minsk. Mabbut had slept a little but was now, frustratingly, wide awake. He felt in the bag by his feet and pulled out the package Miss Lu had given him. For the umpteenth time he withdrew a small white envelope and unfolded the letter inside. It was handwritten and on the top were the words 'Foreign and Commonwealth Office, Whitehall'. Crossed out.

Dear Keith,
Forgive me for being so flagrantly discourteous, but the verdict on Astramex, while great news for us all, is only a temporary reprieve and I want to do everything I can to make it permanent. This involves calling in a lot of favours and making a lot of visits. I wish it were otherwise and that I could settle down in one chair and one bed for more than a night but believe me this work is never done, and keeping one step ahead means always having a bag packed.
It also means working under the radar. As

I think I told you round one of our camp-fires, as soon as I become the story, then my work, not just here in India, but in all those other countries where communities are at risk from the Astramexes of this world, becomes much harder.

Now to my point. I have spent many years fighting off the attentions of those who want the Melville story, and I have no regrets. My life will tell its own story one day, and there is still so much to do that I don't have the time to nostalgise. (Is that a word? Should be!) At the same time I'm aware that public curiosity is stronger than ever — Wendy will tell you just how many television companies come barking at the door each year — and I know enough about these things to recognise that if you don't play ball, admiration eventually turns to suspicion, and suspicion to speculation.

In short, I think the time has come for a pre-emptive strike and this is how it could work. You get your book. I collaborate with you, exclusively, and in so doing I get everyone else who is sniffing about off my back. The two of us can use the book to highlight my work — which we both know is more relevant than my life. I can give you contact details for those closest to me and I'll assure them that you're completely kosher. Wendy will give you information on the campaigns we've been engaged in, and I've enclosed a purely factual biography which has some of the early personal stuff that I'm sure Mr

Latham will be looking for.

All I ask is that you leave me to get on with my work and that there be no attempt to involve me in the day-to-day research for the book or in interviews of any kind. All contact must be through Wendy, who will pass on to me any serious queries or problems.

I will fully understand if you choose not to go down this path, but I'm afraid it's the only thing I can offer while remaining true to what I do. We talked enough about the world as we see it for me to sense that we think the same way in many respects. Forgive me if I'm wrong, but I think we share a common desire for justice and truth, we identify with the weak rather than the strong, we believe, as a wise man once said, that 'there are no superior or inferior cultures, there are just cultures which satisfy the needs of their members in different ways.'

This is a message that seems self-evident yet everywhere it is under threat as each country and each religion seeks to promote its own interests at the expense of others.

So, Keith, there is a risk on both sides. You must believe in me, and I must believe in you. It would be too much to say that together we can make the world a better place, but we can, perhaps, add a little to the sum of human understanding.

I'm sure we will meet again some time but until you have completed your work I'll leave you to it. It'll be better this way. We can be

*friends, but it's much better for both of us
that the outside world shouldn't know this.*

*So farewell. And good luck. Whatever hap-
pens, I've enjoyed our time together. And if
all else fails we could use you out here. No
money, but job satisfaction guaranteed!*

Your friend,
Hamish M

There was no question in Mabbut's mind that
he could now write the book. A book about a
remarkable man, remarkable for his achieve-
ments certainly, but also for his modesty, his
carelessness of reputation. Mabbut could show
the rest of the world that these unfashionable
talents were something not just to be celebrated,
but emulated. It would be a handbook of how to
make things better, how to change the world
from the bottom up, how to do good without
being a do-gooder. Such was the tide of positives
on which he was riding that he took out his
notebook and began to scribble down the
opening lines. He paused and checked the flight
map. They were approaching Warsaw.

PART III

Everything Else

1

They had agreed on a delivery date of the end of April, which gave Mabbut marginally less than six months to complete the work Ron Latham had decided to call *Melville: The Real Life of a Legend*. This came with the dangling carrot of sixty thousand pounds on delivery and another sixty if the book made it to publication. This in addition to the sixty thousand Silla had already secured for him on signature, most of which had gone towards repaying the last few years of household debts. Mabbut had never been a conspicuous spender and the promise of financial abundance was as bewildering as it was welcome. It certainly improved his frame of mind as he sat down at the laptop and tried out the title for the first time. It also helped to assuage the sharp pang of guilt he felt as he cleared *Albana* away into a box which he stowed in a bedroom cupboard where Krystyna had once kept her dresses.

Though meeting Melville may have been something of an epiphany for Keith Mabbut, he knew that he owed it to his subject to remain clear eyed and avoid the trap of sanctifying or sentimentalising him. To remind himself of this he found a photograph of Mother Teresa, which he stuck on the wall in front of him and across which he drew a thick red line.

He started by typing up the notes he'd taken

235

in India, for this had to form the central core of the book. This was the seam of gold. This was what only he knew and what only he could deliver. From here there would be flashbacks to different parts of Melville's life. The more he investigated the contacts Melville had given him over the weeks that followed, the more convinced Mabbut became that this was the right approach. Interesting as the memories and anecdotes might be, none came as close to revealing the essential Melville as the information he had culled from his ten days in India.

Miles Cardish, a friend from Melville's schooldays, had been charming, telling stories of how the two of them got into frequent trouble as a result of Melville's devotion to practical jokes. Chamber pots on top of flagpoles, collapsible bicycles, glue on walking sticks. Cardish and his ailing wife had been quite surprised that such a persistent offender should end up 'saving the world'. And no, they didn't see him much nowadays.

Friends of the family up in Cumberland had not been as surprised by young Hamish's later career. They reminded Mabbut that Melville's parents had been members of the Humanist Association and that he had been brought up in a passionately irreligious household. The only substantial contact had been a man called Charley Murray, a friend of Melville's from his university days, still a bachelor at seventy, who lived amid an erotic art collection in a fourth-floor flat beside the Albert Hall. They'd talked over tea as the first snow of winter settled on Kensington Gardens. Charley was a delight. A fine raconteur, full of keen insights. On many dark evenings Mabbut replayed the recording he had made to remind himself of the essence of the young Hamish Melville.

I suppose I knew him as well as anyone, which is not saying much. Hamish was always a loner. We played a lot of sport at university. He was a half-blue in athletics and a very fine cricketer too. Could have played for his county, but as soon as he'd mastered something he'd drop it. He tried for the Foreign Office but didn't get in so we both headed for banking. He worked for Cazenoves for a while. Did very well. He had a talent for cultivating the right client. Usually foreigners. He'd go out and spend time with them. Whereas most of his colleagues sat about in London having long lunches, he'd be off to Nicaragua or Swaziland or wherever his client lived. He preferred being abroad, I think. And he picked up languages just like that. Used to say that you only need to know five hundred words to speak any language fluently. I suppose that's where it all started. He was in the army briefly. He once told me he'd quite like to have been a regular if he hadn't had to kill anybody. I think it was the training and the discipline he admired. Extraordinary man. Doing what we all ought to be doing, eh?

It was Murray who told Mabbut about Melville's short, tragic marriage to a South African heiress called Zena Carlsson. They had met in Kenya. She was very beautiful, but had a wild side. Their fights and arguments were famously fierce. They'd been together for only two years when she was killed in a plane crash on the Kenya-Tanzania border while trying to photograph the wildebeest migration.

He came home for a while and tried to pick up his old life, but he was never comfortable staying in one place. Then both parents died within a few years of each other and that freed him to become this sort of international guru. Thing is, Hamish could do pretty much whatever he wanted, wherever he wanted. He was incredibly well connected, but always hated the establishment. That's the thing.

Much of Mabbut's time was spent at various libraries and learned societies such as the Asiatic, the South American and the Royal Geographical, getting himself up to speed on the world through which Melville moved so energetically. He'd become a regular on eco-websites. Wendy Lu was helpful, checking and cross-checking all the facts and supplying information.

There were opaque areas. Apart from the stories about his short, sharp marriage to Zena Carlsson, Mabbut could find disappointingly little evidence of women in Melville's life. Charley Murray hinted at a healthy interest in the opposite sex but not much more. One source mentioned rumours of a royal liaison but the trail led nowhere.

It had been equally difficult to unearth much detail as to how Melville financed his worldwide operations. Those who knew him gave the impression that he had never been short of funds. Mabbut had the names of some good contacts in the City, but this was the world of old money where handshakes were more important than written records and it was almost impossible to get enough material to use. When he had pressed Wendy Lu to ask Melville for more information on possible backers and supporters, she had assured him that Melville's costs were 'on a Third World scale' and that those who worked for him were more interested in principle than price. One of Mabbut's own contacts in the financial world had, under the strictest confidence, spent many hours at Companies House before concluding that if Melville had money, it wasn't in a UK account. Which, for an international operator living abroad for eleven months of the year, seemed more sensible than sinister. Even Rex, when asked, drew a blank on Melville's arrangements.

For Mabbut it was just good to be a journalist again, using his old skills to decode a challenging subject in a ridiculously short time, and by and large the book moved forward at a steady pace. And as he pursued his research into the real life of Melville, his own life began to take a clearer shape. Forced to confront someone else's motivations he was better able to face his own. Self-defence was no longer eating away at his confidence. Pride, however tentative, was seeping back into his life.

Krystyna seemed to notice this. For the first time in almost two years she was the one who got in touch with him, rather than the other way round. They went together to the opening of Sam's new play. Initially it seemed to confirm all his worst prejudices. The play was set in a prison and involved a group of gay men who were approaching the day of their release. But once Mabbut had got the central idea that none of them wanted to leave and that the action revolved around their various strategies for staying, he realised, with considerable pleasure, that his son had real talent. For comedy, of all things.

Jay was still with Shiraj. Whether it was through love or pity or love and pity he wasn't sure, but she spent most of her time with the boy and Mabbut got on well enough with him. Shiraj was a serious character, and once he'd got over the embarrassment of living with an unmarried girl in her father's home he became good company, forever wanting to engage Mabbut in kitchen-table debates. Mabbut, in turn, took a certain amount of pride in being able to extend a helping hand to the persecuted. And he had never seen his daughter happier.

For himself Mabbut had never thought of happiness as a natural state. To him it was just the postponement of unhappiness. But now he was beginning to think rather differently. By accepting a looser, more general definition of the word, meaning things being not too bad for a significant amount of time, happiness was perhaps not such a far-fetched proposition after all. So, bit by bit, as the book crept forward and winter faded into spring, Mabbut came to accept the unfamiliar feeling of being, by and large, predominantly, content.

2

The last day of April was a Saturday, but Mabbut, as a point of pride, turned in the disk and a crisp hard copy of *Melville: The Real Life of a Legend* one day early, on the last working day of the week. The hard copy had been Silla's idea.

'I know it's old fashioned, but I still think publishers like to see a book that actually looks like a book.'

'Not Ron Latham's style, I wouldn't have thought.'

'You'd be surprised. Ron's more impressed by tradition than you'd think.'

Mabbut raised an eyebrow.

'Well, here's to Hamish.'

The book had gone off to Urgent that morning and Mabbut and Silla were celebrating in Goldings, to which Silla remained loyal despite its almost perverse lack of glamour and its clientele of office workers and exhausted Oxford Street shoppers. Mabbut asked her about this and Silla admitted that with some of her clients she might have to go a little more upmarket.

'But not the ones I like.'

She raised her glass of house Cava with such genuine warmth that Mabbut felt an unaccustomed sense of closeness to this fierce, erratic, indomitable woman, who'd guided his own erratic career with such loyalty.

'To Hamish. And to you, Keith.'

Their glasses clinked. Two men from the postal depot next door, in to collect a takeaway, looked round. Celebration was a rare event at Goldings, especially at lunchtime.

'And to you, Sill. For everything.'

They clinked again.

To Mabbut's regret, the comely Croatian waitress had moved on, as they do, and in her place was an English girl. Quite chubby, straight hair, thick mascara. Hint of a West Country accent. She took their order abstractedly, staring out of the window, as if that was where the real world began.

Silla's mobile rang. She picked it up and Mabbut reconciled himself to staring into space for a few minutes. But with a brief look at the caller's name, Silla switched it off and dropped it into her bag.

'I don't want to be disturbed.'

He'd never known her do this before. From the moment she'd given up smoking, the mobile had become Silla's digital substitute; rarely, if ever, out of her hands.

'It might be Latham,' he said. 'Wanting to know if we'd like the money in twenties or fifties.'

Normally he'd have expected an earthy laugh in response, but Silla looked surprisingly serious. She leant back and stared briefly out of the window, before turning her eyes on him.

'You know, dear boy, that I don't do bullshit with you, so you have to believe me when I say that this is one of those moments when this whole shitty business seems worthwhile.'

For the first time in a long while, Mabbut really looked at Silla. At her broad prison-warder's shoulders, the inverted triangle of holiday sunburn running down to a well-chosen cashmere sweater; her wide, round face, her hair taut at the forehead and descending in a skilfully dyed auburn mane. Though her skin-tones were Scandinavian, everything else reminded Mabbut, suddenly, of the Gyara village and the women who lived below the sacred hill.

'I've had so many bad days, you know, Keith. I mean genuinely bad days when I had to sell crap to people. They know it's crap and I know it's crap but neither of us can admit it because we all need the money. So when something like this comes along, totally out of left field, you have to thank whoever's up there for showing you there can be good days too.'

'I never thought of you as having bad days, Sill. I thought that was just me.'

Silla threw her head back and gave a bark of laughter.

'Oh, for God's sake. Listen to the pair of us. Les Misérables!'

Two portions of pasta arrived. Silla brushed a wisp of hair from her eyes and called for two glasses of red wine.

'Large or small, madam?'

'Enormous!'

She took two rapid forkfuls of pasta, dabbed at her mouth and pushed the bowl to one side.

'Believe it or not, Keith, when I started out, all

those years ago, I genuinely thought I could change things. That I wouldn't be one of those 'See you Monday', lunch-at-the-club sort of agents. That I would go out there and find new authors. Go to universities and schools even. Visit writers' groups. Find someone who had something fresh and original to say and help them say it. So that's what I did. I went out and looked and listened. But no matter what I did or who I found there was always this undercurrent of disapproval. Why did I think it was more important to go to Newcastle to meet a new author when I should be at a book launch at the Savile Club? Especially as the author I was going to see had just completed three years for armed robbery.'

Another hoot of laughter. The wine arrived. Silla took a sip and let out a satisfied sigh.

'Mmm! Same old shit . . . I had to put up with all sorts of weird stuff in those days, Keith. That I was having affairs with all these boys — and girls. That I was on some mission to corrupt the purity of the English language. At talent meetings I'd be treated as if I was someone on work experience. Then came Abigail Morris, do you remember her?'

'*Counting the Dead*?'

'Still one of the best books about the drug scene. True and honest. No bullshit. A one-hit wonder as it turned out, but still a wonder. One hundred K in hardback, two hundred K in trade paperback; film options, foreign sales. And all at once I was taken seriously. Given a partnership at Nathan Bowles and a nice fat expense account. Suddenly everything seemed so easy. Why go bowling up to Glasgow on a wet Saturday evening when they could come to you? I did pretty well. I had a good table manner. I gave a good lunch.'

Mabbut looked around at Goldings and grinned approvingly.

'The money came in. Good money. I bought a flat in Marble Arch, hired a chauffeur to take me shopping in Sloane Street. And I didn't really notice that the so-called authors I was bringing in were people just like myself. Successful people, leading the same successful lives. And, as you know, there was and is an insatiable appetite for the lives of the successful. How they dress, where they eat, who they fuck and where they go on holiday. None of which is very interesting.'

She took a gulp of wine.

'But being the nice sociable gal I am I listened to them and I *encouraged* them and the next thing I know I'm the celebrity publishers' darling. The first port of call for overpaid footballers, models and chefs. And I'm persuaded, not that I took much persuading, to leave the agency and set up on my own. 'Silla Caldwell Associates'.'

She shook her head.

'No, I didn't know why I needed the 'Associates' either. I think it meant my mother. Anyway, along came the nineties and the economy went belly up and suddenly everyone was reining in, looking after number one, and of course it was only the big boys who had the money to ride it out.'

Silla drank again, swallowed and winced.

'Those were the days before you knew me, Keith. And if you'd known me then you'd probably have been ever so polite and raced off in the other direction. I was a loudmouth drunk and I lost the will to give. I just took whatever was offered and that included authors.'

She threw back her head.

'Anyway, out of the blue came Sir Galahad, Ronald Arthur Latham.'

'Ron *Latham*?'

'The same. He was going up, I was going down. We met on the stairs.'

She held his gaze. Her eyes were defiant and apologetic at the same time.

'Don't look so shocked, Keith. This is a story with a happy ending. Remember?'

She clinked his glass.

'Ronald had his golfing stars and a budget to bring them in, but he didn't know how to deal with celebrities 'from the wider world'. He wanted to learn from me, and he was the first person in a long time who'd wanted to do that. We spent a lot of time together. We got on pretty well but ultimately we weren't the right gender for each other, and he was far too ambitious to want to come home at night and watch television. But I saw something of the younger me in him and I was happy to see him succeed. In return, he looked after me. Got me back on my feet. We did business together every now and then. Thanks to him I was able to keep the brass plaque and the chauffeur, and I began to look around as I had in the old days, to find things that other people didn't. Which is how I met you. I'd read your newspaper articles. I thought you could write. Remember? After the arsenic leak story. I knew then that you had something else in you.'

'So you put Ron Latham up to this?'

Silla shook her head emphatically.

'Ronald, for all his big talk, is one of nature's conservatives. I've been on to him for years to do something with some class. I've suggested subjects but at the last minute he always plays safe. Then out of the blue, this Melville idea comes up. And stubborn as he can be, I knew that, at last, some of what I'd been banging on about had finally got through.'

'So what prompted the Damascene conversion?'

'Because he's done bloody well with his golfers' memoirs. He's made a lot of money but I think now he wants 'his place in history'. I know what you think of Ronald, but he's not that bad. He lacks charm because he lacks confidence, especially around people like you.'

'Like *me*? A hack for hire?'

'You've been to university. You've taught a creative writing course. He's always been embarrassed by what he thinks of as his lack of education.'

'Hardly seems to have done him much harm.'

'That's why I give him credit. I know you hate everything he stands for, but he's come good now.'

Silla drained the last of her red wine with a flourish.

'Enough apologies! Ron's come good and you've come good and I've come good. I call it the Melville Effect. Another glass?'

* * *

When they parted, shortly after three, Mabbut felt lost. He crossed Tottenham Court Road. There were buses and trains that would have taken him home, but instead he followed a vaguely northerly route, walking through the back streets around the university and the big sober squares south of Euston station. Something was nagging at him and he needed time to pin it down. The fact was that beneath the elation of having completed the book there was an element, quite a strong element, of fear. Fear that deep down nothing in his life had changed. That these last few months had merely been a happy aberration before normal service resumed.

Sullom Voe, with all its compromises and inadequacies, had taken up almost two years of his life. The Melville book, during which he had rediscovered the joy of doing something relevant and valuable, hardly seemed to have started before it was over. It had brought satisfaction, but was it enough to change him permanently? Had it been enough to rout the despair gene? Or whatever it is you do to genes?

Mabbut found himself in Gordon Square. He remembered that Virginia Woolf had liked to sit in Gordon Square Gardens. Virginia, the doyenne of despair. He had read her diaries from cover to cover and advised all his students to do the same. Her books were classics, yet for her too the fear of failure had been stronger than the solace of success.

He carried on across Euston Road, past the British Library and the curious Levita House, an incongruous public housing block inspired by the architect's trip to Vienna in the 1930s. It had turned into one of those fresh spring evenings. A clear sky, a wind from the north-west and even the most mundane buildings seemed dramatised by the evening sunshine. Mabbut noticed things he'd never seen before. A modern art gallery tucked under a railway bridge in Kentish Town. A Somali barber's shop, full of tall graceful men arguing fiercely, an old-fashioned ladies' dress shop, squeezed between two supermarkets, a young man, grimacing wildly, being patiently accompanied down the road by what looked like a grandparent. His mind went back to India and the people he'd passed on the sacred slopes of the Masoka Hills. He'd been lucky enough to feel some sort of connection to these people. To be touched by lives so utterly different from his own. Which was another reason why, despite the long hours and the eye-aching research, he'd enjoyed writing the book so much. It was his way of paying something back to those whose way of life had been saved by Hamish Melville. He wandered along the back streets of Camden and Tufnell Park and it was nearly six by the time he turned into Reserton Road.

★ ★ ★

250

The house was quiet, and threatened to darken his mood, so, after a shower and a celebratory glass of wine, Mabbut scanned his notebook, found a number and, after a moment's pause, pressed 'call'.

'Hello?'

'Hello, Mae.'

For a moment there was silence. Then a voice, guarded at first.

'Keith?'

'How are you, Mae?'

'Oh, I'm fine. Just fine. How are *you*?'

'I'm very happy, Mae.'

'That's good.'

'I just wanted to ring and tell you that. You used to worry about me.'

'Oh, aye. The despair gene.'

He heard her laughter down the phone.

'I'd be much better company now.'

'You were always good company, Keith. You were the only one who didn't think so.'

'I've finished a new book, and it's quite good. I'd like to send you a copy. See what you think.'

'Well, that'd be an honour indeed.'

Outside he heard a booming noise, deeper and more resonant than the usual passing plane. It sounded like thunder.

'I might bring it up to you. In person.'

'Are you serious?'

'Why not? I've handed it in today. I'm due a fair bit of money, so I could afford the crazy airfare. And I'd like to see you again.'

'What sort of book is it?'

'It'll be a surprise.'

'There's no oil terminals in it, then?'

'No. There's an aluminium refinery, though.'

Mae laughed again.

'Unputdownable!'

There was a pause, as if neither of them knew exactly where to go from there.

'I'd like to be up there with you, Mae,' Mabbut said cautiously. 'I've been going stir crazy here. Eyes locked on a screen twelve hours a day.'

'Tell me about it.'

'A bit of Shetland air's just what I need.'

He realised that this had come out with more of a slur than he'd have liked.

'You sound as though you're celebrating, Keith.'

He peered out of the window. It had begun to rain and two figures were racing across the street towards the house.

'Now how could you tell that, Mae?'

With some relief, he heard her laughter again.

'This, if you must know, *is* my first,' Mabbut protested. 'Since four o'clock, that is. And the strange sound you can hear in my voice is happiness. And when I think of happiness I think of you.'

He heard a key in the front door.

'I'd better go. I'll call you again, Mae, if that's all right.'

'OK. Bye! And congratulations.'

He put down the phone as his daughter and Shiraj came in from the hallway. They had one umbrella between them and it didn't seem to have done much good.

'You look cheerful, Dad. And dry.'

'I am, my dear daughter. This has been a good day. How about you?'

Jay threw down her bag and shook her wet hair. Mabbut, sensing something in the air, looked at Shiraj, who had collapsed the umbrella and laid it carefully by the door. The boy smiled back, politely, inscrutably, but Mabbut could see that something was bothering him. Jay headed for the kitchen.

'Tea, Shiraj?'

'Yes.'

Mabbut followed his daughter, rummaged in the kitchen drawer for a towel, then went back and handed it to Shiraj.

'Sit down. You look tired.'

Shiraj dabbed himself with the towel.

'The news from home is not good.'

'Ah.'

In the kitchen the kettle began to hum. Mabbut looked at Shiraj, expectantly.

'What's happened?'

After a moment Shiraj spoke, quietly, almost reluctantly.

'We have heard that two more of my family have been arrested. My uncle and my younger brother. We don't know where they've gone or what they have been charged with.'

Despite the physical appearance of youth, there was a remarkable maturity about Shiraj. He was a tad serious, sometimes over-earnest, but bearing in mind the trauma he had endured he remained remarkably self-assured. It was a characteristic he shared with Mahesh and

253

Kinesh. And like them, he had brought Mabbut face to face with a very different kind of life.

Jay had filled two mugs with tea — both, he noticed, bearing the imprint of the NorthOil canteen at Sullom Voe. She set one down in front of Shiraj, lightly brushing her hand through his hair as she did so. He made a quick movement away with his shoulders, which Mabbut noticed.

'So you've heard the latest?' Jay asked her father.

Mabbut nodded. 'About the family? He's just told me. I'm really sorry.'

'The latest about Shiraj?'

'No.'

'He has to go before another review panel . . . If he doesn't get an extension he'll be sent back.'

Mabbut moved towards her and put a protective arm around his daughter's shoulders. She took a breath.

'He'll be sent back . . . '

She stopped, reached for a tissue and blew her nose.

Shiraj looked away, his expression showing a mixture of embarrassment and wounded pride.

'I'm sorry,' Jay blurted through her tears. 'This is so stupid.'

'There must be something we can do,' Mabbut said soothingly.

'I asked Rex to help. He knows all these people on committees and stuff.'

Jay sniffed and reached for another tissue.

'And . . . ?'

'Well, you know. Mum's not seeing him as

much, and if I try to ask her if he can do anything for Shiraj, she just sort of, well, she gets quite snappy. So I don't *know*.'

She drew out the last word like a wail of desperation.

'Look, I'll have a try,' said Mabbut. 'I may have a contact or two myself.'

'Whatever you can do, Dad.'

'In the meantime, is there anything I can do to help your family, Shiraj?'

'No, thank you, sir. You've been very kind already, letting me stay in your home.'

Jay exchanged a glance with him.

'There is something . . . ' she began.

Shiraj shook his head firmly.

'What's that?'

'It's nothing, sir. Thank you.' He rose. 'I think I shall go and do some study. The immigration people will ask me many questions.'

When he'd gone, Mabbut looked with concern at his daughter. He hadn't seen her like this for a long time. When the children were growing up, it was always Sam who had the crises.

'Come on, love. What can I do?'

'I can't tell you. He won't let me talk about it.'

'He doesn't have to know.'

Jay puffed out her cheeks. Her eyes were red rimmed beneath the blotchy mascara. She cast a quick look out into the hallway then spoke softly and urgently.

'The only way that they can get any information about what's happened to his uncle and brother and where they've been taken is to pay money to the local prosecutor's office.

Everyone does it, but Shiraj has this stupid male pride thing about being different from everyone else. He says paying bribes keeps a bad system going. But if it's that or never seeing your family again, what would you do?'

'How much does he need?'

'I don't know exactly. It's something like two thousand pounds for each of them. But it's no good, he won't take charity.'

'I'll give him four thousand.'

He raised his hands, anticipating her reaction.

'I want to! I'm in the money, darling. I handed in the book today.'

'Dad, you don't understand. There's a huge amount of pride involved.'

'Just tell him it's a loan and he must pay every single penny back. Or else!'

Jay took his arm.

'Are you sure?'

'Absolutely.'

Then she giggled.

'Down payment on the wedding, Dad.'

'What?'

'Well, you never know. I do adore him.'

She left the room with a little skip of happiness. It was infectious. As Mabbut poured another glass of wine and pulled open the fridge, he marvelled at how different the world looked when you could give something back. From now on he was going to stop worrying and learn to enjoy good fortune. He scattered a few biscuits in Stanley's dish, filled up his water, and settled down to watch football.

3

It was the start of the weekend and Reserton Road was as quiet as the grave, save for Mabbut's exercise-obsessed neighbour, Grant, who emerged into the street in shorts and a tight yellow running vest. He rolled his head this way and that, stretched first one leg, then the other, against a low brick wall, then set off up the hill towards Archway. A milk float purred across the intersection, then all was quiet again.

A short, sharp buzzing noise woke Mabbut from some rambling dream. He opened his eyes and squinted at the clock. It was a quarter to eight. His first thought was one of surprise and pleasure — for the last six months he'd have been well awake by now, worrying about the book. The phone rang again. He pulled himself up on to one elbow and picked it up.

The voice was familiar.

'*Mister* Mabbut.'

'Mr Latham.'

'Did I wake you?'

'I was sort of dozing . . . What can I do for you, Ron?'

'I've read your book.'

'Oh, that was quick. I wasn't expecting — '

'There's a lot of work to do.'

Mabbut transferred the phone to his right ear. 'I'm sorry?'

'The book's not there yet. There's work to do.'

257

'What do you mean? I've been putting in eighteen-hour days to finish it, Ron. You're the one who gave me the deadline.'

'I can see you've put in the hours. It's impressive. India's very good. But it's a one-note book.'

Mabbut was wide awake now. He pulled himself up and leant against the headboard.

'What d'you mean?'

'I mean it's a one-note book. The guy's a saint.'

'With respect, Ron, I've met the man, I've worked with him. You haven't. I've spent six months researching every fact about him, meeting all his friends, talking to anyone who knew him. The fact that he comes out as a good guy doesn't mean I haven't done my job. It means he might *be* a good guy.'

'Calm down, Keith. I'm not disputing what you say. It's just that we have a lot of money riding on this, so we have a say as well. You know that. Your contract is very generous.'

'So? I got the man who has refused every biographer, every interview, for God's sake, for the past forty years, to talk to me. Isn't that good value for money?'

There was a shout from outside. A door slammed and Mabbut heard footsteps briskly receding down the hill.

'The book business has changed, Keith. A nice book about nice people doesn't sell because people don't want to know about nice people. Or if they do, they want to know that they have struggled to be nice. Had to sacrifice one of their children or ordered a contract killing. Stolen from their own mother on the way to becoming nice. Redemption justifies a lot, Keith. Melville comes across as Mr Right from day one. OK, he's a little unorthodox, doesn't brush his hair, sleeps on a hammock with the natives, turns down knighthoods, hangs out with guys who put pots on top of college spires, but that's about as non-nice as he gets. There is no light and shade. No dark side . . . '

'It's a biography, Ron, not a lighting catalogue!'

'And a dark side is what we need to shift this thing in the numbers we planned.'

Mabbut caught sight of himself in the mirror. He was staring distractedly, like a hospital patient.

'Why didn't you tell me this before I started? Then I could have lied and we'd all be happy.'

'Steady on. What we asked for was a rounded picture — 'every aspect of the man' — remember? Those were my exact words.'

'I'm a journalist, Ron. I look for information that will lead me to the truth. That's what journalists do. If there were bad things, they would be in the book.'

There was a brief pause. Mabbut could hear the sound of tea being sipped.

'Your last book, Keith, the one about the oil terminal . . . '

Mabbut frowned. What had that to do with anything?

'I'm told it's pretty good.'

'Thank you,' Mabbut replied cautiously.

'NorthOil must be pleased.'

'Yes, they like it.'

'I'll bet. No mention of the *Braer* disaster, I'm told.'

Mabbut experienced a short, sharp convulsion.

'That was pretty nasty. Thousands of tons of oil spilled.'

'The *Braer* was nowhere near the terminal at the time.'

'Thirty miles away? It's not *that* far.'

'But it had nothing to do with the terminal.'

'Unlike the *Esso Berenicia*. That was very close to the terminal. In fact, a little too close. It smashed into a loading jetty and there was no oil-spill procedure in place. Clean-up cost the company two million, nearly four thousand birds killed. Is that in your book?'

Mabbut's brain was racing. There were no copies of the book around, apart from on his shelves and in NorthOil's offices. How on earth had Latham got the information?

'What's the point you're making, Ron?'

'My point is, Keith, that it's horses for courses. I've no doubt that you, a campaigning journalist, would want to tell the truth — about oil spills and fights with the council when they tried to protect their profit share — but the ball isn't always in your court, is it? The oil boys pay the piper. The piper plays the tune. What I'm getting round to is that you were paid — I'm guessing here — fifteen thousand all in. Plus expenses?'

Astonishingly accurate.

'To produce the book that NorthOil wanted you to produce.'

'And?'

'If Urgent Books is paying you nearly two hundred grand, then surely you must feel some sort of obligation to produce the book we've asked you to produce?'

Neither spoke for a moment. Mabbut tried to calm himself enough to give a sensible reply.

'So what does Urgent Books want, Ron?'

'Why don't you come in and we can discuss it.'

'I'm happy to discuss anything. I can do Monday — '

'This afternoon. Two o'clock?'

'I can't do that, Ron. I'm going to the football with Sam. It's the first time in weeks — '

'I'll see you at the office. Ring the night bell if there's a problem. Oh, and I've warned Silla there might be a delay in the delivery payment.'

The phone went dead. Mabbut sat in a mess of bedclothes, trying to control his rage.

★   ★   ★

Mabbut had decided that one of his top priorities, once he'd finished the book, would be to restore good relations with his son. There was a lot of ground to make up: sibling rivalries, maternal propaganda . . . The football had been his masterstroke. He and Sam hadn't been to a match together for years, and he'd leant on a few contacts to get tickets for the local derby with Tottenham. Tickets to die for. And there they

261

were, in the kitchen, pinned up on the board in front of him. Latham was a cunt. An absolute cunt. He could bloody well take his money and shove it. Mabbut didn't need it. He'd got by before. All he wanted was never to see the man again.

Jay appeared at the door. Behind her came Shiraj, his usual air of deep seriousness replaced by a cautious, almost embarrassed smile. He came towards Mabbut with his hands together in front of him. He gave a short bow, transferring his right hand to his heart.

'Believe me, Mr Mabbut, as God is my witness, I do not deserve this.' He bowed his head again. 'But thank you. Thank you, sir. And may God bless you always.'

Mabbut smiled uncertainly. He'd never seen Shiraj look so happy. Come to think of it, he'd never seen him happy.

'Jay told me what you offered to do last night. Believe me, your generosity towards my family will never be forgotten.'

Jay took her father's arm and squeezed it.

'I am unhappy that this should be the way my country works. It is a far from perfect place, sir, but God willing, with the help of people such as yourself, we can change things.'

Shyly, tentatively, Shiraj held out a piece of paper.

'This is the bank here in London to which the monies should be paid, and here is my full name and the name of the account. I am sorry to be so forward, sir, but time is of the essence.'

Mabbut nodded, aware of Jay beside him and

262

her hand on his arm.

'Thanks, Dad.'

She reached up and kissed him.

★ ★ ★

It was half-past one. Silla's car had collected him fifteen minutes earlier but the traffic was bad because of the football and Hector Fischer was not happy.

'Soccer is not my game. Soccer is a game for the proletariat. I'm a ruggerby man. Twickenham.'

He gestured at the crowd streaming across the road towards the stadium.

'Look at these people. They are the common herd.'

But Mabbut wasn't listening. He was still in shock. He spoke to Silla in a muttered whisper.

'What does he mean, 'one note'. He's a golf publisher, for God's sake.'

'Was.'

'He doesn't understand people. All Ron understands is a business model.'

Silla sighed.

'I'm sorry,' Mabbut went on. 'I know you and he . . . but, I mean, you've read the book.'

'I skimmed it, old boy, and I thought it was great. I loved the India stuff. But Ron will have gone through it with a fine-tooth comb. He'll have been up all night. That's the way he works.'

'Maybe he'll be asleep when we get there.'

Silla gave a short, hollow laugh.

'Some hope.'

'You know what they do, these people?' said Hector, sensing a break in the conversation. 'They take a newspaper, roll it up and wee-wee into the pocket of the man in front of them. And he to the man in front of him. At Twickenham nobody pees on anybody.'

Mabbut looked out of the window. The sea of red-and-white scarves was a painful sight. He'd called Sam twice, left messages about the tickets, but had heard nothing. Sam knew all about the weapon of silence.

It was well past two when they turned off Southwark Bridge Road and into the car park of Urgent Books. It being a Saturday there was no one on the gate, but there was notification of an emergency number to ring. By the time the barrier had been raised and the rising kerbs lowered, a further five minutes had elapsed. Hector dropped them off at a side door which led into the glass and marble reception area, empty save for an Asian man wearing purple overalls who was making slow, sweeping passes over the marble floor with a rotary polisher. Ron, looking fresh and sharp in navy polo shirt and jeans, called down to them from the gallery above.

'First floor, coffee's on. Lift's out of action.'

As they climbed the strangely old-fashioned curving staircase, Mabbut slowed down, aware that his pace was a lot faster than Silla's. When she reached the top of the stairs, she had to stop for a moment to get her breath.

'You all right, Silla?'

264

'Fine, thanks, old boy. Stairs are best when they go down, I find.'

★   ★   ★

Latham picked up coffees from the dispenser and carried them towards his office. He gestured at the lines of unattended work-stations and sadly shook his head.

'Never understood weekends myself.'

In the office, he motioned to two leather chairs then settled down behind his desk. Through the window, Mabbut caught a glimpse of light reflecting off the distant Thames and it gave him some hope. Latham snapped the blind shut.

'Sorry about that. It's the only problem with this office. Lets in the sunshine.'

'Have you any water, Ron?' Silla asked.

Mabbut looked over at her. She seemed to anticipate his concern and made a rude face, which partly reassured him.

Ron reached into a fridge and found a small bottle of water. The manuscript lay open on the desk and Mabbut could see Ron's scribbled notes, even on the title page, for God's sake.

Ron licked his forefinger and turned the pages back and forth.

'OK, guys. You know my problem with this. It's well written.'

He looked across at Mabbut as if this were his first big mistake.

'And if I were Melville's mother, or the head of Amnesty International, this would press all the right buttons.'

Silla gave a short, involuntary cough. Mabbut caught her eye. Latham leant back, interlocking his fingers.

'You've been on the oil rigs for too long, Keith. Lost your sense of perspective.'

Mabbut opened his mouth to protest but no words came. Latham assaulted a few more pages before picking up the manuscript in both hands, as if weighing it.

'If you don't mind my saying so, this is like a note to a new lover.'

Mabbut coloured. Silla stared at Latham. He met her eyes briefly, then they both looked away.

'All right,' Latham continued. 'I've made my point. I'm not going to say any more, other than this is not a book I can recommend to my board.'

Mabbut felt very weary, like a man slipping back into quicksand when all but the tips of his toes were clear.

'Look, all I did was fulfil everything I had been asked to do. Believe me — '

Latham leant forward and raised one finger.

'Yet.'

Mabbut paused. 'What?'

'This is not a book I would recommend to my board. *Yet.*'

Silla coughed again. It sounded worse this time. Ignoring her, Latham went on.

'There are things that can be done.'

Mabbut rolled his eyes. 'I have covered the ground, Ron. I have talked to thirty, forty people. I have followed up every lead. This is not a portrait I dreamt up myself. This is a consensus. I'm sorry if you don't like it, but that's the way it is.'

Latham tapped a key and looked at his computer.

'With all due respect, Keith, I think there may be some stones that remain unturned. I asked the boys and girls in my research team to look at some of the grey areas again and . . . yes, here we are.'

He pressed another key and a printer began to hum.

'They've come up with something you might have missed.'

He pushed his chair along the desk and retrieved two newly printed sheets of paper. He held one out to Mabbut and one to Silla.

'This, in my humble opinion, is worth pursuing. I don't need to tell you both that it's highly confidential information. It just might be the sort of thing our book needs.'

4

When they reached Silla's apartment building, Hector had to help her from the car. Apart from delivering a short diatribe about Japanese tourists wearing face masks — 'Who's sick? Us or them?' — he had been strangely subdued as they drove home. Mabbut and his agent had barely spoken and, for once, Hector seemed to catch the mood.

Mabbut held open the brass-handled doors as Silla, resisting any form of support, straightened up and walked into the lobby.

'Are you sure you're OK?'

'Yes, I'll be fine. It's just some kind of fluey headache.'

'D'you want me to come up?'

Silla shook her head vigorously.

'No, no, no, dear boy. Quite unnecessary. I shall have a hot toddy, go to bed and watch *The X-Factor*. I'll be fine in the morning.'

Mabbut pressed the lift button.

'What's his game, Silla? What's this all about?'

'How should I know, old boy? He has people on his back. Urgent have put a lot of money behind this project and they want something that'll be talked about. It's the way the business is, believe me. And he may be right. There could be something you've missed. No one's perfect. Not you, not Melville.'

'Should I do what he says?'

268

'No option, dear boy. The publisher's approval clause is a tough one. They can lead you round the ring for a lot longer.'

She suddenly looked very drained but managed a wan smile.

'Don't sulk, darling. Six months ago you couldn't believe your luck. Now you're behaving like Ernest Hemingway.'

The lift slid down in front of them.

'Talk in the morning?'

Silla nodded and with a peremptory little wave she stepped into the lift. Mabbut was aware of Hector's pumped-up frame filling the doorway behind him.

'She don't look well.'

'No.'

'I drive her four year. I never see her look like that.'

Mabbut nodded agreement.

'Once I drive another lady. Much younger. Always laugh. Then one day she don't come down.'

'Well, I'm sure she'll be fine.'

'Dead. Two days dead! I had to break in. She was fifty-one.'

'That's sad.'

'Oh yes. Sad. Where you go now. That place you live?'

'No, I've . . . I've some shopping to do.'

For some reason Hector winked.

'OK, sir. I understand.' He gestured towards the lift. 'Look after the lady. She's good woman.'

★　★　★

Mabbut walked away from Silla's block and took a turning that led to a small garden dominated by an expansive London plane tree. It was tucked away, a relic of an eighteenth-century churchyard, and few people seemed to know it was a public place. A woman and her daughter were feeding a flock of fat, fidgety pigeons. Two Asian girls in headscarves sat on one of the benches, giggling. Otherwise, people passed by without stopping. Mabbut found a wooden bench as far away as possible from the others. He leant back against the words '*In memory of Mifanwy Dell, who loved this place*', and took out the sheet of paper Latham had given him. At the top, in bold, was the name and address of one Victor Trickett. *Sir* Victor Trickett. Latham must have cut and pasted the rest of the contents, presumably from his researcher's report.

Therefore, following extensive enquiries, we have ascertained that this is the same man who had dealings with Melville back in the early eighties, an episode which does not reflect well on Mr Melville. VT has agreed to talk to your author provided his identity is protected. He has never spoken about his relationship with Mr Melville before, but he's now ready, for a [something cut out here] to put the record straight before it's too late. We recommend that the author make contact with a view to a visit asap.

At the bottom of the page Latham had added, in his own handwriting, '*Strongly recommend follow-up. For any help with arrangements, contact me personally 24/7. RL.'*

Mabbut folded the note and slipped it into his inside pocket. A strengthening wind rustled the branches of the tree that sheltered him. The last months spent criss-crossing the country in search of contacts, doing research in libraries and news archives, had reminded him why he had once been good at his job. He was thorough. He took pride in following up every lead, knocking on every door, making sure he missed nothing. Now, apparently, he had missed something significant, and an all too familiar feeling returned; that sudden, swinging collapse in morale to which he seemed so fatally susceptible.

He read and reread the single sheet of paper. There was something that worried him about it. It was not so much that it showed him up, or even that it had appeared so late in the game, collected by some anonymous figure from an equally anonymous informant. What made him suspicious was the apparently uncritical way that Latham had endorsed these findings. His shifty, conspiratorial 'contact me personally' approach smacked of something more than a mere desire to get at the truth. If there was a separate agenda to rake up bad news on Melville, then perhaps Mabbut's failure to find it was less culpable. The difference between honest and dishonest reporting.

A light rain began to fall, marking a circle of dry ground beneath the shelter of the tree. A smartly dressed woman hurried by, holding her dog as if she were afraid of it getting wet. The

Asian girls stood and walked cautiously out of the park. They checked their mobiles. One gave a high-pitched squeal and they set off rapidly up the street.

★ ★ ★

'Hi, Dad.'

Mabbut shut the front door, dropped his bag to the ground and made wearily for the kitchen. Jay and Shiraj were at the table, cups of tea in front of them, eating something wholesome from foil containers similar in shape and size to those that littered the approach to his Underground station every Saturday night.

'Did they like the book?'

Mabbut stopped himself from telling the truth just in time.

'Pretty much. There's a few things they want me to look at before it's all signed and sealed. How about you. Had a good day?'

'Yes, really good.'

Jay smiled and reached for Shiraj's hand.

'I was able to speak with my mother and my cousins this afternoon and they are all very happy and send blessings to you for helping us in our time of trouble.'

Mabbut cleared his throat, and unhooked a mug from above the worktop.

'I won't be able to get it straight away, I'm afraid. They're delaying the delivery payment.'

Jay's face clouded. 'But you've delivered the book?'

'Technically, yes. But they want some new

interviews to be done. It'll take another week or so.'

Jay looked embarrassed. Shiraj shook his head and turning to her, spoke softly.

'It's fine, Jay. I will tell them.'

Mabbut still had his coat on. He turned and went out into the hall to hang it up. By the time he came back he'd made up his mind. Of all those around him at the moment, Jay was the least compromised, the one most open and dependent on him. This was the one family relationship he had not messed up. And most of his debts had been paid off.

'Don't worry, Shiraj. I'll authorise a transfer right away. The money should go through first thing Monday.'

'Please, sir, I do not want to take from you what I cannot pay back. Believe me, my family will honour any amount you can find for us. You have already given me your hospitality and your friendship. This will never be forgotten.'

Mabbut looked at Shiraj. His troubles were of a far, far greater magnitude than anything Mabbut had ever had to deal with. These were matters of life and death and yet the boy accepted them all with a stoical calm. Whatever Urgent Books wanted was insignificant compared to what might befall Shiraj or his family. He felt not only a warmth for the decent young man his daughter had brought into his life but also gratitude for the opportunity he had been given to right some wrongs. He extended his hand. Shiraj stood, and as he did so, Mabbut reached out and hugged him close.

273

5

Sir Victor Trickett wasn't easy to find. His address, 'Lees Hall', had no accompanying number, only the name of the village where it was located — 'Great Brenham, Norfolk'. Mabbut had taken the Norwich train, hired a car and had already got lost twice as he negotiated the back roads where signposts were still shaped like pointing fingers.

Great Brenham was the largest of a cluster of villages that also included Little Brenham, Brenham Till and Brenham Magister. Though it had once boasted three medieval churches, the present-day population of the Brenhams was probably in the low hundreds. The only thing approaching a centre was a small village green with a single multi-purpose shop. Mabbut received directions to Lees Hall from the elderly proprietor.

'It's been empty for quite a while,' she added, encouragingly.

Mabbut bought a steak pie and ate it sitting in the car. As he stared out at the two or three flint-work cottages with their creeper-clad walls he found himself hoping beyond hope that this would be a bum lead. He tidied away the remnants of the crumbling pie, took a swig of water, then scrutinised the directions he'd been given and turned on the engine. A mile or so down a country lane a track led off between

274

stony fields until it dipped and entered a small wood. He slowed down when he came to a timber pile marked on the map and a few yards beyond that was a stout but mildewed five-bar gate, securely fastened. He got out of the car and was examining the rope knots when he heard a voice and the gruff bark of a dog.

'I'll do that!'

Down the overgrown driveway came a short, barrel-like figure. The man was wearing a beret and a trenchcoat and looked to Mabbut to be about his age. An elderly retriever shuffled along behind him.

'You must be Mabbut.'

On closer inspection the man was clearly much older than his visitor. His skin, though firm, was deeply lined and mottled around the neck. He had a thick grey moustache and wisps of white hair curled out from beneath the beret. On the front of it was a badge which caught Mabbut's eye.

'Eighteenth Royal Hussars. Light Dragoons they call them now.'

The man's voice was harsh and croaky, his tone petulant. The classic outsider, thought Mabbut, as he watched the man work deftly through the knots and slip the rope over the gatepost.

'You can bring the car in. Just be careful of the dog. She's half blind.'

Lees Hall was little more than a large Victorian villa. Ivy grew across its plain red-brick façade, and with the woods hemming it in on three sides, there was a sense that nature was close to reclaiming the space. There was one open aspect, through which could be glimpsed a low hill, on top of which were what looked like outbuildings.

'Used to be a farm,' said the man, who Mabbut had to assume was Victor Trickett. He led Mabbut through a porch into a large dark hallway that smelt of dogs and damp.

'Want a beer?'

Mabbut declined. 'D'you have any coffee?' he asked.

'No.'

'Tea, perhaps?'

There was an unmistakable hiss of exasperation. 'Bag do?'

'That's fine.'

'You should find one in the cupboard.' He indicated a long narrow kitchen, off the hallway. 'Above the basin. Kettle's full.'

His voice receded and Mabbut found himself alone. A fine layer of grease on the kitchen surfaces put him off any further exploration. Checking that he wasn't being observed, Mabbut emptied and refilled the kettle, then selected a mug, washed it carefully and set it down on the one empty space on the worktop.

'So what d'you want to know?'

The voice came from a room next to the kitchen. Mabbut peered through the door and found his host in a cluttered drawing room which was full of good-looking furniture, but too like the back room of an antique shop to be completely comfortable. Trickett settled himself into an armchair and poured a bottle of beer into what looked like a regimental mug.

'I haven't got long,' he said to Mabbut.

The kettle was barely whispering, so Mabbut abandoned the idea of tea and perched himself on the edge of a chair, reaching into his pocket for the voice recorder.

'Do you mind if I use one of these?'

'Rather not.'

'It's purely for accuracy. Protects you as much as it protects me.'

'Don't you people have notebooks?'

'I use one of those as well. The recorder's just for back-up.'

'Notebook'll do me.'

Mabbut put away the recorder and took out his pad and a blue Pentel.

'You're certainly off the beaten track here.'

'Suits me.'

Mabbut cleared his throat. 'Sir Victor, I believe you know Hamish Melville.'

'Used to. Haven't seen him in years.'

*　*　*

This proved to be the tone of much of their conversation; Mabbut having to prod, Trickett playing it straight back. He claimed they'd met in the army, when Melville was a captain in the Royal Engineers. That, at least, corresponded with Mabbut's own research. Both had been involved in the Suez invasion of 1956 and both were highly critical of the way the operation had been bungled. They'd kept in touch. Neither of them had been tempted by civvy street, both by nature 'a touch stroppy'. Then, without warning,

Melville had left the army and started to make money in the City. Trickett had stayed on in the Hussars for a while but seeing how well Melville and some other ex-soldiers were doing he too had resigned his commission and gone into business. Melville was a wheeler-dealer, had good 'what they called people skills'. Trickett admitted he was the opposite: an inventor, someone who was happiest at the drawing board, or in the lab. In the early days of heart surgery he had worked on a pioneering set of MHVs, mechanical heart valves, and was experimenting with a new type of plastic anginal valve. Development was expensive, however, and he had approached his old colleague Melville to come in as a partner.

To get this far had taken a couple of beers, and it was when Trickett returned with a third that the story took a very different turn.

'Did the partnership come to anything?'

Trickett wiped a finger across his upper lip before he spoke.

'Yes. But not exactly as I'd hoped.'

His voice had lost some of its military briskness and for the first time he seemed a touch unsure of himself. The dog wandered in and sniffed the air before collapsing at his master's feet.

'I've never spoken about this,' Trickett began, looking up sharply at Mabbut, 'and your people did promise me that — '

'My people?'

'The chap who rang. Said he was working for you.'

For a moment both men looked confused. Trickett made to get up.

'I wrote the name down somewhere. I can find it for you.'

Mabbut motioned for him to stay in his chair.

'Anyway, I made it clear to this chap that I didn't want to be named.'

'Any special reason?'

'I'm a very private man, as you can see. I'm not interested in settling any scores. But if a story is to be told then it should be the truth.'

'Absolutely.'

'Well, I'll tell you. Hamish and I fell out over a woman. It seems no big thing nowadays but it cost me a lot of money and a great deal of credibility. At the time my wife was also my colleague. She was Yugoslavian, Slovenian. She'd heard about my work on the anginal valves and was doing similar work herself, so we corresponded. I went over to Ljubljana to meet her. We became . . . '

Trickett cleared his throat and his eyes went down to the carpet.

' . . . we became very fond of each other. Bettina came to London in 1976 and we married the following year. She was a clever woman. And she was beautiful.'

He gave a short, rueful laugh.

'I didn't really stand a chance. I had my head down, literally, going over the designs again and again, testing and retesting, to prove beyond a shadow of doubt that they would work. Bettina was doing the work alongside me, but she was less . . . single minded than

279

me. She liked to mix work and play.'

The dog let out a sudden high-pitched exhalation and stretched its legs out across the carpet. Trickett did something similar, pulling himself up, bracing his shoulders, and looking Mabbut full in the eye. When he spoke the military precision had returned.

'To cut a long story short, Melville seduced her, and took from me not only my wife but the money we'd invested in the development of the valves. Three years later, someone else came up with a suspiciously similar technology. I thought of taking legal action but what was the point? Bettina never came back to me. I returned to medical research. Developed a lightweight heart — lung connector. I was given a knighthood in 1989 so I've nothing to complain about. But when I was told that Hamish Melville was about to be portrayed as the saviour of mankind, I felt it was time to tell my side of the story.'

There was silence in the room. Mabbut scribbled furiously. His shorthand was rusty, and it took him a while to catch up. By the time he'd finished, Trickett had got to his feet and it was clear that he was not keen on having Mabbut in the house a moment longer. Mabbut noticed that his eyes were misty, owing perhaps to the effort of recall.

'May I ask you — ?'

'If you don't mind, Mr Mabbut, I've many other demands on my time.'

'I'm sure. Your long experience must be valuable.'

He waved his hand as if swatting a fly.

'Yes, there are always people who want to get in touch.'

He shuffled across the hall.

'Still busy?' asked Mabbut, following.

'This and that. Brain like mine can never stop thinking.'

They had come to the front door.

'Well, thank you for seeing me.'

Mabbut felt in his back pocket and handed Trickett a card, more out of duty than expectation.

'That's my number, Sir Victor. If you ever need to call me.'

Trickett took it without a glance, and dropped it into a dusty bowl beside the telephone. Then he drew aside a heavy protective curtain and pulled open the door.

They squeaked across the gravel towards the car.

'I'll go ahead. Open the gate for you,' said Trickett.

'May I ask you one more thing, Sir Victor?'

Trickett stopped and turned.

Mabbut was aware that he was on delicate ground. He couldn't just say he thought the man was a confused old fraud.

'You'll understand that I need to be very thorough when dealing with accusations such as this. Is there anyone else who can . . . corroborate your story? Your wife, maybe?'

Trickett shook his head.

'My wife died ten years ago.'

Mabbut closed his notebook and was about to get into his car, when Trickett said, 'There is someone who knew her.'

Mabbut sighed inwardly and pulled out his notebook again.

'And who would that be?'

For a moment Trickett stared down at the gravel. Then he looked up, but not at Mabbut, at a point somewhere behind him. He moistened his lips. 'Her daughter. Ursula's her name. She's not in this country. Last thing I heard she was in Czechoslovakia.'

Mabbut wrote this down, and looked back at Trickett.

'Second name?'

'Galena.'

'Ursula Galena,' he repeated, writing it down. 'Well, thank you.'

'Don't you want the surname?'

'I'm sorry, I thought that was it.'

Trickett shook his head and his face betrayed the merest glimmer of a smile.

'Ursula Galena Melville.'

6

The spa town of Karlovy Vary sat prettily in a steep wooded valley. It had been known as Carlsbad for most of its working life, but was renamed at the end of the Second World War when the Germans who had lived there on and off for five centuries were expelled, and the town became part of Yugoslavia, then Czechoslovakia, now the Czech Republic. As Mabbut walked down from the station he had a feeling of unreality, of having walked into a Grimm Brothers' fairy tale. The houses huddled steeply together; the onion-domed towers, the deep-pitched roofs and pink-washed walls could all have been made of gingerbread. The place reminded Mabbut, quite poignantly, of a holiday he had once enjoyed with Krystyna in the mountain villages of southern Poland. It was the first time they'd left the children since they were born. Out of the context of work and home, it had been a magical week. Krystyna used to say that she never wanted to go back to Poland, because she'd never be as happy there again.

He reached the fast-running river that twisted along culverts through the town and walked across a bridge to a picturesque riverside strip filled with tourists. Some were shopping for glass and trinkets, others were being carried round in coaches drawn by ponies with red caps on their

283

ears. Portly waitresses in big skirts brought trays of coffee and chocolate to those who were taking late lunches or early teas outside on the café terraces. Beneath a long classical colonnade, groups of the elderly were waiting in line to take the famous healing waters.

Mabbut found a table and ordered a coffee. He still had Krystyna on his mind, so he took out his notebook and flipped through the last few pages, trying to concentrate on the job in hand.

It was twenty-four hours since he'd seen Trickett. It was a visit he'd found disturbing, for many reasons. That the man had failed to show up on his radar was clearly an omission on his part. On the other hand there had been something odd about it all. Why had this highly confidential, and potentially explosive, information surfaced only now? He'd missed it, but then so, at first, had Latham's team of researchers, who'd supposedly been working on the Melville file for six months.

The coffee arrived, a plume of milk still vibrating gently on its surface.

Mabbut had never met any of Latham's researchers. He'd been told they were interns, young graduates hoping for a permanent foothold in the publishing business. On the odd occasions when he'd wanted information from them, he'd had to go through Latham. And then there was Trickett himself. Hardly the most convincing witness. A sad, bitter old man who didn't want his name to be mentioned. Mabbut's hunch was that there was some chicanery here,

284

something that fitted uncomfortably well with Latham's determination to change the tone of the book. Mabbut felt he had to catch up, to try to win back the initiative before it all got out of hand. He had to check out the credibility of Trickett. And he had to check out the existence of this Ursula Melville before anyone else got to her.

There had not been much to go on. A name and a country. Apart from an eighty-five-year-old radio actress called Ursula Melville, Mabbut had drawn a complete blank. He'd been about to give up when, after tapping in her full name, Google had asked whether he'd meant 'Galena Health Products'. Mabbut had idly clicked again, and this time he sat up. Galena Health Products were produced at a clinic in the Czech Republic. The address was Stara Louka, Karlovy Vary. No telephone or email was given. It was a wild card, a hunch, but he hadn't been able to let it go.

Mabbut finished his coffee, left the money beneath the saucer and walked across the plaza to a quiet street of boutiques in tall nineteenth-century houses painted in vibrant shades of green, red, pink and blue. It wasn't a long street and at number 19 Mabbut found the nameplate he was looking for. 'Galena Centre for Health and Beauty'. It was in English. He buzzed and was admitted.

Inside everything was cool, white and minimalist. He'd heard about these private sanatoriums. Largely catering to wealthy Russians, they capitalised on the publicly available

285

mineral waters to offer highly private therapy: expensive, exclusive, exhaustive and dedicated to making the rich feel better. Stairs led up to a first-floor reception area.

Mabbut found himself in a long bright room with tan leather sofas and walls hung with framed photos of bodies beautiful. It was an anaesthetised, strangely depersonalised environment which could hardly be more different from anything one would associate with Hamish Melville.

Through force of habit, or perhaps just to make it quite clear that he was not here for a beauty treatment, Mabbut reached into his pocket and took out his notepad. As he did so, he caught a glimpse of himself in the tinted mirror behind the reception desk, looking old and furtive, like some elderly detective on his last job. The receptionist was impeccably complex-ioned, with the pale, immaculate face of a doll. She smiled as best she could.

'Good morning.'

'Good morning. I'm looking for a Ms Melville.'

'I'm sorry?'

'Ms Melville. Ursula Melville?'

'We don't have anyone of that name here.'

'This *is* the Galena Clinic?'

'Centre. Yes.'

'I was told that Ursula Melville worked here.'

She looked puzzled.

'I don't think so, no.'

Mabbut was treading water now, about to kick himself for the whole absurd adventure, when the receptionist's face showed a glimmer of recognition.

'There is an Ursula *Weitz*.'

'Can I see her?'

'Who shall I say is calling?'

Mabbut was about to reply when he experienced an almost out-of-body experience. The door behind the receptionist swung open and he found himself face to face with a tall, imposing woman with a head of golden hair. Instantly he knew who it was. The shrewdness of the eye, the briskness of the glance, the effortless composure. It was as if Hamish himself stood there, albeit white gowned, full bosomed and forty years younger. So when the woman spoke in a soft German accent he was momentarily confused.

'Yes, sir, how can I help?'

The receptionist gestured redundantly. 'This is Ms Weitz.'

★ ★ ★

'It's pine extract with the zest of lemon, Mr . . . what was the name again?'

'Mabbut. Keith Mabbut.'

'Do you like it?'

'Very nice,' Mabbut lied, as he took the first sip of the tea. They were sitting together in Ursula Weitz's office. The walls were lined with photographs of those who had been treated there or, rather, those who had been treated and were happy to have their photographs taken. Mabbut recognised one or two world leaders, and others he was less sure about: actors, sportsmen and women, television celebrities. All wearing the same impenetrable smiles. Smiles like masks, concealing the anxieties that had brought them to the clinic in the first place. Loss of looks, loss of attraction, loss of the power to seduce and beguile.

The awkward initial introductions were over and despite the fact that her existence was a potentially lethal discovery for his book, there was something about Ursula Weitz that gave Mabbut hope. An openness, perhaps. A lack of Trickett's bitterness.

'I know who my father is, but I don't have any contact with him. I must have met him when I was a baby, but I don't remember anything. My mother, Bettina, she married my stepfather, Felix — '

'Felix Weitz?'

She nodded.

'Yes. They married when I was five years old. I have two step-sisters and a stepbrother and we are all one big family. But my mother always told me the truth. She had to. I was half a metre taller than everyone else!'

Ursula laughed. A loud, unladylike laugh, bracingly out of place in such a controlled environment.

'And your stepfather? Did it worry him?'

She shook her head vigorously.

'He was too busy making money. He loved to play the markets. He was like a child. When Germany reunited, he bought everything he could in the East, companies that no one else would touch. Within ten years they were all making a profit. So he sold them, and went looking around the old Soviet republics.'

She chuckled at some memory.

'He had this energy, you know. He would come home from, I don't know, Azerbaijan, and tell us how he had bought an oil company because he was the only one who could drink and stay awake.'

'Is he . . . ?'

'Still alive? No. He was quite a bit older than my mother.'

Mabbut hesitated.

'I . . . I'm probably out of line here but do you ever think about meeting up with your real father?'

'I have my business to run here. We're opening a spa in Berlin next year. I have a partner who I've been with for five years. My life is my life. Why complicate things?'

'Yes. I understand. May I ask, did your mother talk much about her first husband?'

'She talked about my father. A lot.'

'Only, a man called Victor Trickett claims that not only did Melville steal your mother, he also stole some important designs for heart valves which belonged to Trickett. Did she ever mention this?'

Ursula frowned.

'What was the name again?'

'Victor Trickett. Sir Victor Trickett.'

'I don't remember her saying anything, no.'

'She never talked about artificial hearts, heart valve patents. Anything like that?'

She shook her head.

'I'm sorry. That means nothing to me.'

They talked for a while about this and that, but then a buzzer went on her desk. Ursula spread her hands apologetically.

'It's my oligarch. He's on his way.'

She slid open a drawer, took out a card and examined it.

'Four hours. Four therapists.'

She got to her feet.

'That sounds good for you.'

'It's good money, but he thinks it entitles him to put his hands wherever he likes. And our therapists don't do that.'

'So what do you do?'

'I bring in some girls from outside. I give them an hour's training and tell them that if they keep quiet they can keep the tips.'

'And what d'you tell him?'

Ursula shrugged.

'He never complains. He's ninety-four. He won't be coming here much longer.'

Mabbut smiled at her and held out his hand.

'Thanks for your time, Ms Weitz. I'm sorry to have to ask you these things.'

'I understand.'

'He's a great man, your father. It was a privilege spending time with him.'

He was halfway through the door when Ursula called after him.

'Mr Mabbut?'

He turned.

'How about a realignment massage? On the house, of course. You look as though you could do with one.'

290

7

Mabbut had never felt particularly comfortable in private clubs. He'd been lunched at the Garrick once, and one of his better sources in the arsenic story had been a member of the Reform, but he'd never been invited in. On this bright spring morning, as he turned off St James's and walked up the steps to the bow-windowed façade of Whites, he tried hard to remember that all men were equal. And some women too, as his father used to say. Rex Naismith, dressed in a light grey three-piece, was waiting for him at the bottom of a wide curving staircase, his bulk disguised by excellent tailoring.

Rex greeted Mabbut and suggested they go on up to the dining room and have a drink there. At various tables Mabbut recognised the broad backs, well-filled stomachs and faintly familiar profiles of political life gone by. Rex ordered two glasses of the house white and they ate herring and beetroot salad. They talked, neutrally, about the club, its history, the portraits on the walls and the impossibility of finding a restaurant as quiet as this anywhere else in the centre of London. Then there was a good but slightly tough New Zealand lamb to be dealt with as Rex effortlessly spun gossipy anecdotes about some of their fellow diners. It was not until the table had been cleared and the cheese trolley dismissed that Mabbut began to explain to Rex why he'd asked to meet him.

He described, as fully as possible, his predicament over the Melville book, and the recent revelations about Sir Victor Trickett, though of course he didn't mention him by name. Rex, it was said, knew everything about everybody, so Mabbut asked whether he was aware that Melville might have had secrets, been involved in adulterous affairs and business betrayals. Rex was confidently dismissive. Melville was undoubtedly competitive and astute in matters financial but he was absolutely not the sort of man to have taken a penny that didn't belong to him. On the other hand he couldn't deny that Melville had always 'had an eye for the ladies, and they for him'. Mabbut said that this was also the view of all his sources. Charley Murray had heard rumours of a love-child, maybe even two. Mabbut smiled as he thought of Ursula. She'd turn a few heads in here.

Emboldened by Rex's candour, Mabbut steered the conversation closer to home.

'I gather you and Krystyna are . . . well . . . seeing less of each other.'

Rex seemed taken aback.

'Not at all. We see each other regularly.'

'My daughter seemed to think otherwise.'

For once Rex had no reply. He pursed his lips and looked sideways at Mabbut for a moment.

'Your daughter and her mother are seeing less of each other. That's certainly true.'

'Oh . . . ?'

Rex loaded a spoonful of sugar into his coffee and stirred. There was clearly more to be said.

'I hope I'm not speaking out of turn here.' Rex tapped his spoon on the rim of the cup and laid it carefully on the saucer. 'But there's a little friction between them at the moment.'

'Friction?'

'Over the boyfriend.'

'You mean Shiraj?'

'Shiraj, yes. Krystyna feels that Jay, and you to a certain extent, are being, well, a little over-indulgent with him. Does that make sense?'

Mabbut gave a sigh of exasperation.

'I'm afraid Krystyna and the National Front have never been sworn enemies.'

'That's not entirely fair.'

'Well, put it this way, she's never had unlimited tolerance for non-nationals. It comes from being Polish.'

Rex ignored the jibe.

'I still think it's worth talking to her about it. Julia does belong to you both.'

Mabbut bristled. He was not going to be told how to treat his own daughter by this man.

'If she wants to talk to me, she knows where I am,' he said briskly.

Rex, ever calm, checked his watch.

'Well, I hope you didn't mind my passing the message on.'

He held up his hand for the bill.

'I'll ask around, about your informant,' he added. 'Sounds pretty harmless to me. I wouldn't worry.'

* * *

Mabbut stared at the computer screen. He was left with an adulterous affair and an illegitimate child, and given what passed for sensation these days it was pretty thin stuff. He could quite easily feed this into the text, but would it be enough to get Latham off his back? He set to work that night and by half-past four had come up with something that felt right. He would revisit it in the morning and, all being well, send Latham the relevant pages over the weekend. Then, hopefully, the whole thing could be put to bed and he could get back to *Albana*.

* * *

First thing on Monday Silla rang as Mabbut was emerging from the shower. Latham had read the latest version and wanted to meet them both as soon as possible. Unfortunately one of her most promising new discoveries was at the Madrid Book Week so she wouldn't be able to accompany him this time.

'Are you all right, Sill?'

'Much better. Call me tonight. I should be in the hotel around nine. And good luck, dear boy.'

Mabbut treated himself to a taxi down to Urgent Books, arriving in good shape and, despite his earlier qualms, feeling quietly confident about the way he'd dealt with the Trickett story. Instead of talking in his office, Latham led Mabbut through to the boardroom. He motioned him in and briskly shut the door behind him. There was no offer of refreshment. He slapped the rewrites down on the table and indicated a row of chairs on the nearside of the table. Mabbut sat down while Latham remained standing, his back to Mabbut.

'You've been busy, I gather. Trips to the Continent.'

Mabbut shrugged. 'Just doing my job.'

'I could have organised it all for you if you'd asked.'

'I was lucky, got a cancellation.'

'And?'

'And I now know that he does indeed have an illegitimate daughter. I should have found that out earlier, but as you will have read, I've now included it in the text, with her name changed at her request.'

Latham snorted. 'And her story practically undetectable.'

'There's nothing to it. It's no big deal.'

'Well, that's a matter of opinion. What I'm more interested in is Trickett.'

'I was down there first thing on Monday. Interesting man. A hermit knight.'

Latham tapped his finger rapidly on the pages before him.

'Did you listen to what he said?'

Mabbut paused a moment before answering.

'He specifically asked not to be recorded, but I kept full notes, yes.'

'Did he at any time mention anginal valves?'

'He didn't go into technical detail, but, yes, he mentioned that he had worked on something like that.'

Ron took a piece of paper from his jacket pocket and adjusted his glasses.

'He designed the first ever set of plastic bileaflet valves for use in heart operations.'

'But as I remember, he told me he couldn't finish the work.'

'Because he didn't have the money, right?'

'That was it, yes. Melville offered to help him.'

Latham nodded. 'That was kind of Melville, wasn't it?'

'Very much in character.'

Latham pulled a chair from under the table, and sat directly opposite Mabbut.

'What he did next was not in character, though, was it? And going off with Trickett's wife?'

'Having an affair? That's hardly a character flaw.'

'What about running off with a woman who took all the work her husband had done for the last four years and helping her sell it to the highest bidder?'

'That's not how Trickett described it. He said they worked jointly.'

Latham shook his head angrily.

'That *is* what he said. You just didn't hear it.'

'How do you know? You weren't there.'

'And you didn't hear it because you didn't *want* to hear it, because it looks bad for the man you hero-worship!'

'Look, I've written about his infidelity. I've written about his illegitimate daughter, who, incidentally, has never even met him. And who has never heard of Victor Trickett either. I've taken all that on board and I delivered the rewrites to you in three days flat. I've kept my side of the bargain.'

Latham took a deep breath and leant forward once again. In the hard light of the halogen spotlights Mabbut noticed a few drops of moisture on his forehead. When he spoke, he spoke slowly.

'You have missed the big story, Keith. Whether Trickett deserved to lose his wife or not is not what matters. What matters is whether he deserved to lose his life's work. Whether he deserved to see the man who took his wife grow rich on the proceeds of his genius. That's what matters.'

'He didn't exactly say that.'

'Well, he *should* have done!'

The room rang with the sound of Latham's hand hitting the table. Then there was silence. Latham straightened up and ran a hand across his brow.

'My sources tell me that Bettina Trickett took the designs for the bileaflet anginal valves from her husband and gave them to Melville. Melville helped her to sell them on to a big international pharmaceutical company, making a lot of money for himself in the process, which he then invested in becoming the world's environmental con- science. *That* is the big story, and it should be in the book.'

'Well maybe your 'sources' should have written the book!'

Latham sighed. He sounded tired.

'Keith. You're a good writer. Silla was right

297

about that. The book is yours and no one else's. I just want it to be the best book possible, and if that means facing a few unpalatable truths, then that's the way it has to be. The company is committed to this book. All they ask is that you revisit this area, check your notes, and give Trickett's story the credence it deserves.'

He picked up the manuscript.

'They've given us a one-week extension.'

'Who are 'they'?'

''*They*' are my board. '*They*' pay my wages. And yours!'

His voice dropped.

'Keith. I *need* those facts in there. You said to me yourself that a journalist will always look for the truth. Don't resist it, Keith, when it's under your nose. You're a good writer, now prove that you're a good journalist.'

★　★　★

There was, of course, only one person who could definitively scotch the Trickett allegations, and that was the one person Mabbut had agreed not to contact directly. But if he was to have any chance of saving the book as he had written it, he realised he had no option.

He called Wendy Lu at her number in Singapore. She greeted him with her usual infectious enthusiasm, and before he could say anything she had launched into a panegyric about the book, a copy of which had reached her less than a week ago and which she had immediately sent on to Melville. Mabbut felt

298

compelled to tell her everything that had developed since then. At first Wendy tried to laugh off Trickett's accusations, but it was clear from the increasing silences that she was taking it all in. When Mabbut had finished she was all briskness and efficiency, asking for clarification on certain points, such as dates when things had happened and the people who had brought this information to Urgent Books. She promised to contact Melville and said she'd get back to Mabbut with an explanation. Mabbut made it as clear as he could how important it was that he learnt the truth from the man himself. His personal access to Melville was still his trump card.

Tuesday and Wednesday came and went. In addition to Rex's testimony, Mabbut re-interviewed his other contacts, none of whom could recollect any dealings between Melville and Trickett. He spent a day at the Patent Office, painstakingly checking for any submissions Trickett might have made. Trickett had indeed been a fertile inventor and his name appeared, often with that of his wife, on a number of applications, mainly to do with medical equipment, but there was no mention of bileaflet valves. Interestingly there had been no applications from him for anything since the mid-1980s.

The rest of the week did not go well. Daily calls from Ron Latham and nothing at all from Melville. Silla Caldwell was uncharacteristically elusive. All he got from her hotel in Madrid were brusque assurances that his messages had been received. On Friday afternoon, an old, rather grubby envelope arrived in the post. It seemed to have been reused several times. Inside was a single sheet of notepaper headed 'Lees Hall' and a short message which appeared to have been composed on a very old typewriter. It read, '*Dear Sir, I have remembered the name of the man who first spoke to me about Bettina. It was a Mr Latham. Yours faithfully, V. R. Trickett.*'

Mabbut felt paralysed, caught between his desire to be done with the book and have his fee safely banked, and his increasing suspicion that he was being deliberately manipulated by Latham and Urgent to distort the truth. Nevertheless, the very existence of Trickett and Ursula had shaken him and sown doubt where none had existed before.

At home, there were other doubts creeping in. Mabbut had been hurt more than he'd expected by the news that Krystyna and Rex's relationship was not only alive and well but seemed to be cementing itself around some formless mistrust of his daughter's choice of boyfriend. This only made him more thankful that he had found the money to help Shiraj and his family, and determined to find more if necessary. He knew that Krystyna wouldn't like it, but that was one of the differences between them. He saw duties; she saw practicalities.

It was now Saturday and Mabbut was sitting, stock still, in front of his computer, staring at the back of the house opposite where what had once been a messy green garden had now become a neat paved patio, on which a circular drying device slowly rotated. The doorbell sounded. He

300

walked downstairs. At the door was a young man in well-pressed overalls holding a small computer terminal. Behind him a delivery van was double-parked in the street. A car behind it hooted angrily, but the young man seemed in no hurry. He handed over an envelope and requested Mabbut's signature. Mabbut signed, bade him farewell, and was already tearing the envelope open as he pushed the door shut with his foot.

To his relief and joy, it was from Melville. At last. Handwritten, as before, on old Foreign Office notepaper. With a surge of relief, he took it up to his workroom, shut the door carefully and sat down to read.

Keith, greetings.
Wendy sent me the book. I'm afraid I could only speed-read it on my way to South America, but it looked pretty good to me. I skipped most of the stuff about my early days but appreciated the space you gave to my more mature work (!) and our time in India (I've suggested a few trims of the more personal stuff. Do I really 'bark orders'?) But by and large I'm happy and I congratulate you on an impossible task well executed. This story could make a difference, believe me.
Saw Kumar before I left. He sends his best.
Hamish M

Mabbut turned over the paper. The other side was blank. He peered into the envelope, running

301

his finger deep inside. It was empty. He looked for an indication of date or place but there was neither.

He checked his watch. It was four o'clock. It would be 11 p.m. in Singapore. He took a deep breath and dialled Wendy's personal number. It was on answer. He left a message, impressing on her as strongly as he could the vital need for up-to-date information from Melville. He had just finished when he was distracted by a shout from downstairs. He opened the door and looked over the banister. Jay had come in. She sounded anxious.

'Have you seen Shiraj, Dad?'

Mabbut shook his head. 'Not since this morning.'

'It's odd. He doesn't usually go out without me. And his bag's not here.'

'He's probably gone to the shops. Or on one of his marathons.'

'We always go running together.'

'Have you rung his mobile?'

She nodded. 'No answer.'

You and me both, Mabbut thought. And for once his tolerance of Melville's lifestyle tipped over into irritation. He might be saving tribes from extinction but why this obsession with being reclusive? How difficult could it be to make one phone call, for God's sake?

'I'm sure he'll be back,' he shouted down, automatically.

Jay didn't reply. He heard her go back into the kitchen. He returned to his workroom and sat staring out at the back gardens again. A pigeon clumsily manoeuvred about his hedge, beak full, looking for a nesting site. He banged on the window and it flew away.

The sound of the phone made him jump. He picked it up quickly but then his heart sank. It was Ron Latham, and worse still, he sounded happy.

'How's the writing going?'

'Fine,' Mabbut lied.

'I have some very good news!'

'Oh?'

'Our picture desk has tracked down some shots of Trickett, his wife and our man together.'

'Melville?'

'We're pretty sure it's him. It's a formal photograph at some function. Circa 1980. Resolution's not great but we're working on that.'

'I thought you said that Trickett's name wouldn't come out.'

'We don't have to say who he is.'

'But everyone will be able to see him. That's not what you promised him.'

'Whatever my boys promised him is their affair. I'm a publisher. I have a book to sell. And it's your book too, remember that.'

'That's why I'm worried.'

'Well, don't be. This is just what we need. The camera doesn't lie.'

Unlike you, thought Mabbut.

'Oh, and we sent someone over to that Czech place I can't pronounce — '

'Karlovy Vary?'

'That's it. So now we have an eye-catching

choice of pictures to go with your stuff on the daughter. She's a handsome woman, Keith. Did you get a free massage?'

'Ron, I don't know what's going on here. She had nothing to say. There's no story there! And as for Trickett, I think he was told what to say.'

'Come on, Keith, let's not get into your paranoia. Just put what Trickett told you in the book, and let the reader judge for himself.'

Mabbut was aware of a mounting anger, desperately trying to find somewhere to settle.

'And the photographs?'

Latham was trying to sound relaxed, but his voice was high pitched and brittle.

'They're part of a very full book. There's a lot of other stuff in there. Some people may not even notice them.'

'Which is why you want to put the photos in, I suppose. Ron, you know as well as I do that this stuff is exactly what the papers, the media, will pick up on. They're not going to be interested in Indian or Brazilian tribes he's saved from extinction. If there's a picture of a beautiful blonde outside a health club that's what they'll print. And once Melville has been discredited by association then anyone who wants to do some good in the world is going to find it that much harder. Is that really what you want?'

'Look, no one's talking about discrediting anyone. It's about bringing in the widest audience.'

He heard Latham clear his throat.

'Monday morning, Keith. Full meeting of the board. I have to show them what we've got. This is our last chance. Finish the story the way they want it and have it with me by Sunday night, or the deal is off.'

Mabbut lowered the phone. He felt his heart thumping. This was turning into a nightmare. Everything he had feared from the first moment he'd set eyes on Ron Latham was coming true. He was slipping into a morass and he had no idea how to climb out of it. He pulled the window open and took some deep breaths. He had walked into this unholy deal with his eyes wide open, believing somehow that goodness was irreducible. That what Melville stood for was as near as humanly possible to what everyone should want to stand for. Now it had come to this. Melville was a good man about to be mugged. And he was one of the muggers.

He called Silla in Madrid. This time he didn't even bother to leave a message. Then he returned to his desk and stared out of the window until the dark clouds came and the light began to fade, and finally he set himself to the unwelcome task.

It was thoroughly unpleasant work. Having originally written the book in the spirit of Orwell and Norman Lewis, he was finishing it in the style of a Sunday newspaper in a circulation battle.

After an hour or two his motivation evaporated. He persisted but eventually set it aside, shut his laptop and went downstairs. No sign of Jay or Shiraj. The house that had once given him so much comfort now felt cold and inhospitable, as if it too disapproved of what he

305

was doing. He looked around him. He hadn't bothered to switch the lights on. All he felt now was an overwhelming desire to be somewhere else. He picked up the phone and called Tess.

8

Mabbut awoke with a sense of foreboding. Grey daylight drizzled in through half-drawn curtains. He eased himself out of bed, gathered his things and was out of the flat before Tess woke. There was little traffic on the road, and he half walked, half ran along the slumbering back streets till he found a twenty-four-hour corner store on Hornsey Rise. He bought a pint of milk and some orange juice and jogged back to Reserton Road, where he unlocked the front door and entered the house as soundlessly as possible.

He held his breath. The house felt different. He went upstairs and on to the landing. Jay's bedroom door was open, so he looked inside. The bed was tidy and hadn't been slept in and the curtains were open.

'Jay!' he called as he went downstairs.

There was no answer.

So they'd both been out for the night. He felt hungry all of a sudden. Hungry for something very basic. Bacon, egg, sausage, anything bad. He walked into the kitchen, taking out his mobile to see whether there had been any word from Singapore. Nothing. Instead he found two missed calls from the previous night, both from Krystyna. That was unusual enough to raise a ray of hope.

Finding, to his disgust, that there were none of the high-cholesterol ingredients he craved, he made himself a large mug of coffee and a tomato sandwich then, checking the time, he called his wife.

'There you are!'

Never a promising start to a conversation.

'Where have you *been?*' she asked.

'In bed. Asleep.'

There was the briefest of pauses.

'It's Jay . . . '

His stomach lurched. 'What's wrong?'

'Her little Muslim friend.'

'Shiraj? What's happened to him?'

'You'd better come over. We're at Rex's flat. Fifteen Wilton Gardens. Knightsbridge.'

Mabbut grabbed his phone, keys and wallet and ran out into the street. Sunday morning. No cars, let alone a taxi. Maintenance work on the Underground. He ran back inside and dialled the local minicab firm. A polite, incurious Somali got him down to Wilton Gardens in twenty minutes.

Number 15 was a three-storey stuccoed Victorian cottage, with a black front door and matching railings, in a modest but discreetly expensive terrace not far from Harrods. The doorbell nestled in a circular brass cavity, which had been kept well polished. Krystyna answered the door. She met his eyes briefly, then led him along a narrow hall. Mabbut heard his daughter before he saw her, her whimpering sobs echoing from the kitchen. She was sitting at the table, head bowed; a heart-breakingly fragile figure. She looked up as Mabbut entered, trying and failing to smile.

'Dad.'

He sat down at the table and took her hand.

'What is it, love? Whatever is it?'

Rex appeared behind him in a polo shirt and baggy jeans. He looked almost naked without a tie or a jacket. He smiled briskly at Mabbut and moved towards the kettle.

'Cup of tea?'

Mabbut nodded. Rex put his hand lightly on Krystyna's shoulder.

'Another one, darling?'

Krystyna was seated on the other side of the table from her daughter. She was looking at Mabbut with ill-disguised scorn.

'Could someone tell me what's going on?' he asked, looking from face to face.

Jay took a deep breath, then shook her head and looked imploringly at Krystyna. But it was Rex who spoke.

'The boy's gone.'

'The boy? You mean Shiraj?'

Rex was at the sink, filling the kettle. He turned and nodded.

'Gone? Gone where?' Mabbut's voice rose. 'Don't tell me. It's the Border Agency. They've shafted him, haven't they? It's my fault. My stupid fault. I was supposed to drum up support for him. Oh, Jay, love, I'm sorry — '

Rex cleared his throat.

'It's not the Border Agency. We don't know what's happened to him. He left a message to say he was sorry, but he had to leave and that he'd explain one day, but not to try to find him.'

Jay gave a low moan. Krystyna reached across

the table and took her hand.

'Is he in some sort of trouble?'

'Jay's mother always had suspicions about him,' said Rex, 'so I made a few enquiries and one of my contacts, a perfectly trustworthy source, I promise you, warned me that there was a criminal ring operating within London in the Iranian community, obtaining money under false pretences. One of those on file matched Shiraj Farja's description.'

'No!'

Rex nodded.

'They believe his real name is Anek Mertha and he is an Iranian Kurd.'

'Are they sure?'

'Almost certain.' Rex coughed and cast a quick glance at Jay before going on. 'There's a warrant out for his arrest.'

Mabbut shook his head in bewilderment.

'Do they know his background? What he's been through?'

Jay spoke at last. 'He lied to me, Dad, and he lied to you.'

She hung her head. The tears came again and this time there was no stopping them. He put his arm around her shoulder.

Krystyna's eyes were hard and cold.

'Jay says you gave him four thousand pounds.'

'Mum . . .'

'Is that true?'

'Yes, it's true.'

'You should be able to get it back. When he's apprehended,' said Rex. But Krystyna was still staring at her husband.

'Four thousand pounds! To someone like that?'

Mabbut returned her contemptuous gaze.

'And I would have given him more if I could.'

'Oh, well, of course, now you're a best-selling author, what's four thousand pounds? A drop in the ocean!'

'I gave him the money because I believed him. Just as our daughter believed him. And until I hear a lot more about this, I still believe him!'

Krystyna gave a desperate toss of her head.

'Keith, why do you always believe anything except the truth?'

Rex took two cups off their hooks above the kettle.

'Look, why don't we all adjourn for breakfast. Tea's ready, and I'll put on some toast.'

Mabbut thanked him but declined. He gave his daughter a kiss on the top of her forehead. She took his hand for a moment, and then looked up, as if remembering something.

'How's the book, Dad?'

'Nearly there.'

'That's good. At least that's one thing I didn't mess up for you.'

Krystyna moved protectively towards her.

'Jay's going to stay here with us for a while. She doesn't want to be in the house.'

Mabbut nodded. 'Of course.'

Rex led Mabbut to the front door.

'There's no point in my staying,' said Mabbut on his way out, 'not with Krystyna the way she is. She's in shock. She'll calm down. Perhaps you could give me a call then?'

Rex gave a backward glance then stepped out too, pulling the door almost shut behind him.

'Keith, I'm to blame as much as anybody. I should have spoken up much earlier. I've seen a couple of very similar situations. Plausible young chaps with poise and charm. Perfectly decent people taken in. I had doubts about the boy the first time I met him, but as soon as I voiced them Jay took it personally, and because of my situation with her mother, she and the young man didn't come round much any more. She compounded the problem by telling everyone it was Krystyna's fault. All those stories about us splitting up, that sort of thing.'

Mabbut looked up the street. Two elderly ladies with bulging green shopping bags were getting into a taxi, giggling like schoolgirls. A group of young men with wayward blond hair were walking three abreast, fighting each other for possession of the pavement. An immaculate Jaguar XJ turned out of a side road. This was not Mabbut's London and he wanted to get away.

Rex held out his hand.

'Ring me any time. If you need to.'

They shook. Mabbut paused and looked at Rex.

'I still don't believe he was a bad man.'

Rex sighed.

'That's the skill of these people, I'm afraid.'

★   ★   ★

Back home, Mabbut made himself a cup of coffee, then called Wendy Lu. Her machine said

312

that she was out of the office until Monday but left no other number. Mabbut thought briefly of ways to poison Ron Latham, or even of running away and leaving his clothes and a note on a beach somewhere. Then, fortified by a second, even stronger cup, he returned to the distasteful task he now had no option but to complete. By late afternoon what had to be done was done. He read through the rewritten pages without satisfaction. There could be no doubt now that the subject of his book was an all too ordinary mortal; a man who at one time in his life had reportedly stolen not just another man's wife, but his life's work as well. No matter how much he used the word 'alleged', or the well-worn phrase 'some say', the damage was clear. Innuendo would do the rest.

So now, his side of the contract was complete. Mabbut sat back, numbly, staring into the middle distance. The whole process confirmed that, despite all his grand pretences, nothing had changed. He remained a hack. A pen for hire. The Melville effect had made fools of them all. His delusions of transforming himself into some latter-day Hamish, helping the helpless, spreading the truth, slaying cynicism in its lair, had turned out to be no more than that: delusions. And who was he to presume to slay cynicism anyway? A little more cynicism on his part and his only and dearest daughter might not have ended up sobbing over a kitchen table in Knightsbridge. Stanley, with his unerring sense of occasion, leant against the doorpost and purred with pleasure.

At six Silla called. She apologised for not being around during the week. She was glad to hear he'd revised the book. Things had gone well in Madrid, and now she was back she'd promised Ron that she would come over, collect the new version from Mabbut and deliver it to him personally. She was just glad to hear that it had all worked out.

9

When Silla rang again to say that she would
not be with him for another hour as Hector
Fischer was unavailable — it was Sunday night
and Hector was evidently a devout churchgoer
— Mabbut's misery was merely prolonged.

He poured a whisky, vaguely aware that this
was the sort of thing he was doing far too
regularly these days, checked for the
umpteenth time that the envelope was ready
on the hall table and was about to distract
himself with the evening news when the door
buzzer sounded. He looked at his watch. It
couldn't be Silla already. He half hoped it
might be Jay, but she'd have her own keys.
The buzzer sounded again, impatiently.

'All right. I can hear you!'

He opened the front door. A stocky figure
stood at the top of the steps holding a package.

'Keith Mabbut? Sign here, please.'

He reached for a terminal and marker and
held them out to Mabbut.

Mabbut signed completely illegibly, then
grabbed the package, slamming the door far
harder than he meant to. Inside the Jiffy bag
was another white envelope. He tore it open.
The now familiar handwriting, the Foreign
Office notepaper. The lack of an identifying
date or place. He had difficulty holding it
steady.

Keith,

I've just heard from Wendy of the problems you are having. All I can say is that I'm not surprised. This is why I don't do books. This is why I don't give interviews or go on chat shows. They all have an agenda which is very different from my own. As you know, I had my doubts about Urgent Books from the start, but I'll come to that later. First of all, the allegations. I owe you an apology for not giving you Ursula or Victor Trickett's name on the list of people you should talk to. They both are, or were, part of my life. Ursula is not the only daughter I have either, and I would have told you that had we not both agreed that this was not going to be that kind of book. Bettina wanted Ursula to be brought up entirely independent of me and I have always respected that.

Trickett, on the other hand, is a very nasty piece of work and I would not wish his view of events to go unchallenged. His late wife Bettina was a brilliant woman, a chemist and a physicist with a sharp, highly original mind. I met her through a college friend and although I won't deny there was a physical attraction, I was chiefly interested in the work she was doing. Bettina was from Yugoslavia and she'd come over as a young researcher to Imperial College in '76. She badly wanted to stay and work in London and to help that process she'd married a colleague by the name of Victor Trickett. He was also a surgical researcher, but he was a

plodder; Bettina was the brains. In 1978 she
made a breakthrough that later led to the
development of bileaflet heart valves — that's
a ring to which two semicircular discs are
fitted that open and close to control blood
flow. Without her knowledge, Trickett
approached a big pharmaceutical company
and offered to sell them the technology for a
substantial sum of money, portraying himself
as the one who'd made the breakthrough.
Bettina was — understandably — furious.
She was in the course of developing the next
stage of anginal valve technology, but now,
thanks to Trickett, all her work and her
future ideas had been mortgaged off to a
company called Bell Laboratories. I had been
drifting around the City at the time, as you
know, but while most of my friends were
looking to invest in bricks and mortar I was
more interested in intellectual property.
People doing the sort of things I liked to do,
thinking outside the box. Independent-
minded, difficult bastards. Bettina was one of
those. With her co-operation I raised enough
money to buy back the rights to the work
she — and to a very limited extent Trickett
— had pioneered. Because he had cheated
her in the first place we had to work behind
his back and eventually leave the country to
avoid the long legal battle that he would
undoubtedly have fought. He is not a nice
man, Keith. He sent people over to Prague
to search the apartment. He made sure Bettina would never be able to work in the UK

317

again. To cap it all, he used work she had done with him to produce heart-lung tubing for which he received a knighthood. For a few years he pursued Bettina through the European courts but he got nowhere. He produced nothing more and his career faded into oblivion. I was surprised to hear he was even alive. Bettina worked on in advanced surgical research until she died of breast cancer in 1998. By that time we'd long since gone our separate ways, entirely amicably.

This, of course, is my side of the story, and it's entirely up to you whether you believe it or not. But this you should believe, for it's true. When I heard what they were trying to do to your book I commissioned some research of my own, on your publisher, and the following can easily be checked out — maybe you've even done so? Urgent Books is a subsidiary of Wide Hatt Publishing, wholly owned by the Karlhatt Corporation, headquarters in St Louis, Missouri, and the Cayman Islands. This grand-sounding, if somewhat shadowy, organisation is 80 per cent owned by one Karl Hattiker and his family. Along with a few evangelical radio and TV stations, they also own a cereals combine called Hemisphere Grain Group, one of the big wheat cartels that fix prices around the world. Their domination of the market is now being threatened by Russia and China so HGG are looking to expand elsewhere. One of their biggest, most controversial investments has been to put billions of dollars into the soya fuel market in Brazil. To date they are directly responsible for the clearance of two to three per cent of the Amazon rainforest, and the construction of irrigation dams on the Parcachua river that have already destroyed the cultivable land of thirty local tribes. And Brazil is just the current target. They have eyes around the world, constantly on the lookout for the line of least resistance — the corruptible local politicians, the ambitious state governor, the regime that needs to buy tanks and aircraft. Until last year their operations went almost unnoticed. Then, acting on inside information, my team moved in last August and within a couple of months we had enough evidence to convict the company of fraud, corruption and intimidation. As far as HGG goes I'm Public Enemy Number One. Do you remember those guys out in Bhubaneswar? The ones who came to the hotel? They were HGG heavies, looking for me or my colleagues. And they're becoming increasingly desperate. My guys in Parcachua have had their families threatened. Kids approached at school, for God's sake. Now wouldn't it just suit them if a best-selling book were to come out, showing that the man who has been giving them grief is nothing but a wife-snatching con-man?

Keith, you're the man in the middle. To reel you in they had to play on your impeccable liberal credentials and the attraction of my own impeccable liberal credentials to

someone *like yourself. The problem is that
an impeccable liberal book is no good to
them. You and I agreed on the things we
wanted to say — about the Earth and how
we look after it — and that didn't need dirt.
So they've dug up some dirt for you and left
it on your doorstep.*

*I happen to know that there's a price on
my head now, and being a living legend is
not going to protect me from some unfortunate accident. Whatever happens I shall go
on with my work and hope people will
understand that the past is the past and has
nothing to do with the work I've done since.
The one thing I can thank these bastards for
is that I've had a chance to show you it's
possible to make a difference.*

*You do what you want to do, Keith. I
don't want to drag you any farther into all
this. I appreciate you're being paid well and
I'm sure you could use the money. I'll hold
no grudges if you decide to go ahead. I'm
used to being misunderstood. It's a badge of
honour!*

Regards,
Hamish

Almost an hour later Silla arrived in a cab. She
still had her cough and blamed a heavy schedule
at the Madrid Book Week for impeding her
recovery. They didn't talk much about the book.
She could tell Mabbut wasn't happy with the
situation but at the same time she said she was
pleased and relieved that he'd done what he had

to do. He'd even put the manuscript in a nice red folder.

'Thanks, dear boy. I'll call you in the morning.'

Mabbut picked up the folder. 'I'll come with you. Deliver it personally.'

'If you're sure you want to do that. Ron'll appreciate it.'

At around half-past seven they drew up outside Latham's glittering apartment block beside the river in Battersea.

Silla paid the fare and they walked towards the lobby. Automatic doors slid aside to admit them. Mabbut looked around.

'I thought he lived in the office.'

Silla laughed. 'He takes Sunday evenings off.'

She announced their names to a bored security guard, who queried the name twice before buzzing Latham's apartment. Once inside the lift Silla pressed the button for the twentieth floor and with a breathy hiss they were swept upwards and disgorged into a silent, carpeted, climate-controlled corridor.

Ron opened the door, raising his eyebrows when he saw the two of them. He was wearing a white towelling robe and his face was bright pink.

'Keith! What a nice surprise.' He stood back to let them in. 'I hadn't expected the author himself.'

Mabbut caught the quick exchange of glances with Silla. He stepped into the room. It was what he'd expected: modern furniture, a lot of appliances. Speakers, screens, things in aluminium. Framed certificates on the wall. More surprisingly, a lot of books, on wall-to-ceiling shelves. Some novels among them.

'Drink?' asked Latham. 'I've been breaking my back down in the gym, so I'm on iced water. Silla?'

She chose a juice and Mabbut a beer and Latham went to fetch them from the kitchen.

'That's a view,' said Silla, walking across to the window. The size and height of the plate glass made Mabbut feel slightly queasy. A Lufthansa Airbus, sinking towards Heathrow with a mournful wail, passed across their line of vision like something from a computer game. She made a face. 'I can never get used to it.'

Mabbut just had time to pick up on the remark when Latham appeared with the drinks on a tray.

'Heineken all right?'

'That's fine. Thanks.'

They sat down on either side of a low glass-topped table, Mabbut and Silla together, Latham opposite. He raised his glass.

'So, bang on time. Cheers and thanks all round.' Latham smiled magnanimously at Mabbut. 'I know it wasn't easy for you, and I apologise about the pressure, but I appreciate what you've done, Keith. I think it's something we'll all be proud of.'

Latham pulled his robe tighter around him and eyed the red binder.

'So, do I get to have a look?'

He and Silla laughed, and he reached forward. As he did so Mabbut put his hand on the manuscript.

'I just wanted to say a few thanks of my own, Ron. If I may. Now that the book's finished.'

Ron nodded. 'That's nice.'

For some reason, Mabbut noted the time on the digital clock on the sideboard. It was 19:38. Another airliner, lights flashing, cruised across the window.

Mabbut raised his glass.

'Ron, Silla, I want to thank you both for giving me the chance to do this book. I also want to thank Karl Hattiker and the Hattiker family for enabling the Hemisphere Grain Group to continue their good work in clearing the rainforests of the world, and for generously donating some of the profits to fund the activities of Wide Hatt Publishing, without whom there would be no Urgent Books. I should like to thank you, Ron, as my publisher, for encouraging me to look at all aspects of the life of a previously honourable man and to you, Silla, for standing by me when I wavered. And to Hamish Melville, wherever he is, I say thank you for all you have done to open my eyes and the eyes of the world to what is really going on.'

No one moved.

'Hamish, I hope I've kept my side of the bargain.'

He drank deeply, set the glass down on the mirrored table, and only then did he take his hand off the folder and push it across the table.

'Goodbye, Ron. Bye, Silla. Thanks for the drink. Enjoy the book.'

And with that Mabbut stood, collected his coat, and left.

323

Silla sat staring at the door as if she was expecting it to be opened again and the whole scene rerun to a different script. But it remained closed. Latham pulled the file towards him. He loosened the elastic at either corner and drew out the manuscript.

'Well, at least I don't have to be nice to him any longer.'

Silla flashed him a look of irritation.

'Come on, Ron. He gave you what you wanted in the end.'

She paused.

'Ron?'

Latham was staring down at the title page, his face immobile. His left hand beat hard and fast on the top of the table.

'What's the matter?'

Latham said nothing, but shot the manuscript across the table towards her.

'Take a look.'

Silla gasped. She ruffled through the first few pages as if they might offer some explanation but they only confirmed her worst fears. There it was on the title page, in sixteen-point bold Times New Roman:

Triumph in Adversity. The Official History of The Sullom Voe Oil Terminal.

10

The terminal came into sight as Mabbut drove down the immaculate road that ran alongside the company's airstrip. A private jet was loading up and a line of stooped figures in high-visibility jackets, heads down into the wind, were hurrying towards the aircraft steps. High in the sky, white clouds were dashing across from the west. A moment later the dark waters of the Voe appeared to his left. With a twinge of nostalgia, he glimpsed the four familiar piers jutting out from the terminal complex. A Norwegian-registered crude carrier, the *Olaf Kohner* of Bergen, was offloading oil from one of the newly opened deep-water fields out in the North Atlantic. On higher ground, behind the jetties, stood the rows of crude-oil storage tanks. Sixteen circular drums, each one capable of holding 600,000 barrels. Mabbut once knew this world well. This thousand-acre city squatting on damp and windswept hills where not much more than thirty years ago there was nothing but isolated crofts and grazing sheep.

Mabbut pulled up at the barrier to the car park. There was a new man on security, someone he'd not seen before. He handed over the permit he'd been given.

'My name's Mabbut. I'm here to see the head of External Relations.'

The man consulted a list carefully, moving his

lips as he read through the names.

'Have you any means of identification?'

'Apart from the letter with my name on it?'

The man, whose complexion was so smooth it was almost babylike, simply nodded.

Mabbut dug around in his wallet and handed over his driver's licence. A flock of herring gulls wheeled around a garbage truck that was emerging from the service entrance.

Once inside the compound, Mabbut cruised the long rows of parked cars until he found a space close to the administration building. He reversed in, as was required by the regulations. To one side loomed the tall walls of the terminal's own power plant. The largest building on Shetland, they proudly used to say, as if that made up for the way it looked. Behind him was a ten-foot security fence topped with coils of razor wire. Behind that, rabbits were playing on the hillside.

It had been only a month since he'd walked away from the book deal, although it seemed more like a year, so profoundly had his life changed. For once, he hadn't looked back, had second thoughts, or sought compromise. Instead, he had stayed at home, cleaned the house, painted the front doorstep, washed down the garden chairs and enjoyed the summer evenings. He had realised, with some surprise, that his self-respect and confidence, far from being shattered, were enhanced. There would always be the Sillas and the Lathams of this world who would tell you what you should do, but however persuasive, understanding and even generous they might be, they were ultimately acting on their own behalf. He, on the other hand, had been very bad at acting at all. Silla was right. He had too often been passive; full of thoughts and ideas and opinions but always waiting for someone else to tell him what to do with them. But through Melville he had acquired a confidence in his own judgement that he had never known before. He was not a fool. He knew that, true or false, Trickett's evidence was always there, and he could hardly deny that Ursula existed, but from the moment Latham and Urgent decided that these should be key ingredients in a book about an inspirational environmentalist he knew where they were going. And he knew that he must not accompany them.

It was now up to him to make sure that the story Urgent wanted to tell would never see the light of day. In the days that followed his last meeting he had consolidated this position. Not only had he refused to do Ron Latham's rewrites, he had threatened that if anyone else did, he would produce a full account of Ron's part in the whole affair. Lawyers locked horns, threats were made, dust was raised, but within a couple of weeks the deadline for meeting a Christmas publication schedule passed and by the end of the month Mabbut was able to share with Wendy Lu the good news that Urgent had quietly put the book to one side.

Krystyna had been predictably unforgiving about his decision to abandon a small fortune, but he no longer felt vulnerable to her taunts. Nor was the money as important or necessary. Rex, that decent man, had stepped in to bankroll the family while demanding nothing back. Apart from Krystyna.

So here he was, back on the island where the news that Krystyna wanted to finalise their separation had first hit him like a sledgehammer. Now, with hindsight, he was able to accept that if it had not been for his stubborn refusal to let Krystyna go, much unhappiness would have been avoided. Last week, with the approval of all the family, he had agreed not to contest the divorce.

Almost exactly on the dot of one o'clock he saw Mae Lennox leave the building. He opened the door and waved. She grinned, waved back and made her way to the car. He leaned over to kiss her. She offered both cheeks, formally, as if they were still at work.

'You're cold,' she said.

'I've had the window open. I thought we could go to that new place in Brae,' he said as he drove towards the gate.

Mae seemed breathless, as if she'd run from somewhere.

'That'd be nice. I mustn't be longer than the hour, though. There's a bit of a crisis on.'

'Oh?'

'There've been gales all week out in the Atlantic and one of the loading tankers hit the rig. Could have been a whole lot worse but they've closed the operation, which of course makes everyone a wee bit twitchy.'

As they turned on to the road towards Brae, Mabbut was aware of Mae fiddling with her clothing. Opening her coat, adjusting a scarf, tugging at her tight grey jacket.

'Well, hey, what a surprise!'

Mabbut laughed. 'I told you I'd come up, didn't I?'

'Have you brought your new book?'

His face clouded. 'No . . . it didn't exactly work out.'

'I was looking forward to that, Keith.'

'So was I, but it wasn't meant to be.'

'I'm sorry about that. You must be gutted.'

A sharp squall blew in from nowhere. Mabbut flicked on the wipers as the rain spat against the windscreen.

'Oh no. It was all for the best. I promise you.'

Sammy's Fish Bar had a well-scrubbed white-wood feel to it. There was a takeaway section that was busier than the tables, so they found themselves sitting beside a big picture window with room to spare. Over fish and chips, Mabbut told Mae the whole story, about the book and how he'd walked away from it, and about Krystyna and the divorce.

She looked at him with a concern that he tried to brush off.

'I feel so much better, Mae. I've started to make decisions rather than avoiding them. I won't have a wife for much longer and I won't have an agent either, nor a publisher. But what I hadn't expected is that what appeared to be the worst thing that could happen to me would turn out to be the best.'

He took a sip of beer.

Mae raised her eyebrows and nodded in agreement.

'So why did you decide to come all the way up here?'

Mabbut smiled. He stared out of the window, scanning the dark bays and the low, close-cropped hills running down to the sea. Then he turned back to Mae.

'There are times in your life when you're so busy doing a job you don't see what's going on around you. When I was up here trying to get my head round prefabrication policies and oil-flow anomalies, I just took it all for granted. This was my workplace, like any workplace anywhere. But I've not been able to get it out of my mind, Mae. Not just the islands and the peace and the beauty of the place but the people too. What I sometimes mistook for them being closed up and defensive was just a different way of looking at the world. When people didn't talk much I thought they were trying to tell me something.'

'I like that.'

'Now I realise that they don't talk unless they've something to say. There's a constancy to people here. It reminds me of what I saw in the hills in India. Among the tribes there. Constancy is something very precious.'

Mae looked towards the door, so Mabbut called for the bill.

'I also realise how much I took your help and friendship for granted. I don't think I ever stopped to think how close we'd become. You have a fundamental honesty that is so incredibly rare and it chimes with everything I've learnt from working with Melville. It's not pious, or pompous, it's just a straightforward truthfulness

330

that I know is right and good. If I decide to go and work with Melville, would you ever, just possibly, consider coming with me?'

They were both silent for a moment. Then Mae slipped a glance at her watch.

'Keith, I have to go. You've all your plans and it sounds so exciting, but for me reality is a damage limitation meeting at three o'clock. You've the chance to do something good in the world. I have to look at the implications of a company losing over a million pounds a day if we shut down the rig.'

She got to her feet. Keith hurriedly stood up too.

'Think about it. That's all I ask. You don't have to decide now.'

There was not much more to say as they drove back, and as soon as they reached the terminal gate Mae pushed the door open and ran off towards the admin block.

'Tonight!' he shouted after her. 'Eight o'clock. I'm at the Stratsa House!'

She nodded briefly, then pushed through the security turnstile and was gone.

★   ★   ★

He stood in front of the mirror. A blade of evening sunshine cut between the houses and caught the side of his face, reminding him that he was now in the latter half of his lifespan. His skin, always taut and trim, seemed paler than usual. He ran his fingers along his jaw, wondering whether he should shave before meeting Mae.

Earlier, after leaving her at the terminal, he'd checked in to the hotel and as the wind dropped and the clouds cleared he'd walked into the centre of Lerwick. He'd sat on the Victoria Pier and watched the comings and goings of small boats and the unhurried approach of the ferry from Bressay, revelling in the smell of salt and tar and the cries of fat gulls quarrelling over territory. He could easily just stay here, he thought. Buy an old crofter's cottage. Do it up. Move in with Mae. He could write, she could commute to the terminal. They could run a B&B. Take in guests. Maybe buy a small boat like the ones moored up at the pier side, waiting to take tourists to see the puffins or the colonies of gannets. The blast of a ship's horn had broken his reverie. An offshore maintenance vessel cast off and moved slowly away from the pier, heading south.

★   ★   ★

At half-past seven Mabbut walked into the bar that occupied one end of the Clickimin Suite, to find Mae already there. She wasn't alone.

Kevin O'Connolly rose to his feet, smiling broadly and extending one of his big, red hands.

'Keith! Whatever brought you back to this blighted land?'

Keith was about to kiss Mae, but something in her body language held him back.

'I came to see Mae.'

'So I hear. Took her to Sam's for a gourmet lunch. What are you drinking?'

332

'A glass of white wine, please.'

O'Connolly waved his arm airily.

'I'll get a bottle. We can drink it with the meal.'

While he went to the bar, Keith sat down, and gave Mae a puzzled look.

'What's he doing here?'

She didn't have time to reply before O'Connolly returned from the bar. He was grinning broadly. Like the cat that had eaten the cream, thought Keith.

'I've made it champagne,' he said, squeezing in beside Mae. 'In celebration of your return to Ultima Thule.'

Keith forced the smile that O'Connolly clearly expected. He tried to catch Mae's eye for some sort of explanation, but she was studiously looking away. Then O'Connolly put his hand on hers and grinned at Keith, almost bashfully.

'And our wee bit of good news, too.'

Finally Mae did look up, and when her eyes met Keith's he felt as if he had been pushed off a cliff.

O'Connolly squeezed Mae's hand.

'Are you going to tell him or am I?'

☆ ☆ ☆

Ironically, the meal that followed was saved from total disaster by the thing Mabbut least liked about Kevin O'Connolly — his total absorption in himself. There was simply no time to get on to any bruising personal ground as Kevin relentlessly revisited his childhood. The absent, drunken father, the tough streets, the pride of the men at the Clydebank shipyards and the bitterness as their industry shrank to almost nothing. They were the kind of 'Gorbals boy makes good' stories he'd heard many times before, but Mabbut was grateful for them now. A constant, almost soothing background music to his torment.

★ ★ ★

The next morning, as if in sympathy with his mood, the islands were shrouded in fog. No flights were coming in and out of Sumburgh until the afternoon, so Mabbut had time to walk into town. The mist turned everything Dickensian and his footsteps sounded unnaturally loud on the damp flagstones of Commercial Street. Mabbut bought a half-dozen bottles of wine at some horrendous price, and left them at the hotel reception with a note and a card for Mae and O'Connolly, wishing them a happy married life. He called Mae's number at the terminal, but she wasn't answering. He left a message and after an early lunch took the winding road to the airport for what he knew would be the last time.

11

A month had passed since Mabbut had told Wendy Lu the good news about the book, and it was over a week since he'd emailed offering his services, if Melville had indeed been serious about his invitation. He had hoped to have heard something, even an acknowledgement. Whenever he rang, Wendy had apologised. Melville was doing something very hush-hush. As soon as it was over he would be in touch.

With Krystyna, Mae and Melville receding into the distance, life was simple again. Not perfect, but simple. The mist had parted and the future was clear. As he restored his *Albana* books and papers to the desk and the shelves and re-pinned his maps and time charts to the wall, his gaze lingered over a photo of Melville. On anyone else the craggy features, the high cheekbones and the wild hair would look merely old, perhaps a little sad. A portrait of a life running out. But even on this small and curling photograph the big deep-set eyes carried such life and strength that it was difficult to tear oneself away. Mabbut looked at the image fondly and pinned it to the top corner of his board. What was it he'd said to Mae? About constancy? This was the face of constancy. Even if he were never to see this face again, it would be the one part of his old life to remain here as he finally settled down to write *Albana*.

So deeply had he immersed himself in the plains of Uyea and the escape of Stion and Eris from the rivers of fire that at first he failed to hear the doorbell. When it went again it was loud and long enough to jolt him from his reverie and Stanley from a deep sleep. It was mid-afternoon in June and the only other sound he could hear was the distant shouting of children in a nearby playground.

Mabbut ran down the stairs and opened the door. It was a delivery man again. This time quite middle aged, with dark circles beneath his eyes and what used to be called a Viva Zapata moustache. He held out an envelope. Mabbut looked at it curiously. The address was handwritten, but not in a hand he recognised.

He took it and signed, the delivery man belying his mournful appearance with a broad smile.

There was a letter inside, written on thick, expensive notepaper. There was no address on the top, just a single name, in red, and embossed: 'Ursula Weitz'. Her message was short and to the point. Something important had arisen and she asked whether Mabbut would come out to Karlovy Vary. She was holding a hotel room for him and had booked him a club-class ticket to Prague.

Mabbut stood there holding the letter. He was confused. Why her? Why now? Just as he had clambered out of that world he was in danger of being dragged back in. Which was absolutely not what he wanted.

It was Friday night. Quiz night at the Dog and

336

Feathers. He hadn't been there for weeks, and it suddenly seemed the perfect place for a soon-to-be-official bachelor. He dropped the letter on the kitchen table, finished his day's work, fed Stanley and went out.

★   ★   ★

Mabbut laid down his book and gazed out of the window. The train from Prague was wriggling its way through steep-sided cuttings thick with pine and birch and alder. It was high summer and the beams of late afternoon sunlight threw long shadows across the forest floor.

He had been booked into the Hotel Victoria, a three-star place on a steep hill called Stare Mitska. There was a note from Ursula saying that his room and dinner had been paid for and suggesting they meet at the clinic at 9.30 the next morning. The hotel seemed to have been hijacked by a noisy Russian wedding party, so Mabbut ignored the free meal and walked down into the centre of town. Everywhere was busy, but he found a freshly vacated table outside the Café Alefant, and despite repeated attempts from the waiter to get him inside he tenaciously clung on to it. For the next couple of hours he watched the noisy throng of tourists passing by, and ordered white wine spritzers to keep the waiter happy.

When he returned to the Victoria, the Russian party was in full swing, the lift was broken and he felt slightly ill. Mabbut collected his key and walked up to room 416. On one of the landings

337

he passed a couple enmeshed, hands inside each other's clothing.

The next morning he set out for the clinic. A bell was tolling in the church of Maria Magdalena, stalls were being set out on the street and the first groups were already gathering to take the water. He crossed the Tepla river, a thin shadow of when he was last here, and walked along the line of boutiques and gift shops to the Galena Centre. He was buzzed in. It was still early and cleaners in green overalls were sweeping the stairs. Picking his way round them, he climbed the stairs to the reception area. He pushed open the door and spotted Ursula instantly. She was bent over, her back to him, arranging flowers on a low table. She was not yet in her pristine white uniform, and wore a loose-fitting pink tracksuit. She turned and smiled as he came towards her. She was wearing no make-up and her face seemed older than he remembered.

She shook his hand warmly, thanked him for coming and, giving instructions to one of her assistants, led him through to her office.

'Coffee?'

Ursula was clearly in off-duty mode. Indeed, her behaviour as a whole was very different from his last visit. She seemed relaxed, but preoccupied. As the espresso machine went about its work, she reached into a cupboard and took down a packet of Lucky Strikes.

'Would you mind, Mr Mabbut?'

'Of course not.'

She took out a cigarette, lit it gratefully and

338

flicked a switch. There was a soft hum from above the alcove where she stood. With a wry smile, she pointed upwards.

'The rewards of running a health clinic. Your own private extractor fan.'

She poured the coffee, helping herself to two lumps of sugar before offering the bowl to Mabbut. Then she sat down at her desk. She looked tired. That was it, that was what was different. She looked tired and she'd made no attempt to disguise it.

'Thank you for coming at such short notice.'

'Thank you for making it so easy for me.'

'I'm sorry I couldn't put you in the Hotel Pupp. It's the best one, and you should see it before you go, but last night they were having a big wedding. A Ukrainian. Hired the whole place, and three orchestras. He's the second-richest man in Kiev.'

She pulled on the cigarette, inhaled as if her life depended on it, then blew the smoke up towards the fan. She took one more pull then stubbed out the cigarette and dropped it in a bin. She looked hard at him for a moment.

'Mr Mabbut, my father and I are very grateful for what you did.'

'For what I did?'

'Yes. For being a man of principle and not letting them bully you over the book. We are both very grateful.'

'You've heard from him, then, your father?'

She nodded.

'Well, that's good to know. I thought you had no contact with him. I've been going through

Wendy Lu in Singapore.'

'She's nice.'

'You know her too?'

Ursula picked a strand of tobacco from the end of her tongue.

'Oh yes.'

She stood abruptly and reached again for the packet of cigarettes.

'There are a few things you are going to learn today that will surprise you. Maybe shock you. First of all I must apologise for misleading you.'

'About what?'

'You asked me if I ever saw my father and I said no. Well, that was because I didn't want to give out any information. To anybody. For reasons you will soon understand. I am in touch with my father and have been for a while. He came to me for help.'

'What's wrong?'

She looked up towards a small window high on the wall which provided the only glimpse of the outside world.

'I am telling you this in the strictest confidence. My father is in trouble.'

'What kind of trouble?'

She tipped the packet and took out a cigarette.

'Every fight my father joins, every cause he supports, makes him new enemies.'

'I can imagine that.'

'These enemies are now very powerful. And they are trying to destroy him once and for all. They have tried various ways to discredit what he does — we think the book you were paid to write was one of their strategies. But thanks to you it didn't work. Now they are trying less sophisticated ways of silencing him.'

Mabbut took this in. It seemed oddly melodramatic to hear such a thing from Ursula and this worried him.

She raised a cigarette to her lips, but didn't light it.

'A week ago they put a grenade in the cabin where he and his team were working. Three of his men were killed.'

'My God. Is he OK?'

Ursula laughed. Bitterly.

'He was unharmed. Dodged the bullet as usual. But it shook him. Shook him hard. Made him stop and think.'

'D'you know where he is? I've been trying to contact him.'

Ursula glanced at her watch, then she walked to the door and beckoned to him.

'We're about to open. I'll take you somewhere quieter.'

He followed her back through reception — by now spotless, tidy and expectant — and out on to the small landing. She pressed the call button for the lift, and turned to him, both businesslike and apologetic.

'I must get into my uniform. Fifth floor. I'll join you later.'

The lift went only as far as the fourth floor, from which a short flight of steps led up into the eaves of the building. The decorative scheme was very different up here — cosier and more colourful, with big rugs in the corridors and Impressionist prints on the wall. A slim woman in her thirties with a blonde ponytail stepped out from what Mabbut could see was a small office. A half-dozen clipboards hung from hooks on the wall. Above a worktop was a bank of monitors.

'Good morning, Mr Mabbut, my name is Tabitha.'

Seeing his quizzical look, she smiled and added, 'Israeli.'

She opened an artfully concealed cupboard and produced a flat plastic-wrapped package.

'You will be in a treatment area so I would ask you please to wear the protective clothing, and to wash and disinfect your hands before entering.'

She indicated a line of cubicle doors to her right.

Mabbut donned the garments, which included an overall and plastic covers for his feet and head. Tabitha checked him carefully, then led him along a corridor and through a door with a thick rubber seal. Here the carpets and the cosiness ended, the temperature dropped and the walls were plain white again. She paused at another door and peered in through a small observation window. There was a name beneath it which Mabbut didn't recognise. Then she pushed open the door, showed him in and left.

The only illumination in the room came from dim halogen lamps above a bed, from which hung a cluster of cables. These were attached to computer screens and monitors arranged on a glass-topped unit. On the bed lay a figure with a thick white dressing around the top of the head and a thickly bandaged right arm from which a red wire protruded.

The head turned towards him, catching the light from one of the lamps above.

'Keith!'

The voice was weak but unmistakable.

'Did I frighten you?'

'Hamish?'

The bandaged head nodded.

'I didn't expect we'd see each other so soon.'

'Are you hurt?'

'Oh, could be worse.'

He gave a low chuckle, raised a hand and pointed.

'There's a chair over there somewhere. In the corner, I think.'

He pressed a button and the bed slowly raised him into a sitting position. Mabbut found a small metal stool and squatted on it, wanting to stare, but feeling able to take in what he saw only in quick, furtive glances. Melville's biblically long hair was gone, and what he could see of his face was entirely clean shaven, giving him a look of gaunt asceticism. A black and purple mark spread out from beneath the bandage and there was a butterfly dressing across the bridge of his nose.

Melville attempted a wide, reassuring smile, but it was clearly uncomfortable for him.

'I hope you don't mind coming here. I asked Ursula to organise it for me. One of the few compensations of this . . . unfortunate business has been that I get to spend some time with my daughter.'

He indicated the instrument table by the bed.

'D'you mind? There should be some water there.'

343

Mabbut found a plastic bottle with a stack of paper cups beside it. He was about to pour some out when Melville raised his hand.

'Not yet!'

Melville felt beneath his pillow and produced a dark green quart bottle. Unmarked.

'Scotch in first.'

He unscrewed it expertly and tipped a little into the cup.

'Now the water.'

As Mabbut poured, Melville gave a rueful grin.

'Another advantage of having your daughter on the case.'

He took a careful, almost laborious sip.

'I asked her to contact you because I felt I owed you some thanks. You did a very difficult thing, walking away from that book, and I wanted to show my appreciation.'

'The book was a smear job. A million miles from all those things we talked about together. I couldn't have put my name to that.'

Melville nodded and then caught his breath sharply, as if in sudden pain.

Mabbut was alarmed.

'Are you all right?'

'Yes. It passes quickly.'

'Ursula said you weren't hurt in the attack?'

'No, I wasn't hurt, but three of my best boys were killed outright.'

'So why . . . ?'

His voice trailed off as Melville raised a hand towards him.

'Keith, what I'm going to tell you will be

difficult for both of us. All I ask is that you hear me out.'

'Of course.'

'It's about the book.'

Mabbut edged a little closer.

'As I said in my letter to you, Victor Trickett was indeed lying. Bettina was a saint.'

Mabbut nodded.

'I sensed that. I sensed it all along.'

Melville took another sip of whisky, which provoked a short, hard cough. Then he turned his unnerving gaze towards Mabbut.

'There were, however, quite a few other things that you missed, Keith.'

Mabbut felt that the room had grown perceptibly cooler. He caught the sharp smell of antiseptic.

'I'm not sure what you mean . . .'

A brief smile flickered at the corner of Melville's dry lips. When he spoke again it was softly and quickly and carefully.

'For the past twenty years I have been paid money by a number of international interests — both governments and private companies — to monitor the depth of feeling among local communities in resource-rich areas. My job was to gauge how antagonistic or otherwise these communities might be to resource extraction. I also undertook to facilitate geological and other surveys in their area and to actively encourage and promote the interests of those local people deemed to be sympathetic to exploration and investment. This does not mean that I was oblivious to the welfare of the people I worked

345

with. Quite the opposite. My instincts were always anti-establishment and I was never happier than in the company of different societies in distant countries. The farther from my own, the better. Nevertheless, there were times when, if you like, I worked for what might appear to be mutually exclusive interests. And there were times when, if I was unable to persuade either side to do the right thing, I pulled out, knowing I was leaving vulnerable people to their fate.'

'Who . . . who were these — '

Melville held up his hand and spoke sharply.

'Let me finish, then you can say anything you want. Or simply walk out.'

He took a deep breath and went on.

'Things were working well until two years ago, when I took on a project in South America. I was conceited enough to think that I could work for both sides in the Parcachua dam project. It was a very big deal. Eight thousand kilometres, fifty thousand displaced people. I was being paid to get it closed down in favour of another site my people were promoting. Instead I helped to get clearance, simply because the other side offered me more. I was greedy. Not for the money so much as for the power and the influence. I had begun to think I was invulnerable. That I knew best and that I could play the various interests off at will, winning for some, losing for others. I'd built up a formidable team, always coming out on top because none of these billionaires knew jackshit about the jungle or the mountains, or the people who lived there. There was no one in the world who could mix grass roots and Wall Street the way we did. And in my defence, what I did, or what I tried to do, was always to support the local people. If you're feeling charitable you could see me as Robin Hood. Or possibly Che Guevara. If you aren't I was more like Kurtz in *The Heart of Darkness*. But what I hadn't noticed was just how fast the game was changing. With the Chinese and the Russians coming into the market, the sums that these big corporations are setting aside for exploration is staggering. They have their own armies. Lawyers, PR advisers, but also well-trained, highly paid paramilitaries. Over the years I've become used to receiving death threats, but usually from nothing more than arrows or blowpipes. Now they're hiring professional hit-men, trained by the KGB or Mossad.'

He stopped, laid back his head, and moistened his lips.

'Among the many apologies I owe you, Keith, is one for thinking, for a very short while, that you might be one of them. Probably not a hit-man but quite possibly a spy. Hence the less-than-warm welcome when you turned up in India, flattering me in your suspiciously fulsome way about my 'international reputation'.'

He looked over at Mabbut and took in his look of stunned surprise with a hint of a smile.

'As it turned out you were *not* only not a hired killer, you were a genuinely decent man, who reminded me, uncomfortably, of the ideals I had when I first got into all this. And that's why

Kowprah went down the pan, and why I'm here now.'

Mabbut was confused.

'I thought the blockade was a big success.'

'I was being paid to get the Masira and the Musa and the Gyara so angry at what was being done to them that they'd come out of the forest with pipes and arrows and set about the Astramex drivers. This would create a backlash in favour of the company and the issuing of mining permits all round. The double bluff misfired. There was no violence from the tribals, and they won an international propaganda victory and a government decision to stop the mining. Which is why I had to get out of Bhubaneswar pretty quickly.'

'And Kinesh and Kumar and the others?'

Melville's mouth tightened. He shook his head as vigorously as he could.

'They were innocent, like you. They saw it all as something good. I was the only one who knew the bigger story. We'd worked together for years. We were like old friends. Whereas you, appearing out of the bush as it were, with your innocence and your ideals and your admiration, forced me to think my way back to the basics. You reflected back to me the person I once was. And that's when things began to go belly up. Having an idealist like you in the camp reminded me of how far I'd come from what I once believed in. And that's when I decided to water down the Kowprah blockade. Let it be big, threatening, but non-violent. The way Gandhi would have done it. Which is how it turned out. No one got

348

hurt and the tribals looked good and Astramex looked bad and a few weeks later I was attacked with grenades by someone's private army and lost three of the best workers I've ever had.'

There was silence in the room. Mabbut felt a mix of very different emotions: disbelief, embarrassment, anger, betrayal. He reached out a hand and sought the reassuring cool of the stainless-steel trolley beside him. Melville looked exhausted. Yet there were still things that Mabbut needed to know. He cleared his throat.

'Why did you decide to help me with the book?'

It was a moment before Melville spoke.

'Because to start with, before I really bothered to check out who was behind it, I saw your book as an attempt to have one side of my story told, before I was blown up or run over. It would be the best side of the story, the story of what motivated me, once upon a time, before I started playing power games with the environment. There was a risk, of course. You had a track record as an investigative journalist, so I had to be careful. I couldn't let you get too close. I gave you the names of a few school friends that I'd all but lost touch with. People I once knew who were fond of me. A long time ago.'

Something made him laugh.

'It was one of life's little ironies that your admirable idealism and the nasties who controlled your man at Urgent Books combined very neatly to kill off the book.'

Still chuckling to himself, Melville reached under the pillow, brought out the bottle of

Scotch, poured another measure and held the cup out to Mabbut.

'Would you top me up?'

Mabbut poured in some water. He sat for a while, watching Melville as he raised the glass to his lips. He seemed slow and old, as if all the energy had gone out of him.

'Why are you telling me all this?'

Melville took another sip, and when he turned back to Mabbut there was something of the old sparkle back in his eyes, some hint of mischief, some final jag of energy.

'Because I *want* the book to come out.'

Mabbut looked aghast, but Melville raised a hand.

'Only this time I want it to be the truth.'

There was a pause.

'The truth?'

'Yes.'

Mabbut spoke slowly and cautiously. 'You mean the truth as in what you've just told me?'

'Yes.'

'Wouldn't that be a suicide note?'

'Not at all. It would be an interesting cautionary tale. And I trust you enough to know that you would tell it honestly, but charitably too. Everyone, however admirable they appear to be, is simply human. Prone to all the imperfections, temptations and mendacities that go with the territory.'

He smiled.

'Environmentalists are particularly prone to self-righteousness, don't you think?'

Mabbut shook his head.

'I couldn't. I just couldn't do it. The world's stock of role models is low enough. It'd be like telling the world Mother Teresa was a hooker. You'd be hounded by every newspaper and broadcaster on the planet.'

'Suppose I wasn't around to worry about it?'

Mabbut shrugged dismissively.

'The wounds will heal. You're tough. The way you're going I might well have shuffled off before you.'

'I don't think you've quite got the picture, Keith.'

'What do you mean?'

Melville gestured to the bandages.

'These wounds are self-inflicted. At considerable cost.' He chuckled. 'Though my daughter, bless her, has given me a special rate.'

Once again, Mabbut's incredulity seemed to energise Melville.

'I'm taking evasive action, that's all. I'm getting rid of Hamish Melville before anyone else does.'

His playfulness had returned and his voice seemed lighter, less strained. It was, Mabbut realised, this life force that was driving him to plan his own extinction.

'By the time my daughter and her technicians have finished with me — and as you can see, they've already begun their work — there will be no more Hamish Melville. There'll be me, but not a me that anyone will recognise. Don't look so shocked, Keith. Everybody has nips and tucks these days, I'm just having a few more than most.'

351

'You don't need to do this. It's madness.'

'I've never done the conventional thing in my life. Despite everything I've told you, I still do value honesty above everything else. If I can't be a good man I can at least be an honest man. You can tell the world my story and I won't be around to get in your way. But someone very like me may get to read it one day. A retired Brazilian rubber planter, perhaps, or a Tibetan monk, though my preference is for an ancient Swedish fur trapper.'

His laughter was cut short by another grimace of pain.

So hard had Mabbut been concentrating on Melville's words that he hadn't heard the soft swish of the door opening. He looked round. It was Ursula. She said nothing, but looked at her father. He seemed calm now. At peace.

'Mr Mabbut,' she said softly, 'time to go.'

There was a pause.

Melville held out his hand to Mabbut.

'I'm sorry I let you down. But don't you let me down, Keith. Promise me that.'

Mabbut reached across and grasped the long, thin, surprisingly powerful hand. He felt it tighten as Melville looked up at him. Mabbut stared back into those piercingly, irresistibly clear blue eyes.

'I'll try my best.'

Behind him, Mabbut heard Ursula clear her throat. He stood as she pulled the door open for him.

'Might we meet again?'

Melville pulled a last bright smile from

352

somewhere, and shook his head emphatically.

'No. Goodbye, Keith.'

Neither said much as Mabbut and Ursula took the lift back down to reception. She offered him coffee, but he could see she was keen to get back to work. They shook hands.

'My father was fond of you.'

Mabbut couldn't resist a smile. 'Eventually.'

'He said he wished he'd met you a lot earlier.'

'I'm glad we met at all.'

She picked up a package from the desk.

'He told me to give you this. They're transcripts. Something he and I have been working on together. But he asked that you open them only in the event of his death.'

'He's not really going to die, is he?'

Ursula nodded.

'Around the end of September, if all goes well.'

Mabbut walked out into the increasingly busy streets. He sat down at a café across the road, choosing a table from which he could still see the white stuccoed front of the clinic. As he raised his eyes to the decorated frames of the dormer windows on the fifth floor, he had to shade them from the sun. Beside him, in a concrete culvert, the Tepla trickled down from the mountains. The bells on the red-hatted horses tinkled as carriages passed by. Mabbut reached for the bulky brown envelope and slipped it into his bag.

12

Two months later Mabbut was in his workroom wondering whether he should have a second coffee. It was one of those early autumn days that seemed to suit London well. The night had been cool and clear and there had been a light mist when he'd first sat down to write. He'd established a productive daily routine and was deep in the creation of an attack from the Isterians in the land of volcanoes. His decision to abandon the pseudo-archaic language he'd invented for his characters had proved crucial and *Albana* was now moving forward by leaps and bounds. His daughter Jay, now much recovered, had a place at Goldsmiths and was living back at Reserton Road. Sam had a small part in the new series of *Doctor Who*. Krystyna was still with Rex but was finding not having to earn a living deeply unsatisfying and was looking for some new challenge on which to expend her energies. Mabbut had just turned fifty-seven, and in all respects his life had slipped into a remarkably orderly pattern.

The phone beside him rang.

It was a voice he hadn't heard for months.

'Silla! How are you?'

'Keith, I'm so sorry.'

She sounded strained and far away.

'What's the matter?'

'Haven't you heard?'

'Heard what?'

'Hamish Melville. It's so dreadful.'

Mabbut started. His mouth was so dry that for a moment he couldn't reply.

'Haven't you seen the news?'

'No.'

He flicked over to the BBC home page. The story was just breaking.

'Apparently it was the steering.'

Melville had been involved in an accident. His car had plunged off a coastal road in a remote part of southern Argentina.

'He was on his own, apparently. Must have lost control. They're looking for another vehicle that was seen on the same road earlier in the day.'

A helicopter had been deployed, but this was the storm season and the authorities were saying it might be difficult to find the body.

'Apparently he was working down there, on some land rights issue. I suppose that's the way he would have wanted it . . . '

Mabbut found himself both tense and detached.

'Keith. Are you there?'

'Thanks, Silla, I'm sorry, I'm just in shock.'

'There'll be a memorial, I suppose.'

'I guess so.'

'Look, I know it's none of my business, dear boy, but since the book went belly up, how have you been keeping?'

'Oh . . . I'm fine, thanks, Sill. I get by.'

She sounded relieved.

'Well, see you around, dear boy. I do miss you.'

* * *

As the news broke, the media tried to do what they could with background on Melville, but there was precious little to go on. What was above and beyond doubt was that a brilliant if unorthodox man had paid the price for a life of tireless travel across the world, defending the rights of those whose voices might never have been heard.

Shortly after midday, Mabbut returned to the Capital Storage Company in St John's Wood and removed a strongbox. In it lay the package that Ursula had given him nearly three months earlier. He took it back to Reserton Road, and opened it at his desk. There were three sealed envelopes inside. Two of them contained micro-cassette tapes. In the third, a longer envelope, was a letter. The same old Foreign Office heading, smartly struck through with a red pen. Beneath it, in sweeping italic hand, was the message:

For the book they never published, and the book that lies ahead.
Hamish

Stapled to it was a cheque for one hundred and twenty thousand pounds. It had been post-dated to 19 September. The day of his death.

Hamish Melville's body was never found. He was given a posthumous knighthood by the Queen and a hall was named after him at the University of Strathclyde. Two years later Melville: The True Story of a Legend became the most successful self-published work of all time.

The company that issued it, Slow Books, run by Keith Mabbut and his ex-wife, Krystyna Naismith, was set up with £120,000 capital from an anonymous investor.

Their next book, The First Men, volume one of The Albana Trilogy, was published three years later, to universally lukewarm reviews.

At the last count it had sold eight and a half million copies worldwide.

Acknowlegements

The author gratefully acknowledges the help of all at TransIndus, and Wendy and Billy Stove in Lerwick.

AROUND THE WORLD IN 80 DAYS

Michael Palin

The book of the major BBC television series. The story of a Great Twentieth Century Adventure . . . In the autumn of 1988 Michael Palin, actor, comedian and writer, set out from London's Reform Club to circumnavigate the world, following the route taken 115 years earlier by Phileas Fogg. The rules were simple. He had to complete the journey in 80 days and could use only those forms of transport which would have been available to Fogg. Palin's Passepartout was not a loyal French manservant but a BBC film crew who recorded his every move. Fogg brought back a Princess, Palin a lot of dirty laundry and a television series.